GEOGRAPHY OF SHAME

GEOGRAPHY OF SHAME

A Fictionalized Memoir

MARYANN FEOLA

FCP

Full Court Press
Englewood Cliffs, New Jersey

First Edition

Copyright © 2015 by Maryann Feola

Published in the United States of America
by Full Court Press, 601 Palisade Avenue
Englewood Cliffs, NJ 07632
fullcourtpressnj.com

ISBN 978-1-938812-41-5
Library of Congress Control No. 2014959077

*Editing and book besign by Barry Sheinkopf
for Bookshapers (www.bookshapers.com)
Author photo by Elena Olivo Photography
Cover art courtesy of the author
Colophon by Liz Sedlack*

FOR MATHEW

as you right/write the future—with much love

We all were sea-swallowed, though some cast again—
And by that destiny, to perform an act
Whereof what's past is prologue, what to come
In yours and my discharge.
　　　　　　—William Shakespeare, *The Tempest*

PROLOGUE

New York City, May 2014

At the moment, I am happy in my life.

But it hasn't always been this way. For many anxiety-filled years, I only felt centered inside a classroom, teaching literature to students with dreams, separated from the troubles I left in the hall behind the closed door. But after each class, these troubles stood waiting like a stalker determined to have his way.

As far back as I remember, I had been emotionally enmeshed with people who drank, drugged, and abused women. During the course of a typical day, a man who probably thought he was the love of my life brought me flowers, told me I was too fat, cooked us a gourmet meal, struck me when no one was looking, swore that he adored me, and threw the dinner—plates and all—onto the floor. The chaos only ended when he passed out on the couch. I'm convinced my bout with uterine cancer in 2008 was set off by having endured years of unbearable stress.

As with other toxic relationships, I stayed in that one way too long. Explaining away my history of denial by saying, "We love what is familiar," may be clichéd, but for me it bears truth. I grew up in a family where heavy drinking turned laughter and warmth into violence and chaos. Anxiety still sets in when I smell Sambuca or hear ice crackling in a glass of what appears to be a Rob Roy. Writing this book, a fictionalized memoir framed in a family saga, has yielded valuable insights that lift me up when I begin sliding back down the bottomless rabbit hole.

But before I begin the telling, I have to come clean. I too have abused my drug of choice: a reckless concoction of overeating and excessive spending. If your unanswered questions are mounting up, not to worry, dear reader, a detailed road map of my shame fills the twelve chapters that follow.

I trace what troubles me back to life in Rutino, a small hilltop town in southern Italy. The ancestral home of my Longo relations, a humble cottage rented from a local *padrone*, lies fifteen miles from the Amalfi Coast. Good fortune has enabled members of my extended family to vacation in Italy, but no one goes back up the mountain. Their journey ends by the sea in Palinuro or Positano. Rutino beckons one to leave, not return.

Southern Italy is rich with mythology and history and trauma. It has been the imagined site of loss and recovery in Greco-Roman stories, including Virgil's epic, *The Aeneid*. It is also the land that the Greeks, Romans, Lombards, Arabs, and Normans had colonized before it became the plaything of Italian principalities, and then the property of the French, the Spanish, and perhaps most sadly, the northern Italian ministers who governed after the unification of Italy in 1861.

After the unification, my family were among the multitude that awaited the promises made by revolutionaries and politicians. However, like the Spanish colonizers before them, King Vittorio Emmanuele's government denied them land of their own, enough bread to feed their children, and political empowerment. So they became part of the Italian diaspora that yearned to walk America's fabled "streets of gold." They boarded ship in Naples, unaware that, packed along with the few belongings they were travelling with to Ellis Island, was a shitload of post-traumatic haunting, the kind that is passed from one generation to the next. I think of this haunting as the silent partner of our DNA.

I know this familial landscape so well that I feel like those early modern cartographers when they mapped a world previously rendered flat by ignorance and fear. One feature that distinguishes their mapping from mine is that their maps were drawn with sea monsters menacing the borderlands. I have sought to banish a monster I call Shame by breaking my silence and writing this story.

CHAPTER 1
South Of The Border

June, sea pulsed wild, high.
Young girl travels far from home,
Tossed from waves to shore.

Summer 1963

ARI AWOKE LISTENING TO THELMA'S VOICE. Her southern accent was strong, her tone self-assured. It was as if someone had taken a man's voice, added alluring feminine charm, and placed it in Thelma's mouth. At the time I thought she was strange, but good strange. That summer, I compared what I saw in Thelma Johnson, my Uncle Vito's mother-in-law, to my previous experience with wives and mothers and found that *everything* was different.

Whenever she called out, "Arianna, darlin'," it sounded gruff and throaty, with just the slightest touch of Southern gentility. She'd look me in the eye and smile crooked, benevolently dangerous, the way a gypsy woman had when she entered our front garden to convince me that handing over my dolls' clothing would save the lives of poor babies somewhere in Europe. Both encounters took place without interference from those loving sentinels Bella and Ted Naso, my parents.

Masculine approval did not concern her. Thelma had traveled around, experiencing the world beyond her kitchen. Like gypsy women, she had a dangerous reputation. She was the worldly, independent woman my family had warned me away from becoming.

She's different but cool, I thought, probably feeling a queer bond between myself and another *strega*, the "witch" my mother accused me of being when we argued.

My poor attitude—not being afraid to argue with "my elders" and showing early signs of unconventional behavior—had turned me into an Italian witch. I was warned that such defiance would be my downfall: "Your mouth is your worst enemy." Now, on the brink of becoming a teenager and with my hormones raging, Thelma's feistiness appealed to my rebellious nature, although as an adult I'd travel down a different path.

I became the first woman in my family to attend a four-year college. Moreover, I continued my education until I earned a Ph.D. Most guys I dated were Americans, non-Italians whom my parents tolerated the way one tolerates seasonal allergies that pass with time, or in my case, with the arrival of a boyfriend whose ancestors shared our southern Italian heritage. My parents worried that I was wild. But they would have worried more had they known how, for years, I used diet pills to curb my appetite and give me the stamina to run with the bad boys. As a matter of course, I lied about where I went and whom I was with and what I did. Once, I overheard my mother boasting that I had the good sense not to "ruin" myself.

"She may be popular with the boys," she said, "but my girl has the good sense to keep her virginity intact."

I thanked whatever heavenly force was keeping me from getting pregnant. Worry about pregnancy or being too fat or too thin, however, did not interfere with my appetite for books and doing my own thing.

But I never realized how the summer vacation at the Johnson

home influenced my personal journey. The trip took place at a time in my life when I was falling in love with unconventionality. Remembering Thelma's voice and its hint of vagabondage, I understand why I am drawn to singers with throaty, haunting voices. When I hear the music of the "High Priestess of Soul," Nina Simone, I embrace my inner Siren. Other throaty favorites, especially Janis Joplin and Van Morrison, have acknowledged Simone's influence.

Then there are the self-reliant authors whose work I teach to students in women's studies courses at the College of New York City: Aphra Behn, Colette, Diane di Prima, and Dorothy Allison. Was it Thelma who sparked my passion for women who defied tradition and lived to make both peace and art out of the consequences? That quality in memory that leaves you feeling the way you do when you slip the right piece into a jigsaw puzzle tells me she was.

Yet I wish I had been prepared for the fallout that visits women, especially Italian American women of my generation, who do not follow the path their parents paved for them.

As a teenager it was comforting to remember that Thelma too had broken free of the traditional gender expectations set by the "man of the house." And she had done so in the days before anyone spoke of "breaking through the glass ceiling." Now, it wasn't that this woman, born eighth in a family of ten to Ohio sharecroppers, had gotten herself an education or achieved any estimable position. But she had done something even more remarkable: She came to voice her opinions and both fund and manage her life without getting hung up on what "the people would say." (Growing up, my parents' response to my flouting convention or acting recklessly was, "What will *the people* say?" Who, I'd wonder, are these people, and why are we so worried about what they will say?) From day one of my stay in her Lake Worth home, it was evident that Thelma's ways were different from those of the "Italian women," my relatives back home in Brooklyn.

In contrast, my loved ones valorized piety and humility. Loving and lighthearted, the women in my family revered the patriarchy inherent in their Catholicism and Italian heritage. They voiced concern for "good" behavior without questioning religious beliefs and social conventions that had been handed down from generation to generation.

"We wait for the man of the house to sit at the table before we start eating!"

"Get up and get your husband [or your boyfriend, or your father, or your godfather] a clean napkin."

As God was the head of their church, men were the head of their homes.

Even a twelve-year-old could see that Thelma wouldn't give you five cents for piety. And she'd probably laugh at the thought of acting humble. My mother, Grandma Lena, and my Gregorio relatives spoke about Thelma's bossy manner and "hard ways." They warned me about her before I headed south with Uncle Vito, my mother's eldest brother, and his wife, Aunt Lettie, Thelma's only child. Family gossip had established that Thelma was far more brazen than the other "American" women they routinely lampooned.

To begin with, Thelma had changed husbands "about as often as decent people change light bulbs." She had married and divorced four husbands before she "took up" with the latest, Papa Jake Johnson. Years of listening to such stories taught me that "took up with" meant that they weren't actually married. But that wasn't the worst of it.

Papa Jake lived in the house Thelma bought with her savings, not because she needed him there, but because she wanted him there. He may have been first mate, but that 5'1" redhead with an impressive collection of dangling earrings was captain of their partnership. She teased him about movin' like a turtle while he did his chores, often reminding him that the Lord was lucky he hadn't put the building of the great ark into the hands of someone like Jake Johnson. Nonetheless, they lived as a happy twosome, old mates talking about their days on the road as they whiled away the hours on the lanai he had slowly but skillfully built.

Born one-quarter researcher and three-quarters snoop, I studied their interactions. I liked how there was none of that firm authority coming from the man of the house that made things so tense. Even though I was under the watchful eye of Uncle Vito, whose presence stood as a reminder of the way things were done back home, the fact was that he was under Thelma's roof, where there was no bossy man in charge. I felt an inner peace that was new and appealing.

I liked to sit with Thelma and Papa Jake while Aunt Lettie washed the dinner dishes and Uncle Vito walked the Johnsons' dog. The punch lines of their jokes were over my head, yet I was amused by their gentle bantering, noticing how Thelma usually had the last word, something I could not imagine happening back in Brooklyn. I liked the openness in their home. Witnessing altered boundaries, role reversal, and sexual partnership was my brave new world. Yet I did not know its geography. My awareness that change is a complex process was not shaped until my junior year of college, when I tuned into antiwar, civil rights, and sexual liberation struggles. In the meantime, I acted out against authority in a reckless, smart-mouthed way.

After Thelma's second husband, Aunt Lettie's father, packed up and left for parts unknown, she'd returned to the carnival circuit and boarded out her daughter to a home where she encountered the petty cruelties and mean spiritedness that she'd eventually medicate with a lifetime of spending every unaccounted-for cent of Uncle Vito's modest postman's salary. Randolph Hearst may have had his "Rosebud," but Lettie Gregorio had her Easter basket.

The defining moment had taken place in 1931, when little nine-year-old Lettie spent Easter watching the other children in her caretaker's home eat chocolate bunnies and jelly beans sent by their families. "No one, not a one," as she often recalled, "had the decency to offer me a piece. But sure enough, the next day my basket arrived from 'Mother-Dear-on-the road,' and I ate all the delicious candies up by myself, ate them till I turned green."

"Where was your mother that she could not spend Easter with you?" some relative or other always asked. But she'd just clear her throat and continue her foundational tale, explaining how she stood her ground and "gave nothin' to no one, just as no one had given nothin' to me." Aunt Lettie's bravado, however, was a thin mask for many buried childhood traumas. Childlike and fiercely loyal, she delighted in the things she loved. Foremost among them was Vito Gregorio, who had rescued her from carnival life and the "Pop the Balloon" stand one Saturday night. During his stint at Fort Benning, he and three of his army buddies had filled the weekends with as much fun as they could. In three weeks they'd leave for Europe to fight Hitler's army and his allies, including the Italian, Benito Mussolini.

Vito put a quarter down on Lettie's counter and pretended he needed help. Since she was busy with young customers, it wasn't until his fourth game that she paid him any attention. He flashed a big smile and expressed his thanks. "I hope tonight is the night I win the loveliest prize of all." Eighteen-year-old Lettie was naive to his innuendo, but she liked his "Northern style." Vito spent two dollars and fifty cents at the booth before Lettie allowed him to win a felt poodle and her consent to meet her parents. Thelma also liked Vito's looks and friendly banter. Anyway, she had decided beforehand it was time for Lettie to settle down and be taken care of. She worried about her daughter's awkwardness navigating adulthood, often responding with stern impatience and maternal shortcomings that were infused with genuine love.

Before Vito finished basic training and left for Europe, Thelma helped him find an affordable engagement ring. The Protestant South was promptly introduced to the Italian Catholic North in a three-minute phone call. The connection was hampered by static created, not by faulty telephone wires, but by two different understandings of a mother's hold on adult married children. When Grandma Lena said, "My son Vito is my eyesight," Thelma, having had no previous experience with the drama and histrionics of Italian American motherhood, got the impression that Lena was suffering from some form of blindness, and that Vito helped her manage.

Grandma considered it parental abandonment when Thelma remarked that, after the war, the young couple must find their own place in the world. Yet this abandonment might have its benefits, thought Grandma Lena. How sweet the thought that there'd be no motherly and grandmotherly competition for time and affection!

There were tears on the July 1941 afternoon when Vito left Georgia with the US 2nd Armored Division's 41st Infantry Regiment. Since Lettie had not had much of an education, for the next four years Vito did much of the letter writing from the battlefields of North Africa, Southern Italy, and France. Like Othello, he filled his beloved's imagination and deepened her passion by explaining the details of his brave leadership. However, Othello's telling profited from the safe distance of memory and the cadences of Shakespeare's poetry. Vito's stories, set in motion by Hitler's army, pulsated with gunfire from exploding aircraft and the moans of dying men a few feet away.

Upon his return in early 1946, Uncle Vito began making arrangements for Lettie to come to Brooklyn. Six months later, Thelma and Papa Jake Johnson drove up to witness the wedding vows recited before some 150 family, friends, neighbors, and former army buddies. Thelma was upset that her daughter had to walk down the church's side aisle.

"What sort of tomfoolery is this?" she asked Grandma Lena. She didn't care that the church allowed only Catholic brides to walk down the main aisle. "Well, that ain't nothin' but an insult to me and my daughter."

The Church of Saint Mark was packed. Before, during, and after the football wedding reception, the men from the 41st Infantry regaled the other guests with Vito's numerous acts of heroism. His rapid rise to sergeant surprised no one; he was brave, well-organized, and not afraid to give everyone hell when he thought it was necessary. He had been among those who participated in Operation Torch when his company landed at Casablanca in November 1942. The medals he won, his buddies explained, were for the many acts of valor he performed during the summer of 1943 when the 2nd Armored Division landed at Gela and fought their way through to Palermo.

Although she would hear these stories countless times over the years, Lettie never failed to marvel at them and begin massaging the spot that had been grazed by an Italian soldier's bullet. Everyone anticipated her saying, "Imagine you Italians shooting each other up during the war. Just ain't civilized."

Growing up, I noticed how the family listened to Lettie's childhood stories with a blend of empathy, horror, and downright incomprehension. They wondered how Thelma, or any mother for that matter, could be separated from her child because of the demands of work outside the home. "*Disgraziata*," they would whisper among themselves. No child of theirs would ever have to stuff themselves with day-old Easter candy.

In the years to come, while my mother, her sister, and her sisters-in-law became proud parents, Aunt Lettie and Uncle Vito underwent tests until they learned Lettie could not conceive a child. The genuine love they had for me, my sisters, Julie and Baby Nina, and our cousins could not mitigate their anger and disappointment. Over the years, Uncle Vito became sterner, more cynical, and Aunt Lettie more infantilized. The couple's behavior became the focus of endless family discussions.

Listening to the sharp critique of my aunt and uncle, I'd sit at the dining-room table, hand on chin, relishing the gossip and stuffing my mouth with food. The adults never asked us kids to leave the room when they were conducting what might be called character assassinations. So we grew up taking for granted their view of "Lettie and Vito's oddball ways." Often, I was the one who commented on what was being said, only to hear that "children should be seen, but not heard."

I occasionally swallowed my rude remarks, but I was relentless with my questions. For one, I could not understand how these comments concerned the same Vito and Lettie that everyone showered with love and admiration when they were visiting. My questions went unanswered, but the exposure to family drama developed my taste for characterization, mythology, and decoding double-speak.

My FIRST FAR-AWAY VACATION, a trip to Lake Worth, Florida, to visit Aunt Lettie's parents, came in July 1963, three weeks after my graduation from St. Mark's Elementary School. I left Brooklyn excited but expecting to feel a little homesick. My mother reminded me that I had my summer reading to keep me company. Knowing my passion for reading, she knew I found comfort in my books. I brought along two of the four books I had chosen from the summer reading list Fort Hamilton High School had sent to incoming freshmen. For each book, I needed to write a summary and response to what interested me most. No big deal. The nuns at St. Mark's had encouraged what they called my "flair" for writing, so I felt confident I'd do well on my first high school assignment.

During my last year at St. Mark's, my parents and eighth-grade teacher, Sister Thomas More, wanted me to take the Cooperative Examination required for admission into a Catholic high school, but I wasn't having it. Despite many "attempted brainwashings," I insisted on a public high school. Mostly I wanted to get away from the nuns and all their rules. And I yearned for something different, even if I did not know what that something was. I knew there was a better chance of finding it in a public school away from the nuns who ridiculed "sinful" girls like me.

My flaw was that I belonged a rather rude group who sneered at the thought of religious vocation. Once or twice a term, the teachers at St. Mark's, Sisters of St. Joseph, asked if we had experienced "a religious calling." We weren't told how we would recognize one; we were just asked routine questions.

"Have you considered the priesthood? Wouldn't it be nice being a bride of Christ? Which saint's name might you take when you realize your vocation?"

Backs straight and hands folded atop our desks, we answered the nuns' questions about our spiritual calling. Playing it safe, many of my classmates said they weren't sure. But my friends and I seized the opportunity to share our more colorful ambitions. Mine was becoming either an actress or an artist living in Greenwich Village. A sigh and look on my teacher's face let me know I'd given the wrong answer. In the seventh grade, my teacher told me that I was intentionally looking for a life of sin. My classmates laughed. I overheard Sal Lentino say, "With her mouth, she has a better chance of becoming a town crier."

How often has a strict parochial education, like the one in the hands of the Sisters of St. Joseph, backfired, turning little angels into scheming, over- (or under-) eating demons? Ah, the power of staging rebellion or at least speaking your mind to thwart the ambitions of your oppressors! Binge eating and wildly fluctuating weight were my personal revenge.

I'd like to say that I was a sensitive child, although my mother told me I was too touchy. Whatever the case, I self-medicated the shame and anger: Before going home where Mom had milk and cookies waiting for me and Julie, I stopped along 13th Avenue for a slice of Boston cream pie at Otto's Luncheonette. For thirty-five cents, I had a balm to heal the pain from the ridicule I experienced in class.

Otto was the widowed father of two girls a few grades ahead of me at St. Mark's. Whenever I stopped by to stuff my feelings down with pie, Bonnie and Caroline were doing their homework at a table nearby. We'd wave but said little to each other. Many years later, when I began teaching at the College of New York City, we'd meet again. Otto's daughters were staff members in Academic Affairs. I blushed when Caroline recalled my reputation for being a "top student," and my cheeks felt as if they were on fire when Bonnie told the provost how she and her sister remembered me as "the little student who loved Papa's Boston cream pie."

On more than one occasion, Mom had been called to school by the principal because my friends and I—known as "the wild bunch"—had been caught passing around a poetic put down of Sister Thomas More. Sister was a large, stern woman who occasionally took a stab at being witty by pitting her students against each other. She must have listened closely to our schoolyard banter. The insults her students exchanged became her weapon to divide and conquer. In front of the whole class, she'd refer to a student as "Little Miss Four Eyes" or "Mr. Dog Breath."

The short, tight perm that broadened my already chubby face had earned me the schoolyard nickname "Gorilla Head." That year, I wore my winter hat well into the spring, so my hair was covered for at least part of the day. It was too hard for me to talk with my parents about the shame I felt over the name-calling. But I did tell them that I thought my hair looked ridiculous. "This will be my first and last perm!"

"Can't you see that, for once, your hair stays in place? For once you don't look like some *strega*."

My hair is fine and hard to manage, but was this the alternative? How could I tell my parents that Sister Thomas had chimed in about my fat-faced hairstyle? I was tired of hearing that I was too sensitive, "touchy," like some relative or other who had been mythologized as a drama queen. I felt ugly and alone.

But just as academic success was the gift that brightened my adult life, my ability to do well in grammar school often turned darkness into light. One Friday, two of us were left as finalists in the monthly spelling bee: me and Michael Campinello. His mother ran errands for the sisters and priests at St. Mark's and was President of the Altar Society. Sister Thomas made no secret that she wanted him, one of her favorites, to win. I received the next-to-last word "polymorphous." Michael had just sweated out "hegemony" and was patting the beads of sweat from his budding mustache. Both sister and I could see he was feeling the pressure. Before giving me the next word, she turned to the class and said, "The next word goes to Arianna, our favorite Gorilla Head." I told myself the laughter and hoots were meant to cheer me on. Back straight, smirk on face, I belted out: "P-a-r-a-d-o-x-i-c-a-l." Michael messed up on "collegiality," and I won a Sacred Heart medal and some high fives from my friends. But the real prize was the experience of not losing my composure under fire.

Writing became my outlet. I was part of a group who collaborated on poems that satirized Sister Thomas. Lorraine Olofski would write the first stanza and pass it to me, Geri Fiore, or Joanne Healy to write the next. And on it would go, until we got caught. The title of each poem was "Another Adventure at the Happy Hippo Lodge." The subject was a heavy drinking, Bible totting ogre who misquoted passages and ambled about, stepping clumsily on the small creatures in her care. Our work was immature and insensitive, but it also demonstrated the ability to use language that Sister had gruffly but successfully drummed into our brains.

"This, Mrs. Naso, is how your daughter and her friends behave during recitations of the Baltimore Catechism." Back home, I'd meet my father's wrath. He had a short fuse and no sense of how to guide a rebellious preteen.

"Bella, tell me everything they said. Don't try to sugar-coat her craziness." A Linotype operator for the *New York Times*, my father was a loving husband and a skilled craftsman. Patient child-rearing, however, was not among his talents. The youngest child in a prosperous immigrant family, Ted Naso may have been spoiled by his mother, Mamie, and sisters, Clara and Gloria, but his older brother,

Milo, had toughened him up.

"Act like a man" and "Don't take any guff": These were among the life lessons he learned from Milo, who often assumed the role of male guardian while Grandpa Joe spent long hours running his bakery and, later on, his bar and grill. Providing his family with all the comforts that had been nonexistent in the tiny village of San Nicola la Strada, outside Caserta, was Grandpa's time-consuming quest.

Orazio Longo, Joe's father-in-law, had set a high benchmark for the family's financial success. Forgetting his own struggles as an immigrant who arrived in New York in 1892, Orazio always treated Joe as if he had just gotten off the boat and was ignorant about the way business worked in America. Joe Naso was determined to succeed. He had no tolerance for raucous behavior, unless of course it occurred on Sundays after much wine had been passed around the table.

When Dad disciplined me or my sisters, he never thought to ask what we were thinking, let alone what we were feeling. The nuns were to be respected no matter what. The principal's suggestion that I seemed troubled was nonsense. He would handle it. Raising a complex, willful daughter probably scared the life out of him. His coping mechanism was most strange. During the week, I met with stern punishments, being sent to bed early, often after a beating. Then, as if needing some comic relief, at the Sunday gathering, usually over espresso and Sambuca, my father regaled the family with the story of my latest outrage at school. "I can't decide if Arianna will turn out to be a poet or a juvenile delinquent." There I'd sit eating a Napoleon, laughing along, relieved that I was no longer on his nerves.

Three years later, during my sophomore year at Fort Hamilton High, I learned Sr. Thomas More had been transferred to another school for cleaning out a twelve-year-old student's "foul mouth" with brown soap. My friend, Anita Rinaldo, whose aunt was a housekeeper for the nuns, broke the news to our wild bunch. "The worst part," she said, "Is that the boy had a seizure, and Sr. Thomas took her time calling for help."

The news spread quickly though Bensonhurst, but I wanted to be the one who told my father. I wanted to see the look of shame on his face for defending such a bully. That night, I waited until we took our assigned seats at the table; then I shared each and every gory detail, adding a few to intensify the drama. I could see that my mother was appalled, because she kept shaking her head, eyes closed, lips pursed, as she did when she heard about some injustice. Then I struck. Arms folded across my chest, and in the smuggest tone I could muster up, I asked, "Who do you think is crazy now, Dad?"

He slapped me so hard that my right ear rang for an hour.

By seventh grade, I was becoming more outspoken, "bold," my teachers said. My parents' expectations for their children's obedience had been shaped by the traditions, values, and methods of treating unruly offspring that had come over from Southern Italy. Frequently, they responded with the verbal and physical abuse that, as an adult, I spent thousands of dollars and hundreds of hours recalling to a succession of psychotherapists. Dialing 911 to report that my father was threatening to kill me and was hitting me as if he just might, or telling a school counselor that my mother alternated between telling me I was her precious lamb and that I was an ungrateful child who would cause her death, was beyond my thinking.

Anyway, I found that I could restore my power after physical or verbal abuse by hiding a classmate's eyeglasses or kissing a boy behind a neighbor's bush and bragging about it to my Aunt Lettie, whom I knew my parents only took half seriously. Chaos, I thought, was the road to a good time. And for many years to come I traveled down its destructive path

FOR THE TRIP, I PACKED JERRE MANGIONE'S *Mount Allegro: A Memoir of Italian American Life*. Autobiography was a new genre for me, but it shared many of the features in the lives of the saints I'd read at Saint Mark's. Give me a remarkable life filled with passion and purpose, and I'd stay up all night until I finished the book. Those figures, Catholic saints, like the remarkable women's stories I now teach, transcend the ordinary; they live out drama, trauma, or both, and by the end of the story, there is a notable transformation or awakening. So, as I began Mangione's story, I wondered what I'd learn about Italians from a guy born way back in 1909. I found myself enjoying the book, but it was years before I realized the nuances of young Gerlando's conflicted feelings for his family.

We spent the first night in a Howard Johnson's in Virginia. While I changed into my baby doll pajamas in the biggest bathroom I'd ever seen, Uncle Vito and Aunt Lettie were watching television. In the background, I heard President Kennedy's booming voice responding to reporters in Cork, Ireland. Happily, when I opened my book, they turned down the volume. But I neglected to say "thank you," and my uncle let me know it.

I continued reading Chapter 2, "Family Party," where Mangione, through his character, Gerlando Amoroso, recalls the Sunday family gatherings that colored his childhood in Rochester, New York. Our experiences were separated by sixty years, yet I found his world familiar. I imagined myself sitting right next to him, watching.

And so I read on:

> *Sicily was never as large as the United States, but once it was the world's garden of culture. Those were the days before the popes and the priests got a stranglehold on it. The Greeks, the Romans, the Saracens, the Normans, and even the Arabs were among those who planted their seeds in that garden.*

Had to think about that for a moment, so I opened a bag of Fritos and reread the last sentence. After I looked up "stranglehold" in my pocket dictionary, and made the connection to all those people who wanted to run things in Sicily, I moved on to the part where Gerlando's grouchy uncle explains why the family left Sicily.

"Don't fill the child's head with a lot of nonsense about culture," said my redheaded Uncle Nino, who was more cultured than any of my relatives. "Sicily is beautiful, yes, so beautiful, in fact, that I should like nothing better than to return there. But it is also terribly poor. It lies at the end of the Italian boot and some government clique in Rome is always kicking it around. Some Sicilians got tired of that treatment and finally left."

Sitting at the dressing table that doubled as a desk, I decided to use the complementary stationery to jot down a few ideas for my report.

Gerlando wants to know more about Sicily. His family always talks about how good it is there. They really seem to miss it, too. The foods there sound great, and the countryside is so beautiful—like a dream. I think his family came to America (Rochester) because of Sicily's poverty and some kind of trouble it had with Rome. He learns a lot about Italy from his Uncle Luigi and his Uncle Nino, who gets mad a lot and reminds me of someone I know who is sitting on the other bed.

I found a part I decided to quote, even if I did not fully grasp how the same set of circumstances had affected my family.

Gerlando learns that Sicily is at Italy's boot and "some government clique in Rome is always kicking it around."

(Must add a footnote when I get home.)
Description, a quote. . .now I'll add my thoughts.

It seems some Sicilians wanted to go to Rome, but they did not have the money. But many did find the money to come to America, like my family did from Naples. What happened to all the sadness when they crossed the ocean? Did some of it follow them to Rochester? Maybe it did, but the family did not know. I hope I will find out.

This book is teaching me that Sicilians look like Saracens (whoever they are; must look it up in the big dictionary when I get home) and other people. This is because Greeks, Romans, Saracens, and Normans were once there, probably because of all that beauty. Gerlando's Uncle Luigi also tells him that priests and popes wanted to control Sicily. It sounds weird, and I wonder what the nuns at Saint Mark's would say about that. More later.

THAT SUMMER, I LEARNED A LOT about Thelma's past. Papa Jake, Aunt Lettie's third-but-best daddy, told me how at fourteen years of age she'd run away from Ohio and her "mean as hell" mother and step-daddy. "Her upbringin' had been all about slaps on the behind and threats, real mean ones." Thelma quickly picked up a southern accent and the hard ways of the "carny people," as Papa Jake called the migrant workers, who pitched tents from Tennessee to Florida ten months out of every year. The carnival was the place where she learned to draw out her words and drop consonants "mo' quickly than the 'pigeons'" dropped their nickels at the "Wheel of Fortune" stand she worked seven days a week, rain or shine.

"Smart as a whip and stubborn to boot, she was borned with a capacity for endurin' hard work and long hours. In a snap, she learnt the business inside and out."

Papa Jake explained how Thelma began work as an errand girl in 1912. Within four years, she had married the senior partner's son, Sly Jim Baker. Unlike the other carny wives, she managed her own money and gave, rather than took, orders. At night, she sat with the men, discussing business and planning ways to sabotage the competition. "Thelma was always the first one out of her trailer in the morning and the last one to say goodnight." On behalf of the Baker, Hayes, and Applewaite Carnival, she traveled the back roads of the South in search of sites for the following year. When she located a spot, he explained, "She'd argue like a man for reasonable rent."

But Papa Jake could have told more, if I hadn't been only thirteen years old.

He could have told how Sly Jim meekly shook his head when Thelma gave him a tongue-lashing or beat him at cards. Her first husband never said a harsh word in spite of the ribbing he took from the other men. He believed he held the trump card: the better deal that awaited him in the single bed he shared with his feisty wife. Yet for Thelma, the nights in that bed offered little pleasure and no surprises. Having brought more sexual experience to their marriage, she tried sharing her cache of positions and sex play. Sly Jim was not a quick study. Like a child at his mother's knee caps learning a waltz, his moves were awkward, out of step. Not only did he lack the moves, but he had little soul and less passion.

Beneath his taut body, Thelma thought about the swarthy man who worked the Wonder Wheel when the company visited Tallahassee. Boasting he would show her how to "kiss like a woman," he awoke a passion Thelma fought to satisfy for the rest of her life. Nights when he convinced his roommates to sleep in another trailer were spent teaching the fifteen-year-old various ways of giving and receiving sexual pleasure. A master of touch, the man knew how to fan the flames of young Thelma's desire. In bed, evoking the memory of those nights, she'd feel a pulsing where Sly Jim was fumbling about.

Then, riding her like a jockey racing to the finish line, he'd yell, "Hold on Thelma, here I come." When he was finished, it was always, "Damn, honey that was *gooood*." Then, in a show of thanks, believing he had had his way with his woman, he'd fondle her buttocks. But Sly Jim never gave a thought to the roughness of his skin or Thelma's pleas that she needed his hand somewhere else. After three years and two abortions, and with enough money set aside to become a partner in a large traveling company, Thelma left the single bed and husband number one.

I LOVED THE STORIES, and I studied the subject. Did Thelma notice my gaze during those three weeks? Looking back, I see myself watching her at the beach, during the long car rides, and shuffling the deck for our nighttime card games. She was like no woman I'd ever met. She was in charge of herself. And she treated me like an adult.

One afternoon, Uncle Vito took everyone for a drive along Palm Beach's South Ocean Boulevard. "This is where the local millionaires live," he explained. Facing the sea, like cement and stone Titans, each mansion had a name. Moving to the beat of the music from the transistor radio I sandwiched between the car window and my ear, I spotted a marble sea horse with *Sorrento* carved on its frame. "Look, Sorrento. That is my friend Cecilia's last name. I wonder if these people are related to her."

"Cheez, sweetheart, that's the name of the house! The only Italians you'll find in this part of town are working in the kitchen cooking or in the yard planting with the coloreds."

"But, Uncle Vito, what about the rich Italians? Where do they live?" Before my uncle opened his mouth, his mother-in-law laughed, snuffed out her cigarillo, and explained, "Honey, y'all are up in West Palm on the Intracoastal with your front-lawn Virgin Marys and your Eyetlian flag out every chance you get. Folks here would just as soon take in coloreds or those Cubans that keep swimming over like rats before they'd let one of y'all into their midst."

I had heard stories from Grandpa Joe about how he and other Italians had been treated when they came to America. They had taken whatever work was available. As a matter of course, they were paid less than anyone else. Landlords and store owners mistook their unfamiliarity with English for stupidity, and overcharged them for the meager necessities they purchased. Regarded as "colored," they were the butt of jokes: the dagoes, wops, and guineas people welcomed as friends once they got to know them. They might be excellent cooks or tailors or barbers, but their children were held back from mainstream middle-class life by the Anglo-Americans, as well as by their parents' fears that social mobility would distance them figuratively and geographically.

As a child in Brooklyn, I had been too young to notice the subtleties of race, ethnicity, and class that played a role in setting the boundaries of neighborhoods and entrance into colleges and the professions.

Looking at the waterfront mansions, I decided that someday I would be rich enough to live, as Thelma might say, "wherever the hell I wanted." But given my upbringing and exposure to the traditional roles that flashed before me on our 14-inch Westinghouse television, I could only imagine that marrying some rich, cool, and of course good-looking Italian guy would get me there.

It would be decades before I understood that becoming self-reliant is the best way to underwrite success. It took even longer to appreciate that being successful in life must not be confused with owning a mansion on the Atlantic coast that stands like a showy totem gazing at the Old World in some meaningless act of defiance.

WE PLANNED ON SPENDING the last day of our vacation at Palm Beach. Right after breakfast, Thelma ordered everyone to get ready. She was adamant about an early start and finding a good spot. Papa

Jake was outside, watering his herb garden, when Thelma yelled out, "Come on now, move it along, old man." I marveled at how he always did what his wife asked. This would never happen back in Brooklyn! Uncle Vito, who by this time had had enough of Thelma's orders, shook his head and mumbled something about how rowdy volleyball players and bossy women would drive him crazy before noon.

While I changed into my hot pink polka-dot swim suit with matching cabana jacket, I listened to Bobby Rydell on my transistor radio sing about love and the coolness of traditional values. I turned up the volume so high that I didn't hear Uncle Vito banging on the wall.

Immersed in an early teenage fantasy of Rydell's "Swinging School," I pushed my breasts upward to fashion a little cleavage.

> *My days will be filled with studying and writing poetry with the coolest guy in the class. We'll be the top two students, everyone's favorite couple. Being deeply in love, we'll take long drives in his convertible to romantic spots where we'll kiss passionately beneath the stars.*

Into my fantasy crept the nuns at Saint Mark's and my mother telling me what happened to "bad girls," those who didn't listen and liked to flirt. My father snuck in too, fists clenched. I erased them all. Expanding the map of my daydream, I took it on the road.

> *After high school, my love and I will drive cross country in his convertible. We'll study at a college in Southern California. We will work hard and marry right after graduation. He will love me forever, not only because I am pretty, but also because I'm smart. Being his wife and mother of his children will make me so happy.*

Unsophisticated, and with little exposure to educated women, I could not see myself sharing household responsibilities. Trading "bookin for cookin" was the just the way it was supposed to be.

Yet a husband watching our child, while I attended a graduate seminar or prepared a lecture, hid in the shadows of my uncharted future. But on that morning, the radio blaring, the beat "groovy," I longed for the only type of sexual fantasy I could imagine. I may have been brazen, but I knew the boundaries set for Italian American women.

I thought I was the first one ready, but there was Thelma sitting on the lanai, all dressed and packed for the beach. A picture of self-confidence, she was smoking one of her little cigars. She flicked a long ash and winked when she saw me. Gesturing like a swimsuit model, I asked Thelma how I looked. "After all," I confessed, "there might be some cute guy at the beach."

"Sit by me, darlin', I've been meaning to tell you a few things before y'all head back up North, things you should think about during your high school years when your hormones kick in. For one," she said, snuffing out the tip of her cigarillo, "stay away from these things and from booze 'cause they turn you into some croaking babbler before they finally do you in. Watch out for any man who promises to take care of you. Being taken care of is for cats and dogs, not for women. And nothing ever comes for free. If there is anything I learned in life, it is that you need to keep your wits. They are your gold. Make your own way—ain't nothin' wrong with being independent. It is certainly better than being someone's slave or patsy. Hm. . .yeah, be careful of that Adam's extra rib crap they teach in those church schools y'all go to."

Intuiting the struggles that Thelma's advice would create for an Italian girl, I reached for a Devil Dog and ate it up in two bites. Everything she said entered through my ears and went into mental cold storage. Her advice sounded smart, but in my thirteen-year-old naiveté I did not know what it meant. Years later, when I was asserting my independence, my raised awareness helped me retrieve this valuable lesson.

The ride to the beach was unpleasant. Aunt Lettie went on and on about what she had bought with her Green-Stamp collection until Uncle Vito asked her how many stamps he would need to buy a muzzle. In her innocent, unconfrontational way, Lettie laughed, but her mother took up the insult. "Muzzles are for mad dogs, not noisy pups, Vito. My daughter ain't some bitch."

"Mother, Vito is only joking. Leave him alone." The breeze that rushed through the open windows provided little comfort. The heat had less to do with a hot July day in Florida than it did with our three-week stay in the Johnsons' small house.

Aunt Lettie must have thought the subject needed changing, so she asked if I would let her perm my hair again when we got back to Brooklyn. With the perm question came painful schoolyard memories. No more "Gorilla Head" gibes for me. The last of my perm had fallen on the floor of Uncle Lenny's beauty parlor, where Mom took me to have my hair styled for graduation. Now I'd let my hair grow down to my shoulders. I was eager to cultivate the Barbra Streisand look I equated with being "cool," a word my father had forbidden me to use in reference to anything about myself. (He associated "cool" with jazz musicians who were addicted to heroin and lived in Harlem.) That day, however, I decided it was too hot to repeat what I had already made clear. I said nothing.

But silence never stopped Aunt Lettie once she had set her mind on something. "A nice trimming and a good perm will give you a clean look for high school. Can't you see that yet, Ari?"

The warm feeling from the fantasy was gone by now. I mumbled that I was starving and pushed my aunt's hand away when she reached across to where I was sitting. Dangling her charm bracelet in my face was her way of reminding me that, one day, all those sterling silver trinkets would belong to me, her favorite niece. I felt resentful, so I stuck my head out the window to get a wider view of the boats moored beneath the causeway.

"Sure she will," Uncle Vito said with a tense sarcasm in his voice. "After all, our little girl will remember what a good time she had on vacation when she gets back home. She'll want to do the right thing. Won't you, Arianna? And move that thick head of yours back inside the car before someone knocks it off."

"This is crazy. I am blocking them out because none of this matters." I was no stranger to acting defiant, but that day my reaction came from somewhere else: How weak I must have seemed to the strong-willed Thelma. So I sat back, hands folded over my chest, and tried to look like I was in control.

"Hey, young woman, where are your manners? Tell your Aunt Lettie that of *course* she can perm your hair. Or do you always want to behave like some *ingrato*?"

The view of the Intracoastal, sun sparkling on the water and boats gliding past, heading here and there, was a freeing contrast to the oppressive rigidity in the car. I spoke up. "I want to be a part-time model while I am in high school, and models have long beautiful hair. A model wouldn't be caught dead with some short, crappy perm."

"If your father heard you talking like this," Uncle Vito said, "he would give you a good slapping."

Thelma turned towards me, waiting for my response. But I did not answer. My silence angered Uncle Vito more. "Why do you always have to be this way? Why do you aggravate your parents and show your aunt such disrespect? If you were my daughter—" He cut short his tirade, but not before exclaiming the expected, "Cheez, these damn ungrateful kids my sister raised!" I sat back and closed my eyes. I was humiliated that Thelma had heard how I was treated when I displeased my family. And I was irritated and bruised by Uncle Vito's way of making me feel that I was bad and deserved punishment. He loved me, as he did the rest of his nieces and nephews, but he often told us that we were bad, disrespectful, or downright out of control. "If you were my kids, Cheez, I'd let you know who was boss!"

Once, during Sunday dinner at my grandparents' home, Uncle Vito had told me I was bad. He'd called me a handful. Not yet six years old, I hadn't been sure what that meant, but I knew it wasn't good. And the consequences of my so-called badness were horrific. Damaging.

Julie and I had been racing from one end of the hallway to the other inside the railroad flat. Angry that my longer legs were letting me win the pretend race, my four-year-old sister had tripped and begun crying.

"Be quiet! You'll wake your baby cousin," our mother said. "What's happening in there?"

"Ari tripped me on purpose," Julie lied.

"That's it Arianna, go sit by yourself and be quiet."

"Bella, why don't you make her go downstairs and play outside, so she can run around without waking up Butchie?" Uncle Vito had said this in a more-than-asking tone. In later years, I recognized the eldest son in an Italian American family, especially if he is a war hero, is the alpha authority no one challenges.

"Cheez. If I had kids, they would know when to be quiet. And if they forgot, I would give them a good slapping to remind them."

So on that Sunday, I'd played alone outside my grandparents' apartment building. Spinning round and round like a whirling dervish, I had thought I looked so cute because when the man who smelled like Daddy did when he came home from the Rustic Tavern began to chase me, I believed I was having fun. Then "the man who wanted to take Ari," as would be remembered by the family, ran alongside me until he trapped me inside the doorway. My arms hurt from trying to hold the door shut. Then. . . .

I remember nothing else, although therapist after therapist has tried to help the adult I have become retrieve the memory, move past the trauma. Was that the first time I hid pain behind a wall of denial? What I do know is that my struggle with a neighborhood alcoholic child-molester taught me how to fight, how to protect myself, how to hold some door closed until help arrived.

Back in the apartment, my mother had screamed the way she did when she thought I had done something wrong. (Ironically, it was she who had woken up Baby Butchie.) I recall her screams and my cousin crying while I sat on Grandma Lena's lap. She had assured me everything would be all right. "Tomorrow, I will pick you up from school. We'll walk to the West End Bakery for a Charlotte Russe, just you and me." Grandma's plan, like her love for me, was comforting. I had fallen asleep in her arms.

However, things would not be right for a long, long time. I thought about that Sunday a lot, saw the man's face in my dreams. No matter how I tried, I couldn't remember what he did after he trapped me in the hallway. All I could see was me trying to hold closed the front door, and then the sound of my father pounding the man with his clenched fists. Most likely I feared that my father would soon be pounding me.

Whenever the family brought up the incident, my mother cut the conversation short. Consumed with anxiety, I'd stuff my mouth with food and my mind with grandiose dreams. No one thought to shield me from overhearing the story's brutal ending. "Now that the police beat the life out of him, he'll never have the chance to menace children again." Shortly after that Sunday he had a fatal stroke, and I developed a twitch.

The twitch (I'd raise my right shoulder and move my head alongside it) concerned my family and my teachers. Dr. King, my pediatrician, asked my mother if I had suffered a recent trauma. Squeezing my hand to keep me silent, she told him I had not. I gave a double twitch. Too young to connect all the dots, I was old enough to act out my resentments.

I was glad we were heading home the next day. I wanted to love my aunt and uncle as much as they thought I did, and I felt guilty over that. The complexities of their life experiences, and disappointment that they were childless, were beyond my understanding. Absorbed in my own self-preservation, I returned to the swinging school fantasy and chewed on a fistful of Raisinets.

Papa Jake circled the parking lot three times looking for a spot Thelma approved of. "No, not here, Jake. Kids from the ice cream stand will be sitting all over the car. No, not here, darlin'—I think I see something closer to where we're heading. Ah, crap, didn't you notice there was a hydrant?"

Uncle Vito's tolerance for female willfulness was spent. He turned around to register a complaint with Aunt Lettie and noticed the look on my face. "What is it going to take to make you stop pouting?" I wouldn't answer. "If your father was here, he'd give you a good slap to knock some sense into you, young lady."

That was it. I opened my eyes and gazed at Thelma, who was sitting between me and Aunt Lettie. I put on my best faux Southern accent. "Well, honey, just let me say this: Darlin', since there ain't nothing that's good about a slappin', then there mustn't be any such thing as a good slappin'." Thelma turned away, muffling her laughter. Uncle Vito let out another "Cheez," Aunt Lettie shook her head disapprovingly, and Papa Jake asked, "What the hell is going on?"

"I'M GOING TO LOOK for some shells to bring home. I'll be down near the rocks. The other day, I saw some neat ones there."

"Stay off the rocks, Ari, darlin'" Thelma said. "It's high tide, and they'll be 'specially slippery."

Uncle Vito chimed in. "Young lady, don't go near those rocks now. You hear me?"

Looking back over my shoulder, making sure my uncle and the

others were not watching, I walked out more than twenty-five feet before they spotted me and started shouting and waving me back. Uncle Vito and Papa Jake ran towards the surf, but they could not outrun the wall of water coming at me. Its roar drowned their voices and thrust me underwater. Tumbling downwards, my head barely made contact with a rock, yet it was enough to render me unconscious.

As the waves submerged me just below the water's surface, my body and my mind floated down deeper, to where the Nereids, the sea nymph daughters of Nereus and Doris, sat in council. Inside their coral reef, they were discussing the fate of Italian women who had lived at different times, were born in different places, but shared something in common: They had suffered loss, grave loss. While they met, I floated near a corridor, where I saw the faces of two women whose lives were being discussed. Their stories moved the Nereids so profoundly that they asked their sister, Erato, to petition the Fates for mercy. "At least one of these women should be given a second chance to reclaim her life."

As the lifeguards brought my body to the shore, my mind drifted to a place where a dubbing ceremony was about to begin. "Where is the squire being knighted? What country is this? Who arranged such a ceremony?"

"You did," a voice answered. I looked towards the voice and saw a bearded man who looked like a friendly wizard I had once seen in a Broadway play. "My name is Prall. Come here so we can begin."

"Do my parents know I am here?" I asked.

"No," he explained. "You did not want them to know, so we didn't invite them."

Before I could ask him what I did not want my parents to know, Prall handed me a candle. "Here, hold this; you have worked hard for this moment." I looked around, feeling comforted by the stars and books and the golden strands of the tassel bound to the velvet tam on my head. "Here, take the candle, so I can move the tassel from right to left." Somewhere deep inside my mind, in a field where the past, present, and future are one, I became omniscient.

I heard the voices of the two women. The first said her name was Angelina. And although she spoke Italian, I was somehow able to understand everything she said. Evidently she understood some English, because she smiled when I told her she looked like Dolores, my grandma Mamie's niece. Angelina told me that her family had witnessed the making of Italy, an event that promised much but delivered little to the people who lived south of Rome. "You will write about the burdens of our people, who lived like outcasts in their own country. You will tell the fate too of future generations. I am among those who left to make a better life, but the curse on Southern Italy followed me across the ocean." I started to ask Angelina who she was, but she faded away.

The second woman appeared in her place; she was not old, but she was no longer young. Her face resembled mine. Before she began her story, the woman gazed at me. She did not introduce herself.

"Once, I was a given a diamond ring and the promise of never-ending love, but the giver bruised me. I had the habit of loving people who did me harm. There were scars on my face," she continued. "See, now they have faded, but they are not yet gone."

The candle I was holding enabled me to understand things I had not yet experienced. Intrigued, I wanted to hear more. But Prall diverted my attention. He turned the candle into a pen. He told me that I would meet the women again and, in time, learn much about them. "You will give them voice."

"What does that mean? How long will it be before that happens?" But Prall was vanishing as I spoke.

In his place stood Uncle Vito, who despite his relief at seeing my eyes open, sternly said, "Don't ever do that again, damn you."

OF COURSE MY UNCLE LOVED ME and meant no harm. Yet damned I was for many years to come, all through my adolescence and through much of my adult life. It was as if I had fallen victim to some ancient curse, the kind that haunted Rutino, the rural village my great-mother Angelina, her husband, Orazio, and their two young daughters left in 1892. Angelina died long before I was born, but Great-grandpa's stories always ended with a warning about how we should not tempt fate by acting foolishly.

Way too many of us kids were left-handed. "This must be corrected. They must only use their right hand!" But my mother and my aunts saw no reason to tie a string around our left fingers to create right-handedness. Evil Great-grandpa cautioned, was lurking about; we must be careful. My cousins and I laughed.

Now it seems as if there was an ancient curse. It held me hostage in one alcoholic home after another. Vengeful and relentless, it decreed that I remain powerless against the substance abuse that addled four loved ones: my father, my youngest sister, my husband, and my son. I am still recovering from this curse, which my therapist calls "a family disease." For a very long time it played havoc with my happiness. Sometimes I think about Great-grandpa's insistence that we were in danger of some evil force. I no longer laugh about these things; instead, I try to understand them—and a lot more—so I can change, so I can live a better life.

CHAPTER 2

Angelina's Story / Part One
"In Italia"

6 July 2005, London

Dear Jed,

It was good to hear your voice and catch up a bit. As always, I am enjoying London, but miss you and all my NY friends. Glad you'll be back from Santa Fe in time for the Lincoln Center Festival. Listening to Joshua Bell always lessens the sadness of summer vacation coming to an end.

Can't believe I've been gone for six weeks. As I had hoped, the time away allowed me to complete the manuscript. Before I get to the British Library tomorrow, I'll send it along with this letter. Your offer to edit it was more than generous, but that's you. I meant it when I said I don't mind sending a hard copy instead of an electronic file; I too remain a Luddite.

And when we spoke, I forgot to thank you for having Sara send the Italian American literature notes I'd left at school.

They helped me fold in some insightful history of the challenges Italy, Italians, and Italian Americans encountered across the centuries. Earlier today, Jana Sessions at Magnum House requested an overview of the book for their publicity. What I drafted follows; please share your response.

I just called Virgin Atlantic and booked a flight for next Thursday. Looking forward to a day or two in Brighton, breathing in the sea air, before coming home. Writing this book has been an odyssey. I had expected it to challenge and exhaust me—and it has—but the long view of the past also has left me feeling more connected to myself and to the world.

So you're probably wondering what's next. I've decided it's time to tell my own story. I want to experiment with fictionalized memoir, which, as you know, privileges experiences and ideas over strict adherence to fact. Creating events in Angelina's Story was so compelling. Now I'll delve into memory and see how I can recreate myself.

Please give my best to Gary, and hugs to those gorgeous cats. See you soon.

With love,

Arianna

FOR THE PUBLISHER'S PUBLICITY:

Angelina's Story is Arianna Naso's biography of her great-grandmother, Angelina Longo (1870–1933), a southern Italian born into a family that fought against foreign powers to unite Italy. In the Mezzogiorno, the area south of Rome, scarcity and doing without had been as timeless as the hills facing the Amalfi Coast. Angelina was among the millions who emigrated after they were betrayed by the newly installed Piedmontese government. Yet the ghosts of Angelina's losses follow her to Brooklyn, where her husband, Orazio, lives la dolce vita, and her children shamelessly choose modern living over strict adherence to tradition. Tragically, the haunting rears its unrelenting head.

Angelina's Story

—Manuscript for Magnum House, July 2005

Angelina's Story / Part One
1848–1892 : "In Italia"

Women bound by blood,
Grief endured for place, for sons.
Sing muse, weave our tale.

NGELINA LONGO LAY AWAKE IN SILENCE. She swallowed the pills Minnie had brought, her lips struggling to form a kiss. After a few minutes, she feigned sleep, hoping her daughter would leave her bedside and tend to her own life. What a beautiful young wife her Minnie was. Ah, what a treasure, she thought. My girl with eyes like emeralds! So much love in her, so much joy.

Since her stroke, Angelina's family had taken turns caring for her every need. Her three daughters each spent two days a week feeding, washing, and wheeling her from bed to commode to table to garden. On Sundays the entire family gathered, trying to provide an atmosphere of normalcy. However, for three years the Longo home had been the site of unspeakable grief.

In June 1930, the Longos' eldest son, Michael, had taken the life of his mistress and her lover before turning the gun in his left hand to his head. On a sunny day in June, she and Orazio, surrounded by family, *paesani*, and some of their Americana neighbors had buried their son in South Brooklyn's Green-Wood Cemetery. In the days that followed, Angelina had stayed in bed or sat in the garden drinking espresso. She could not understand why a handsome young man left a good wife and beautiful daughter to move in with some *puttana*, who spent his money and brought her *cumpà* to his bed when his back was turned.

This America, this place where living is easier than it was *in italia*, maybe there is too much here, too many temptations. Not like *italia mia*, where people know right from wrong. Here nothing stays the same. One day people are respecting what they must, but the next. . . O, *Dio mio*, I could never understand what my Orazio calls the "modern way." And now this strange way has taken my son.

MICHAEL WAS HANDSOME, he was fun; everyone in the neighborhood loved him. At 6'2", he towered over the other men in the Longo family. He was all Rotolo, more Greek than Italian in appearance. "Like a movie star, a Valentino," the cousins would say when Michael entered the room. Young Joseph might have been the gentler and more constant of the Longo boys, but inwardly he resented his older brother's athletic build and dark good looks. "What a dancer!" was the automatic response when his name was mentioned. Sure he didn't like to work, but that's why Orazio bought the store on Fourth Avenue, to keep an eye on him. Yes, he was often selfish and had his way with women, and if he had done the right thing by his family, none of this would have happened. *Che scorno.* What a shame.

Angelina asked herself questions and explored possibilities that drove her into her final struggle with depression. Why was Michael so obsessed with, how they say. . .these speakeasies? What made him bring that dance-hall floozy back from Chicago? How could he set her up in an apartment just one street away from the home he shared with his wife and daughter? Her headaches and melancholia had become unbearable after Michael left his family and moved in with Louise. This disgrace, and the rampage that ensued, were unfathomable to Angelina's Italian immigrant sensibility.

HER FAMILY BELIEVED THE TRAGEDY had caused her stroke. In the months that followed Michael's funeral, she cried day and night. She rarely slept. One Saturday afternoon, she complained to Orazio that her head was pounding. Her face felt numb.

"You are making yourself sick." No matter how hard she prayed or how much they cried, he reminded her, Michael was not coming back. "Go rest on the sofa while I heat some soup. If you are going to get strong, you must eat." Before he returned with the soup, a jarring pain caused her to slide off the sofa. Initially, Orazio thought the fall had bruised her face. His wife lay there silently, a distorted version of herself.

The stroke left her speechless and without mobility on her right side. After she returned from a two-week stay in Methodist Hospital, she spent her convalescence living inside her mind. The internal chatter was deafening, but no one heard a word. Her family had often told her that, since she understood every word of English, she should speak the language. America was the family's home; she should stop limiting herself to the few words and phrases she infused with Italian. Now they wished she could speak, anything, if they could only hear her voice.

The family made no further mention of Michael, not to each other, at least not in front of their mother. His name went unspoken. He had been unborn. Future generations might never have known of him if curious youngsters had not asked about the girl *Michele* who died young and was buried in Green-Wood Cemetery. For a long time, their questions went unanswered. Who wants to dig up such a story?

Who might be listening? Who knows what the consequences might be? God forbid!

Yet after she was released from the hospital and settled back on 18th Street, Angelina decided she needed to recover for Orazio, and for their remaining children—Mary, known to everyone as Mamie; Joseph; Anna; and Minnie. These children were Americans, and she and her husband had helped them make beautiful lives in this strange country. They were her reason for not closing her eyes and sinking into the hazy world of medication. Her Michael. "*O, Dio*," once again the feeling of profound loss.

But even when she was in the grip of replaying the horrid event in her mind, the sound of her family moving about the house, taking care of things, and loving each other provided her with a reason to recover. She found comfort too when Orazio or one of the children held her hand. From her bed she watched her grandchildren playing in the backyard, marking the ground with chalk or playing Pick Up Sticks. The sight of them never failed to yield a fractured smile.

ANGELINA HAD NEVER ADJUSTED to life in New York. "Thissa pazzo Brookealeen" was the way she responded to stories about the exploits of assimilated Italians who moved about the city and acted more like Americans than Italians. They dressed in the latest fashions. They allowed their women to cut their hair and smoke cigarettes. She had never seen the point of learning much English. And while her children quickly became fluent in the language they learned on the block and at school, they spoke Italian at home. Like Orazio, they were her translators when it came to communicating with the neighbors or store owners along Fifth Avenue. But, following their parents' example, they identified themselves as Italians, though what they knew about the old country consisted mostly of familiar stories about Rutino and local lore and traditions set against a backdrop of memories shared by family and paesani. Angelina believed it was her duty to preserve tradition within the family circle.

Each of her children owned a home and had a spouse and children. Beautiful grandchildren, American children. They wanted for nothing. Through the hard times that began in 1929, each of the men, her sons and sons-in-law, had the good fortune to keep his job and his dignity. Orazio opened a delicatessen in one of the stores in the new garden apartment complex on Fourth Avenue, where Michael and Fred, Anna's husband, worked. Minnie's Lenny opened a beauty parlor next to the delicatessen, so Angelina's family's stability had far surpassed the expectations she had brought from the tiny village of Rutino forty years earlier. "Hope will return," she tried to convince herself. "Once before, I learned to live with unspeakable loss." When the sad thoughts or tears returned, she'd visualize the warmth in her family's eyes and their love. But oh, the loss, the shame.

Like others whose experience of loss haunts their most courageous efforts to find peace, she was not always successful. Often as she lay in bed, her mind traveled back to Rutino, to all she had been left behind. She would close her eyes and recall the smell of the pink, purple, and yellow wildflowers in the field behind *la Chiesa di San Michele Arcangelo*. After a spring shower, with petals heavy with beads of rain, the flowers gave off a fresh scent—new, alive, full of promise. On the hillside, daffodils, violets, and windflowers arrived each spring and stayed until late fall.

Now, lying in bed, her mind's eye saw washerwomen at work by the River Alento, scrubbing while they sang or told stories that grew longer than the shadows cast by the trees on the slope of Mount Stella. At Sunday mass in *la Chiesa di San Michele Arcangelo* wearing their humble finery, these women emblemized the gentleness of the *Cilentani* people.

ANGELINA DELIGHTED IN REMEMBERING the trees with the white figs she and her mother boiled and diced for baking peasant bread, *pane dei poveri.* She knew that, when the fig trees were covered for protection from the winter frost, they resembled aged peasants. But she did not know they had originally come from southern Arabia and been planted over two millennia before by Greek colonizers.

Other times she pictured her family. Frequently, the odd blend of solace, loss, and exhaustion evoked by memory brought her to sleep, where family and Rutino became splinters of meaning. In this state she met herself again, the self she had left behind in 1892.

Precious was her memory of her father, Giuseppe. Many a day after Mamie, Anna, or Minnie left her sickbed, Angelina drifted back to Mount Stella. There she walked with her Papa while he taught her to appreciate the beauty and strength of the chestnut groves and oak woods. "Nature's sounds," he'd tell her, "are made by some divine mandolin."

"If you are quiet, Angelina *mia*, you will see a fox or wild boar hunting for food. In His goodness, God provides them with plenty, sometimes more than he makes available to those who toil with empty stomachs and emptier pockets." From a ledge high up on the mountain, they'd marvel at the clouds above.

"Look, Papa, this one looks like a big heart puffed up with smoke. And that one reminds me of a baby lying on his side, looking for his mother."

As a child, Angelina believed that heaven began at the peak of the mountain at Stella Maris, the sanctuary dedicated to Our Lady. Once aboard carts and donkeys, the extended Rotolo family visited the sanctuary to pray for a young cousin dying of tuberculosis. Before returning to Rutino, they lunched on bread, cheese, fennel stalks, and some wine. The impending loss of their beloved Emilio subdued the characteristic gaiety of such gatherings. Yet their enduring spirit and love for each other made the moment warm, safe. Zi Annuziato sang a song, while her father and uncles strummed their mandolins. Just as the Rutinese did while working in the fields, the family shared their unspoken grief communally. Actions, not words, conveyed their feelings. While they ate and listened to the music, they held hands, humming and stroking each other's cheeks.

But not Angelina. As quick to tears as she was slow to acknowledge anger, she left her food untouched and sat alone at the base of the sanctuary, lost in thought. Once again she felt an unfathomable darkness take hold. She wondered why families had to endure such suffering and pain. Of course God will not allow our Emilio to die. He is just a boy, so young, so good. It would kill his parents.

Still, she found comfort in the sounds coming from the mandolins. And she told herself the sadness she felt was an act of love for her family. To acknowledge grief was selfish. It angered God. Her simple understanding of spiritual morality made self-awareness of personal feelings and needs a sin. Throughout her life, Angelina practiced the Mezzogiorno's rural Catholicism, carrying it from Rutino to New York as the ancient Romans had carried their household gods from place to place. In New York the Italian immigrants' superstitions and lack of understanding of church dogma was looked down upon by the Irish Catholic hierarchy and by priests and nuns in the local parishes. Yet Angelina always held on to the prayers of her youth and ancient rituals, like blessing her family with holy water on Easter.

Her mother warned her that dwelling on disappointments and fears was prideful. "If we walk in Christ's footsteps and put others before ourselves, we will be rewarded in heaven." But Angelina found that, no matter how good you are in this life, there is loss and there is pain. None of this was surprising to her; it was just the way it was.

Michael's death, she thought, had been punishment for his selfish ways. But really he had still been a youth, misguided, not bad. He'd had such promise, so much life. Would a prayer said outside Stella Maris bring her peace? She envisioned herself there with her family, looking down at the Cilento countryside. There things stayed the same. Not like New York, where rapid change was expected for no reason at all.

She recalled the smell of wild mint growing beside the old sanctuary, until the sounds of the Jewish peddlers hawking their wares brought her back to her present state in her South Brooklyn bedroom. Some days she heard Irish children singing "Too-Ra-Loo-Ra-Loo-Ral" and drifted into a world that was both everything and nothing like the one into which she had been born. She loved the words of the Irish ballad of missing home, of missing one's mother. Voiceless, she repeated to herself the words sung in the language she had never embraced. From her deathbed three thousand miles away, she remembered Rutino.

> *Oft, in dreams I wander*
> *To that cot again,*
> *I feel her arms a huggin' me*
> *As when she held me then.*
> *And I hear her voice a hummin'*
> *To me as in days of yore*
> *When she used to rock me fast asleep*
> *Outside the cabin door.*

She dreamt of water rising towards her home and of baby rabbits. Running, running, she and her sisters hoped to catch the rabbits before they spoiled Mama's lettuce patch. Fortunately, the medicated sleep spared her from the memory of the old wound, and of the time before with the little hands and "Santa Lucia."

OENOTRIA WAS THE ANCIENT NAME of the pastoral area east of the Bay of Salerno in the Italian Mezzogiorno, the region south of Rome, whose people northern Italians regarded as their brutish country relations. According to Aristotle, under old King Italus the Oenotrians received laws and shepherds learned husbandry. Meals were eaten communally, and perhaps the locals' love for large gatherings can be traced to this early time.

Today, the region is called Cilento and its people Cilentani. Among the small, medieval-looking communes sits a mountain-top town, Rutino, bounded by the River Alento and Mount Stella. In the late nineteenth century, as soon as the northern governors sanctioned emigration, much of the peasant and artisan population left for the Americas. Its population dwindled to less than one thousand.

The area's natural beauty and proximity to the sea beckoned sixth-century BC Greeks seeking refuge from advancing Persian soldiers. The Greeks raided the area at the rim of the *Mesogeios*, the western Mediterranean. Appreciating the beauty and geographic benefits, they set up temples to venerate their gods. The Romans later named the region Magna Graecia, boasting ownership of the sea they called *Mare Nostrum*.

Eleven miles north of Rutino sits Paestum, the former Poseidonia, the sea god's domain. Doric temples to Hera and Athena stand as testimony to the once-vibrant society. Paestum's loyalty to Rome during its contest with Hannibal was repaid with the right to mint its own coinage.

Further west, on the Tyrrhenian coast near the Bay of Salerno, sits Palinuro, named in honor of Aeneas' pilot. Neptune, the sea god with vengeful and exacting ways, wanted a sacrificial victim before the Trojan Aeneas fulfilled his destiny: founding Rome. He ordered Somnus, the Roman god of sleep, to perform the vengeful deed.

The story goes that Somnus wet Palinurus' temples with the dew from the rivers of the underworld. But the pilot fought off sleep, holding fast to the tiller and swimming ashore. There he met the half-human, half-bird Sirens—"barbarians," Aeneas calls them—who attacked and killed what they mistook for a prize. Once, Demeter had commanded these songstresses to return her only child from Hades' underworld kingdom. But whatever efforts the Sirens made were not fruitful. They fell from grace.

The grieving goddess banished the Sirens to a southern Italian sea-side cliff. From there, they exact their own revenge on unsuspecting sea travelers, countless Palinuruses destined never to reach safety. The Sibyl of Cumae, Aeneas' guide to the underworld, prophesied that justice would be exacted for the dead pilot's unburied state. She told Palinurus, "The neighboring cities will be goaded by the plague, a sign for heaven to make peace with your bones."

Those familiar with the story of the long, tortured history of southern Italy can understand the enduring impact of the Sibyl's curse. But what is harder to discern, especially before setting out to search into the annals of one's family history and crevices of a troubled soul, is how all this wrath hid in a beat-up trunk that landed at Ellis Island and relocated in South Brooklyn. Somehow this cursed legacy snaked its way down to the port and boarded ship. From there it followed the impoverished exiles seeking redemption in a new land.

Perhaps Neptune, Demeter, and the Sibyl of Cumae's curses are here to stay. Whatever the case, it is undeniable that the Cilento region has had its hauntings. And they are beautiful, dreadful, and full of history. Who knows what will happen in the future? Or *chissà*, as the Cilentani say.

THE ROAD TO RUTINO is a steep, rock-filled path. Ancient Greeks traveled up the mountain, as did nineteenth-century revolutionaries searching for soldiers to fight their Spanish overlords. Now abandoned by locals who sailed to America to build better lives, and others who traveled north in search of higher wages and better times, Rutino sits like a lonely goddess left behind by an ancient mariner. Hope of her lover's return is non-existent. Perhaps he met the wrathful Sirens or, like many Italian emigrants, encountered deadly illness at sea. If so, the goddess' man sleeps below the waves, alone with the memory of his last torturous moments.

A history of hardship did not stop southern Italians in the nineteenth century from joining the *Risorgimento*, the fight to unify Italy. Under Garibaldi's leadership, they defeated the Spanish and their supporters, but the benefits of victory proved elusive. From the onset of unification in 1861, they and their children were despised and disenfranchised by the Savoy government and the church in Rome. Although they were Catholics, they knew little about the Church's history and less of its theology. Their rituals seemed ridiculous, if not downright blasphemous. Clergy visiting from the north were stunned by the Southerners' poverty and their belief in what seemed like endless superstitions.

Visiting government officials spoke vaguely about land reform. But projects like irrigation and road building aimed at improving the quality of life failed to materialize in the new Italians' lifetime. Representatives of King Vittorio Emmanuele and his minister, Cavour, regarded these uneducated farmers and artisans as inferior humans. To their horror, the dark-skinned southerners spoke brutish dialects and lived like the animals that shared their ramshackle homes. Reports described them as being no better than Africans.

A desire to end such sorrow and find a better life was the wish of millions of new Italians from the Mezzogiorno, including Angelina Longo. Imagine the chorus of prayers to Jesus and his mother in the steerage compartments of those dreadful ocean liners! Who was watching, listening, believing it was their right to redeem some, but not others?

SMALL IN SIZE, ANGELINA HAD THE REGAL BEARING of a goddess fit for Italy's ancient Greek temples. Eyes and hair the color of night intensified her prettiness to the point where she seemed overburdened by the darkness. The third child in a family of four daughters and one son, she was born in 1870, nine years after Rutino became part of a united Italy. While they struggled to raise their young family,

Giuseppe Rotolo and Carmela Volpe, like other southern Italians, were aware that freedom had not resulted in liberty or prosperity.

Hunger and oppression had not disappeared with the Spanish governors. The northern Italians imposed laws that did not benefit them. Worse still, the new taxes made life more difficult. Many in Angelina's family had fought to deliver Italy from the hands of foreigners. Each story they told made the same point regarding unification: They had been betrayed. Raising their voices or fists in the name of freedom would not make a difference. That course of action had been tried. It had failed. Anyhow, what is freedom without bread? Liberal ideals are meaningless when you are barely managing to feed your family. And who could understand these rich men's ideas, even if you are curious about their meaning?

Angelina's mother, Carmela Volpe, had been born in January 1848, the year revolutions swept across Europe. Looking back at the reformist ideals of the Napoleonic era, as well as its own imperial past, Italians staged a major attempt to oust foreign rulers. Carmela and a new Italy: two bodies traveling through a dark passage into the light of a life shaded by a precarious future. Generations of relatives learned that, as the feisty Carmela moved down the birth canal, regional freedom fighters marched through nearby fields, gathering recruits for a proposed takeover of Naples. Rutino was the next stop after Torchiaro. Word had it that, at 7:00 p.m., Costabile Carduce would speak in Chirico's Inn. All men were urged to come hear the plan for securing Italy's freedom. By 6:00 p.m., the piazza had been filled. The air was tense. Many families suffered from the rent increases resulting from new taxes imposed by Spanish authorities in Naples.

The Volpes later recounted how baby Carmela arrived swiftly and safely, but the birth of an Italy ruled by Italians required twelve more years of gestation.

Salvatore Volpe; his younger brother, Francesco; Carlo, his uncle;

and his father-in-law, Luigi Pinto, sat at a rear table telling old stories of Italians who had taken action against Spanish overlords. Luigi recalled the rebellion of 1820.

"As you know, in '20 a priest named De Luca, a tough *carbonaro*, led a call to action. Rebels gathered at the fortress in Palinura, where they waited in vain for Neapolitan supporters. The unfortunate De Mattia brothers were captured in the Valle della Lucania after royal supporters squashed the rebellion. Their hands were bound; and they were tortured."

"I forget. Why they are buried in Rutino?" his son-in-law's brother asked.

"Well, Francesco, after being beaten with clubs, they died on the hill leading up to our town. Their families were unable to bury their bodies. But some nights later—I hear it was a moonless night—locals took the bodies and buried them in the churchyard of *la Chiesa di San Michele*."

This night, the Volpe and Pinto men had not gone out to seek trouble; they were just following the women's orders to leave the house while they helped Caterina Pinto Volpe give birth. However, much changed after Carduce spoke.

"Italy needs soldiers to fight for its liberty. We must drive out the Spanish bastards who use our land and our daughters without shame. We will meet Commander Poeribo and his men, our comrades, in the Valle Diano, hopefully with our bellies full of salami, mozzarella, and some bread donated by your good Mayor Cuoco. From there we will march to Naples. There we will join columns led by Vinciprova and others. Look well at these colors: white, red, and green. They are the colors of a new nation, our new nation. Italy will soon belong to us and our children. Better days lie ahead. And to match our three-colored banner, we will have autonomy, comfort, and pride."

Salvatore Volpe noticed the listeners nodding in support.

"No longer will our families go hungry and without land of our own. Many of us live worse than the chickens and pigs that share our humble homes. At least those creatures are in the care of people with regard for their worth. You must come with us and fight for what we deserve. We will drive out the Spanish and their Austrian supporters. A new Italy waits."

Carduce wiped the sweat from his forehead. Someone brought him a glass of local wine. Glasses held high, the men shouted "*Per la nuova italia.*" The following night, many local farmers and artisans, including several members of baby Carmela's family, left Rutino with Carduce. But they never reached Naples.

On January 18, in a cart driven by Nino the donkey, Salvatore's cousins, Roberto, Santo, and Pasquale Volpe, traveled to Corleto. The men knew the roads throughout Cilento. For generations the Volpe family had traversed them, selling straw hats, a side business to supplement the few *lire* earned from toiling in fields owned by those more fortunate than themselves. The Volpes were among the four hundred men, including some royalist sympathizers, cheered on by fighters from Corleto. But the momentum was short lived. Slow at grasping much beyond his daily routine, Santo Volpe could not understand why they were not marching into Naples.

Deft at simplifying things so Santo could understand, his younger brother explained. "Listen. There are not enough of us here to win a fight with the king's men. Men from Avellino and other towns did not show up. We need to go back to Rutino and wait for a better time. You understand?"

"Sure, Pasquale, we need more fighters to make a new Italy. We aren't enough to send the king back to Spain. Right?"

"*Si, hai ragione, fratello mi.* We must wait a little longer."

In July, another rebellion broke out in the Cilento, and Roberto and Pasquale were in Paestum when the royalist forces arrived. The battle was swift and bloody. Roberto returned home with Pasquale's body and a deep hatred for all things foreign. When the sheepherder,

Pepe, came by to have his hat mended, he brought news that the king's men were looking for the rebels. The family instructed Santo, "Say nothing to no one." The young man, whose difficult birth had weakened his mind, stopped cutting the hay stalks and shook his head. "When they ask, I'll tell them my brother died of the fever."

"No, you say *nothing*," his mother ordered. "If they question you, we will explain you are a mute who can neither speak nor think."

At baby Carmela's christening, relatives and neighbors spewed their anger over the blood spilled in nearby Laurino. Just as he had done in 1820, King Ferdinand failed to grant a constitution. Feeling powerless, they cursed him, his wife's Austrian family, and any Italian who supported them.

Little Carmela grew up listening to stories of how the leader of the rebellion in Corleto, Nicola Antonio Causale, hid in a cart under bales of wheat destined for Palinuro. She giggled heartily whenever they explained he traveled from Palinuro to Naples dressed as a nun. From there sympathizers helped him escape to Malta.

Every so often, a priest brought news to the village of revolutionaries "waving red, green, and white mischief." He'd remind villagers the Holy Father did not approve. Before returning to Caserta, a visiting chaplain, Father Nardone, part of the Viceroy's entourage at the Reggio, gave a farewell sermon. Valorizing the faithful and the meek whose sacrifices would be rewarded with "heavenly glory," he stepped down from the altar, looking at the parishioners as if he were intent on remembering faces. He pointed a finger at one Rutinese after another. "Before I bid farewell to you, good people of Rutino, I want to remind you to give as generously as you can and pay your loving Father Antonio your deepest respect. He is God's representative here among you. Bring honor to those whose ordained right it is to receive it. You can be guided by the ancient saying 'For God and for King,' and if you take heed, all the blessings of eternal life to come will be yours. Eternal hell fire awaits prideful rebels. Through Matthew, his apostle, Jesus promised, 'Blessed are the peacemakers, for they shall be called the children of God.'"

Every time the story of that sermon was told, little Carmela waited for Zi Francesco and her Papa to clink a glass of wine and shout, "Matthew also says, 'Blessed are those who are persecuted for righteousness' sake, for theirs is the kingdom of heaven.' *A buon' anima Pasquale.*"

During spring 1860, twelve-year-old Carmela joined her mother and aunts at the long table to weave straw hats. Illiterate as the rest of her family, she possessed a natural talent for design. The new weaving and brim patterns she created enhanced the Volpes' reputation. Of course the credit for them was given to her father. He must maintain the position of esteem reserved for the father of the family. Carmela was resentful that her ideas went unacknowledged, but she was a good daughter: She knew her place. As expected, she swallowed her disappointment and did not complain.

Throughout her life, this would be her alternative to confrontation. And although she never voiced her disappointment, she seized every opportunity to display her various gifts: at the table weaving hats, in the garden tending her plants, and, after she married, in the bedroom, creating pleasure for her husband, as well as for herself. Instinctively she knew variety was the spice of life, even for impoverished rustics.

The Volpes and their neighbors were swept up in the cry for a new Italy. Unclear about the northern Italians' plan for liberal reform and national unity, they were however curious about the rebel Giuseppe Garibaldi. Their neighbor Michele Mangione told them how Garibaldi was the hero of *La Giovine italia,* a group of political activists gathered by the Genoese, Giuseppe Mazzini. "Soon Garibaldi will return from America and lead the fight in the south to drive out the Spanish. He is a simple man, someone like us. We must join this fight."

In the Mezzogiorno, the idea of a nation was an abstraction far removed from the reality of daily life. More real was the scarcity of basic necessities and rent increases. That need convinced the Volpes to support the revolt. Salvatore asked his cousins, "What good has come from these Spanish tyrants? Do they care that we are starving? Mangione is right. We must fight for liberty and for bread." In the end many of Carmela's relatives, and those of her intended, Giuseppe Rotolo, joined Mangione and other local reformers in the struggle for Italian unification. No one bothered to ask about the men that would govern the new Italy.

Carmela remembered the night the rebel soldiers arrived, but she never learned the actual events of what occurred when a flash storm muddied the steep path up to Rutino.

Lightning spooked their horses. Some lost their footing and slid into puddles; riders jostled about like sinners in Dante's hell. A scout found a cave beneath some fallen trees at the foot of Mount Stella. The rebel leader reasoned that, if some of them took shelter there, the rest had a better chance of making the difficult climb. Horses were secured and fed before the men entered the cave. Behind a crevice, one of them spied a young woman, who explained she was waiting for her one true love. But her lover, believing his lust had provoked God's thunderous wrath, had turned his donkey around when it started hailing.

Blood heated by the passion of their cause, the soldiers took turns violating their prey. They were convinced she was an enchantress sent by local spirits. Entering her body would transform them into heroes who'd liberate italia.

The next morning, they joined their comrades in Rutino. The young woman considered her fate. Her parents would blame her for the brutal transgression. So, abandoned by her

*lover and ravaged by strangers, she hanged herself from a large
oak tree beside the cave.*

In the Mezzogiorno sacrifice and hardship have a long history. And they exist alongside failed dreams and false promises, a bizarre quartet that offends the gods.

LED BY PATRIOTS LORENZO CURZIO, Filipo Giovanni Vecchi of Corleto, and Mangione, the recruits marched through Cilento, arriving in Salerno on September 7, the same day Garibaldi reached Naples. Two days later, Carmela's uncle, Luigi Pinto, sent a reassuring note to his wife Modesta. He had been charged with guarding Nicola Causale, the hero of '48, recently returned from exile in Malta. "Guarding Causale, I became part of a small group at the meeting with Garibaldi in Sala Consilina. What stories I will bring back to Rutino. We are close to victory!"

Each morning the women prayed for their men's safety and quick return. Since they left, income from the sale of produce had diminished. With fewer hands working the fields, many of the lemons and oranges had died on the vine. Each month, purchasing olive oil and supplies for their hat business had become more difficult.

On the evening of October 26, the villagers' prayers were answered. One of Garibaldi's Red Shirts asked the mayor to gather the villagers. Carmela and her younger brother, Alfonso, sat on a tree stump in the piazza.

"Fellow countrymen, today is a glorious day. Though we must continue the fight to wrest our homeland from thieves and interlopers, I bring news from Volturno. Today, our men, led by the valiant Giuseppe Garibaldi, have defeated the Spanish army and their supporters! Total victory is within reach, and soon we will celebrate the rebirth of Italy! Before I leave to carry this message to Lustra, I urge you to support our cause with food, clothing, blankets, horses if you have any, and of course with your prayers. God bless you and God bless *italia*."

The following year, using scraps of red, green, and white fabric, Carmela and her cousins made a tablecloth for Christmas dinner. The children wondered how long it would be until they met King Vittorio Emmanuele.

ALTHOUGH IT HAD BEEN ALMOST FIFTEEN YEARS since Carmela married Giuseppe Rotolo, their dreams remained unfulfilled. Their wages barely covered the rent for the small cottage that stood close to the one occupied by Carmela's family. But still they hoped before long they would own their own land. Their compare, Carlo Perotta, a fighter with the Red Shirts in Naples, recalled the promises spoken by his captain. "Once victory is secured, the new leadership will make sure farm land is redistributed. All Italians will have a chance at a good life." Yet in the years following Vittorio Emmanuele's coronation, no mention was made of land redistribution. This promise, and others, never materialized.

Spirits lifted when a Turinese official came to town. But in reality all he did was pat villagers on the back and tell Mayor Borrelli that improvements were on the way. Salvatore Volpe and his friends asked the mayor to write a letter to officials in Naples. "Ask them for news about the aqueduct and about land prices, too. For so long, there has been no word." The mayor reported that his letter had gone unanswered. When Salvatore urged him to write again, Borrelli told him to be patient. He was confident that, before long, they would receive good news. It became a stock joke, one born of chronic disappointment, that each January, when Carlo and Giuseppe shook hands and wished each other *buona fortuna* for the new year, Giuseppe asked, "This is the year when we get the land, yes?"

In 1882, the Rotolos, like other Rutinese and Southern Italians, had no prospect of land opportunities, no news about when the aqueduct project would begin, but they were sending their young men to the Italian army and their *lire* to pay various taxes created by the new Northern foreigners, the Italian government. *Disgraziata.*

The Casati Act of 1859 legislated compulsory schooling, so Italian children could read and write. After unification, the act was enforced unevenly throughout the Mezzogiorno; the staggering rate of illiteracy remained. In 1868 there was a rumor that a Northern official planned to visit villages in Salerno and Lucania. Rutino's mayor, wanting to make *la bella figura*, urged the monsignor of *San Michele* to convert the front room of the rectory into a school room. The chipped cement walls were decorated with a tri-colored flag, pictures of Garibaldi and the pope, and a crucifix. The children shared ink wells, pens, notebooks, and used books his deputy brought back from Salerno.

As late as 1881, professors at the University of Naples wrote to the ministers in charge of education, advocating for building a school and educating the children living south of Rome. Such projects, they were told, were of course important. But they were not priorities and, as the saying goes, "Rome was not built in a day."

Carmela and Giuseppe Rotolo were proud when their daughter Angelina learned to write letters and words, and sign her name, during her one year in the makeshift school room. She could even read a little, but more importantly, she could keep an account of the family's expenses and their meager income.

Rutino's makeshift school room was crowded and noisy. The teacher, Concetta D'Orio, daughter of Don Luigi D'Orio, the largest landowner in Rutino, often did more scolding than teaching. Although she spun the story that her "skills" and reputation for "loving children" had impressed the selection committee, in actuality it was her father's influence and the scarcity of qualified candidates. Drills, memorization, and repetition, she was convinced, were the tools of teaching. When they failed, a slap on the back of the head motivated a reluctant student. Barely hidden beneath her reputed love for her students was resentment. "They come in dirty and exhausted, and they are never responsive to anything that makes them think." The townspeople knew her own schooling had been minimal, but no one wanted to offend Don Luigi. Yet despite the horrendous conditions and her ineffective teaching, learning sometimes happened.

The local children took pride in their accomplishments, skipping home to their cottages with tales from the state licensed story books and of practicing the letters that formed the spelling of their names. "A-n-g-e-l-i-n-a. See, Papa? It makes my name! I never knew what it looked like before Signorina Concetta wrote it in my little book. Tomorrow, if you like, I could ask her to show me how to make the letters for your name and for Mama's."

Angelina learned to read a little and write her letters and numbers. She could even sign her name. But when the year ended, she felt relieved. Beyond the basic communication and tabulation skills that had their practical purposes, she had no concept of how an education might enrich her life. Priests, politicians, and the rich—learning suited them. Once the year had ended, she could devote herself to weaving hats and helping her mother run the household. There would be more time to indulge her two passions: stitching floral designs on the *letto* for her dowry, and singing along while Papa played the mandolin.

"Sit still, Angelina. Let me finish braiding your hair. Don't you want to look pretty for the *festa*?" To make sure she stood out among the village girls, Carmela embroidered rosebuds along the neckline and hem of her daughter's one good dress. "Ah, you may be thin and shorter than most girls your age, but those little bumps beneath your dress show you are becoming a woman. Now, unless we hurry, we will not get a good spot at church. After mass, we will join Serafina Longo's family and have a nice view of her grandson, Orazio. He will play the part of the good angel."

Each year on the Sunday closest to May 8, a Rutinese child, made up like the archangel Michael, partakes in an outdoor performance in which he defeats the Devil in a battle of good against evil. Gliding through the air supported by wires and pulleys, the "archangel" evokes a heavenly visitation. Each year, the villagers look forward to the *festa* and cheering on *San Michele* in his fight with the devil in the open spaces near the church named in his honor.

"Good always wins over evil. Yes, Mama?"

Carmela shrugged, remembering the night she and Alfonso had sat listening to the Red Shirt report the patriots' victory. The Bourbons had been devils all right, but since the arrival of a new Italy, there had been no angelic redemption. Wanting to keep Angelina's spirits high, Carmela whispered, "*Si, cara*, that is what I hear. . . . Come, Angelina, if we hurry, we can see his parents escort Orazio to mass. Be sure to give him a warm greeting, and for his mother, Signora Maria, a little kiss on the cheek. During the performance, you must cheer him on. Your father and I think Orazio Longo will make a wonderful husband. And the Longos are better than most at making money. Signor Michele has arranged that, after his next birthday, Orazio will become apprenticed to Don Francesco Altieri, the master barber in Postiglione. We and his parents are in agreement—you will marry once he establishes himself."

Angelina was confused. She had known Orazio as a distant cousin but never paid him any attention when she saw him at the home of a relative or during their year of compulsory education. When she thought of herself becoming a wife and mother, she conjured up a version of herself surrounded by her children listening while she played the mandolin. The husband she imagined was soft spoken and understanding like her Papa, not like some of her uncles or villagers who beat their wives, drank too much wine, or both. *So now*, she thought, *I know the face of my future husband. At least they are not marrying me to the Devil.*

"Now, remember, stand straight when you see him, but keep your eyes down. Never be bold with a man. If you are ever tempted, think about the story I told you of the young woman hanging in the cave after she gave in to her passion."

At thirteen, Orazio was small and lean, weighing in just under the forty-kilogram limit set for the role. The blue dress edged in gold, and the *cartapesta* wings, intensified his handsome looks. He seemed fierce, ready to slay his hellish opponent. And when he swung, from the pulley hook, sword and shield of the angel in either hand, Angelina became anxious. What if he ever came to see her as his adversary? Would he draw a sword on her? What if he made her feel passion? Would she wind up like the girl outside the cave? Angelina's mood turned dark.

Carmela prayed that, once she began to menstruate, her daughter's moods would pass. Instead, her "sad days" increased; she was quicker to tears than ever. Giuseppe had an idea. Next time he brought hats to Lustra, he'd ask Nicola Brigante to reconsider the price for his late father's mandolin. On the morning of her twelfth birthday, Giuseppe told Angelina, "Bring in the package someone left under the lilac bush while we slept."

"I will treasure this gift always, even when I am an old woman with fingers too tired to draw music from the strings." With the devotion of a knight whose sword travels with him over land and sea, Angelina's first mandolin—a gift intended to bring her joy—was among the few personal belongings she'd carry to America. And many years later, when her husband and children gathered around her deathbed, it stood on the wall behind them, blending in like an old friend.

Teaching her to play was easy. She had studied her father's strumming. Noting her talent, he always encouraged her to "try it a little bit." Her long, thin fingers glided naturally along the strings. "Santa Lucia," the first song she learned, remained her favorite. Giuseppe taught her the new tune, "Funiculi Funicula," hoping the excitement over the new cable car to Mt. Vesuvius would somehow rub off.

"Giuseppe is filling the child's head with ideas of seeing Mt. Vesuvius and going to America. He tells her the streets are made of gold and everyone is rich." Carmela believed her husband indulged Angelina more than the other children, not because he loved her more, but because he too struggled with dark moods. Why couldn't her daughter be like her and accept hardship with good cheer?

Carmela confided to her sisters that Giuseppe made himself sick, always talking on and on about how the rest of Italy despised the South. "The Piedmontese dogs," he rants, "deprive us of water, promising an aqueduct they have no intention of building." And the taxes!—he curses the increases before they come. Then after the complaining, there are long silences and sad eyes. Giuseppe's inability to book passage to America for his family was a constant source of irritation.

"I am not like the other men. They go to America and maybe send for their wives years later. That is not the way I am. When, *Dio mio*, will there be enough for my family's escape from this ungrateful land?"

As life became more difficult, as prices rose and the tax collectors became more demanding, Carmela denied her grief. The roof of their cottage begged repair. In the winter, the cold air streamed through the time worn door. "Ah, expect nothing and you won't be disappointed." Her home was ramshackle, and her children often went to sleep hungry, but she did not yearn for much beyond more flour, beans, and olive oil: the staples of the family's simple diet.

"Why should I wish for things I have never seen? *Basta*, Giuseppe. Take your revenge on your mandolin." That was Carmela's advice and Giuseppe's refuge.

Despite her moodiness, the village girls regarded Angelina as a caring friend, the one to whom you went for advice. "Such a big heart in such a small body," they would tease affectionately. Being the one who sat next to her was often the object of their arguments. And once she became confident playing the mandolin for visitors and friends, her company was sought after to the extent that it made her sisters and brother envious. Unsurprisingly, it created an internal conflict, since she saw her own satisfaction as the source of others' misery. At gatherings, everyone would wait in anticipation for her "Funiculi Funicula." Her only condition for playing was that everyone sing along.

When the *festa* ended, Angelina's cousins and friends sang as they returned to their homes. But she walked alone off to the side of the dirt road, lost in thought of marriage and things that might go wrong.

The next week, Signor Michele and Orazio visited the Rotolos' cottage to purchase hats. Carmela handed the thirteen-year-old boy, her future son-in-law, a plate of *pizzelli* fresh from the hearth stove. They were much hotter than Orazio had expected. As the cookie burned its way down to his stomach, his body jerked forward, causing the full platter he held to slip away. Tears welled up in his eyes.

Embarrassed by his son's awkward behavior, Signor Michele hit him on the back of the head with his cap. "You have the balance of a donkey. Tell Signora Rotolo you are sorry."

Sheepishly, Orazio apologized, and bearing the impish smile and easy charm that would prove a blessing and a curse during their forty-year marriage, he picked up the broken *pizzelli* from the floor. That was the first time Angelina noticed he had eyes the color of flaming chestnuts. Warm, mischievous, hungry for the esteem of the good angel, he looked the part of one who had been born to better circumstances. She wasn't sure what life with him would be like. It did not matter. For whatever his quirks and foibles were, on that day in 1882, Angelina learned Orazio Longo was by no means a menace.

FIVE YEARS LATER, AS A YOUNG BRIDE, Angelina began to learn just how complicated her husband was. But initially she experienced only joy, relishing the attention Orazio bestowed upon her: listening intently when she spoke, covering her shoulders if there was a draft, carrying her across a puddle when a storm took them by surprise. Angelina loved that her barber had soft, manicured hands. When he stroked her face and breasts while they made love, she was easily moved to ecstasy by the smooth body of someone Providence had kept from rough labor in the fields.

Because Maria and Michele Longo had recently taken in three children of a widowed cousin, the young couple moved in with the Rotolos. Orazio made it clear that this was only a temporary arrangement: they would soon join his cousins, Giovanni and Filomena, in America.

Whenever she needed reassurance about her future, Angelina reminded herself that her husband was a skilled barber. She colored her imagination with the creams and lotions he worked with, items that signified luxury in the simple village. What America might provide them with was harder to imagine. "How fortunate I am," she confided to her sister Barbara, "to have a husband who takes pride in how he dresses. But it bothers me a little how he rarely passes a mirror without stopping to check his hair or adjust the ends of his mustache."

Inside his older cousin's barber shop, Orazio developed a flair for chatting up customers. Perhaps it was his gentle manner and compassionate remarks that turned him into a repository of village gossip. Ever mindful that trust was essential to maintaining a good reputation, he never betrayed confidences. Yet everyone was aware that he knew a lot, and paid him the respect normally reserved for one's social superiors. He accepted it humbly, secretly relishing the prestige.

Of middling stature, Orazio's suppleness gave him a larger appearance. Each night after supper, he donned his best straw hat for his *passegiata* around Rutino's small *piazza*. There, as elsewhere, people noticed his impeccable style. If anyone questioned how it was out of joint with his place in the world, no one bothered to ask.

He was well liked, although he was outspoken and took center stage wherever he was invited. After few glasses of wine, he'd feign the posture of a beggar and he'd ask, "*Moglie mia, per favore, il mandolino?*"

Politics never failed to bring out the intense, expansive side of his nature. Angelina felt shame whenever this side of her husband's personality surfaced, worrying about how it was irritating his listeners. When the conversation turned to the state of village affairs and how things were worse since the unification, Orazio waxed prolific. Those who said they could only hear so much about the tax collectors from the North, "the mad dogs of the Savoyard bastards, ever eager to empty our pockets," knew he'd soon knock on their door to see if they were ready to listen.

Angelina found him affectionate at one moment, but then he would draw into himself, daydreaming about cutting *la bella figura* in New York, living the life that in Rutino was reserved for landowners and the Northern officials who came and went. During those moments, when "he wanted only his thoughts," she knew her husband was planning their escape.

What the Rotolos' cottage—too hot in the summer and too cold in the winter—lacked in space and comfort was forgotten when Angelina and her father played duets at the table after supper or by Carmela's tiny herb and flower garden on a warm day. On Sundays, Michele and Maria, and the Longo clan, brought some wine that the "new hard times" had forced them to stretch by adding water. If it had been a good week, they brought a little *mozzarella di bufala* for Carmela to place around the salad of sorrel and dandelions Barbara foraged on her way home from the fields. Giuseppe, however, firmly refused the Longos' offer to bring some pasta or bread. The 1876 tax imposed on grinding grain had driven the prices up, but in his home, only he provided the staples.

After dinner on their first wedding anniversary, the young couple walked along the lane beside the cottage. Orazio was quiet. "What are you thinking? Won't you tell me?"

Silence. Then a half smile, index finger over his closed lips, and the familiar, "Later, I am making the plans. *Pazienza.*"

Before they drifted to sleep inside the alcove near her parents' bedroom, he told her what Giovanni had written from Nueva York. Hoping to tantalize his wife and make leaving for *La Merica* easier, he took poetic license. "Trains bring food and so many beautiful things from city to city. No one place goes without, not like here where we are cut off from everyone and everything."

He described the new mammoth bridge that joined Manhattan and Brooklyn. "This East River Bridge has concrete giants rising from the water, holding a metal pathway with cables that touch the clouds. And on this bridge, electric lights that turn night into day! There is plenty of work. We can buy things and make a beautiful home. A home with so many rooms! We will fill it with children, and, if I know you, with music. *Si, bellisima?*"

Angelina was conflicted about leaving; she gave no response. Orazio upped the ante. "And I can tell that this baby pushing against my hand has the fingers of a master mandolin player. Yes? We will have a room with a piano and all the instruments our children will play, a large room just off a *terrazzo.* I will probably learn the violin after we settle in and play it from the balcony outside our bedroom, serenading our neighbors."

"But it is such a long journey, Orazio. First we must travel to Napoli, then board ship for God knows how long."

"Yes, my dear, we will first view Napoli, a beautiful, important city, Giovanni says." Then he stroked an imaginary violin and whispered, "'*O dolce Napoli, o soul beato. . . .*' Yes, you know, like when you play 'Santa Lucia.' Now you will see it for yourself."

Angelina nodded, more in astonishment than in support. The image was too abstract. After all, life in Rutino had not provided her with a frame of reference for Naples, let alone America.

Her husband continued, "No more sleeping like children or animals in a home that is not our own. When this baby comes, we will be three in a space barely large enough for a mule. But before long, my *son* will be an American, dressed like a prince, even though his papa is only a barber. Soon, Giovanni, whom everyone now calls John, will have saved enough for our passage."

"Orazio, how can we take so much money from him? That is a shame."

"Listen, this is how it is done. We get to Nueva York, and before long, our *paesani* will help me get work, so we can find a home of our own and repay Giovanni. Then we will be in a position to help others leave here."

"But if we stay here, maybe we can buy a piece of land that will keep us fed. And even with the baby I can still work on the hats. . . ."

Orazio shook his head in disagreement. "*Basta*. Think about it, Angelina. Who in Rutino has gotten any richer since Italy became one? No one we know. Sure, the Spanish officials are gone, but the Northern politicians take a larger share of our money. For what? To do any good here? No! They want us to pay their soldiers with our *lire* and, should there be a war in Africa, with our lives. You say, maybe we can buy some land. How? There is barely enough to live on after paying their new taxes. *Disgraziata*."

From her father she had learned about the liberators promising much that never materialized. Now, even fewer people could afford even a small plot, and no one was eating any more than before. Angelina wasn't sure America would deliver a better life, but it was clear: Before long, they'd travel to Naples and board ship. Like it or not, this was the decision her husband had made. Angelina knew she must respect his wishes. Yet she had never been further than Castellabate. And she had only seen the sea from the mountaintops of Cilento. Now, with her first child due that July, she dreaded the separation from her mother, cousins, *comari,* and friends.

As a girl, she had dreamed of when she'd show her children the beauty by the River Alento. She'd imagined holding hands and pointing out how the daffodils that circled the grove of chestnut trees on Mount Stella formed a giant ring of gold. Rutino was so beautiful, so home. But this world was a hard world. "Beautiful, yes," she reluctantly admitted to herself, "but always not enough food, not enough room to love my husband without someone hearing our pleasure. Little chance of expecting anything better. And now, with the cholera carrying away young and old, who will come to help?"

Baby Maria Michela Longo was born in July 1890. The week before, the Rotolos had lost three relatives and the Longos five to the sickness of stomach ache and diarrhea, the cholera. Nonna Maria pinned a tiny pouch filled with garlic and herbs to her namesake's swaddling clothes. She hung a larger one inside the cradle's dome.

Angelina hoped it was the figs and melons they'd eaten at the christening feast that was making their stomachs rumble and bowels loose. The possibility that it might be the cholera rendered her a full partner in Orazio's dream. They had hoped to leave as soon as possible, but Giovanni said he needed a little longer to scrape together the money for their passage. Almost two years would pass before he did.

While Angelina wove straw hats with her signature jacquard pattern, or sewed a ribbon around the brim, she pictured her gray-eyed daughter and the baby growing inside her waving hello to the "lady statue, la Libertà" as they sailed into New York harbor. "No, Maria *mia*, do not pull off your pouch. It must stay put so you remain healthy. Be a good girl, and watch what I am doing. One day you will know how to make a hat for your husband." When Maria grew restless watching her mother weave a hat, Angelina sang to her about Naples and the beautiful sea that would take them to a new home.

O dolce Napoli, o suol beato,
Ove sorridere volle il creato,
Tu sei impero dell'armonia,
Santa Lucia, Santa Lucia.

Two months after Giuseppa Anna was born, Giovanni sent enough money for their journey. Angelina convinced herself that, since she was still young, not yet twenty-two years old, there was plenty of time left for reuniting. Maybe if they became rich, as Orazio said, they might return and buy a home where they could live comfortably. "By then, who knows, maybe life here will be a little less difficult. With some extra money, we could raise our family on top of this mountain in the village that has always been our family's home. I need to pray, to believe that this separation is just for a little while."

While she spun possibilities in her mind, she suppressed the realization that those who returned to Rutino had only done so to accompany more relatives to the place where there were wide streets, and work to be had, and the chance of becoming rich. But beyond owning your own home and not going hungry, what else was there? Content enough with her family and music, Angelina had always dreamed small. And, of course, having lived in a rustic world where travelers rarely ventured and where books and newspapers went unread, it was hard to color one's dreams. For such a practical young woman, all the talk about milk and honey running through streets of gold was what in later years she called "bullasheet."

The Longos packed their few belongings and made the rounds to family and friends. Everyone tearfully wished them *buona fortuna*. Talk of Nueva York invariably gave her a headache. Custom deemed it rude for anyone, especially a woman, to speak about innermost feelings, so she always nodded in agreement when someone commented that she was fortunate to have a husband determined to give her and the children a better life.

"Yes, Mama, I will dress them warmly and keep an eye on their pouches. Please don't cry. You will see us all soon when we come to visit wearing new clothes and having some for you. Oh, how I wish . . .God be with you until we see each other again."

Leaving Rutino was traumatic. Zi Mario took them to Agropoli in his cart. When sight of Rutino grew smaller and disappeared as they moved down the mountain, Angelina prayed for the strength to make the journey without losing her mind. Her thoughts raced. "Orazio is acting as if we are on some big adventure. Me, I await the time when I can be reunited with my family and Rutino."

Although some family and friends did eventually come to New York, it was the last time she saw her parents and the place she always considered home. If she sensed this on the day they left for America, it was buried under an avalanche of apprehension and anxiety.

NAPLES WAS EVEN LARGER than Angelina had imagined. Walking along the wharf from the local boat that had taken them from Agropoli, she told Orazio that Vesuvius looked like a lioness waiting to pounce on the city. In the port area near the old marketplace, the streets were, strangely, made of brick and stone. There were people everywhere, so many getting off and on boats, others selling food and hawking items along the Via Caracciolo. Angelina felt a little dizzy. She had never seen so many people in one place. "Orazio, please, no more walking. My feet are sore, and the babies need to rest."

"Sta' zitto—we may never see this great city again. Come, let's take a look at the Castel dell'Ovo."

So on they went, drinking espresso at a café, sitting among others who'd traveled to Naples to board ship for America. "Oh, the tall buildings. . .wait till Mama hears about this." Angelina marveled at how many women were on the streets, walking, eating, shopping, stepping off and on trolley cars. So many were alone, unescorted. Naples was indeed a strange and exciting place, even if it smelled bad and felt a little dangerous.

Some day she would tell Maria and Giuseppa about the adventure they were too young to remember. After hours of being carried through the city, her babies fell asleep in their parents' arms. Maria Michele and Giuseppa Anna slept, oblivious to a new life across the ocean. And as it turned out, the cursed land of their birth, now ravaged by disease, had determined their destiny.

In Naples, the Longos spent two nights in one of the crowded, cheap hotels near the port. They shared a room with their *paesani*, Carmine and Teresa Sforza and their seven-year-old son. The four adults shared a bed, sleeping fully dressed above the blankets. Little Stefano Sforza and Maria Michela slept bundled in a blanket beneath a window. Teresa and Angelina agreed the fresh air would "protect the children from the cholera." Baby Giuseppa Anna lay next to them, swaddled and blanketed in a hat box left behind by a previous guest.

The night before they departed, Stefano woke his mother. He had soiled his pants, and his stomach hurt so bad it was making his head feel fuzzy. Angelina convinced herself that it was probably a case of nerves, too much excitement. But, she thought, it is a good thing I placed the girls' pouches where the herbs will reach their breath, just in case.

Since the *Victoria* was not leaving until 3:00 p.m. and passengers had been told not to arrive before noon, Orazio walked around Naples, stopping here and there to chat with other travelers taking a morning *passeggiata*. The city might look the same when he returned home for a visit, but he was confident that he would look much better, well-dressed and with money, a rich Americana. As the boat pulled away, Maria waved *arrivedici*. Giuseppa rested her head on her mother's shoulder. Later, after they had returned to the steerage sleeping quarters and put the children to sleep, Angelina asked Orazio if he had tossed a coin for good luck in the fountain of the fierce and mighty Neptune.

She did not know the story of Palinurus or Neptune's history of taking victims at sea. Tossing a coin just seemed liked the sensible thing to do. He knew that, if he told the truth, she would reproach him. So he lied and told her he had.

CHAPTER 3

Angelina's Story / Part Two
1892–1911: "Coming to America"

Household gods sail from
Ancient cliffs to streets of gold.
Witness their decrees.

THE STATUE STOOD SHROUDED in a gray morning mist. Angelina and Orazio stared blankly at La Libertà, the symbol of welcome and hope in a harbor so far from home. Before dawn, slipping past the guard stationed near steerage's port-side staircase, they climbed to the deck reserved for second-class passengers. If they were caught, what further misfortune could befall them?

"*La Libertà è bella,*" Angelina whispered in a fragile voice, "*Ma mie figlie. . . .*" Twenty-two days before, they had left the port of Naples on the *Victoria,* carrying Maria Michela, age two, and Giuseppa Anna, barely six months old. But when cholera snatched their children, the young couple had become childless as well as homeless. Angelina felt empty. All her joy had been taken away. Looking towards the statue, she could not have imagined that any good awaited her in this strange land.

On the eighth day at sea, she and Orazio had each carried a feverish child to the common table for the evening meal of bean stock soup and bread. Since the day before, the baby had refused her mother's breast. *Un foco*. Carmela had taught her that cold water reduces a fever, so Angelina had poured water from the jug and dabbed Giuseppa's head and hands. Orazio had tried to feed Maria small pieces of bread dipped in the soup. But the feverish child refused it. Like a worn-out porcelain doll, she rested her head on the table.

"Exhaustion, that's all," Orazio had said.

"No, Orazio," his wife had told him, as if she could cure them by identifying what made them sick, "it is the filth, the stench of vomit and urine they have been smelling. The bad air is getting into their blood. We must move to healthier quarters."

Hiding his own panic, Orazio had spun a scenario of hope. "Angelina, when we arrive in New York, we will find a doctor. He will check them over and give us a tonic to rebuild their strength. And the food there, that will help, too. Compare Giorgio wrote about the many foods he keeps in the ice box he shares with his in-laws. Soon, we will purchase one for ourselves."

A doctor, medicine, foods, and an ice box. Orazio was placing huge expectations on the four *lire* sewn into the lining of his vest. He did not know that his financial worth was less than one American dollar.

Orazio lifted his eldest child's limp body and carried her back to the women's sleeping compartment. The dampness from her bottom he mistook for the fever's effect was actually urine. By time Angelina laid her on the little bunk, her body's warmth had fled. She'd misread the stiffness of Maria's limbs for a deep, healing sleep. And, when neither child could be roused from their place in the morning, it took the chief steerage steward's unimpassioned telling to make death a reality.

"No," he said, "I can not tell you anything else about what caused their death. After all, they were not the only ones to die during the night. With there being no other doctor on board and all this illness, these deaths are becoming unmanageable."

That evening, after a brief service for the day's departed souls, Maria and Giuseppa had been committed to the deep.

Had the Sirens been watching? And had they decided to make little Palinuruses of the two Longo girls? The young couple, he twenty-three, she not yet twenty-two, had been stunned by their babies' unburied state. They were living their own *Aeneid*, and their journey towards a new life was being mapped by loss. They had stood by grief-stricken while deck hands disposed of their children's bodies.

In Rutino, death was followed by sacred rituals performed at *Chiesa San Michele Arcangelo*. Where were the priests with their prayers and incense? There had been no flowers, no music, and no one to wail and walk with to the churchyard. Their prayers, and the comfort of the few *paesani* on board, had to substitute for so much. Almost everything that had been familiar was gone, the children, *italia, la famiglia,* and their room in the back of the Rotolos' cottage that faced *Monte Stella*, where flowers danced as an afternoon storm blew in.

GIOVANNI WAITED IN BATTERY PARK almost a full day before his cousins cleared immigration. The chalk mark on Angelina's arm suggested the health officials suspected she was carrying disease. True, he had not seen them since he left for New York four years before, a few days after the attractive young couple danced at their wedding party in Zi Benedetto's garden. Their faces had not aged, but their grave pallor gave them the look of ghosts. And where were their children? Were they being held in quarantine, or had Orazio decided to settle in first and return for them later? Yes, others who disembarked looked worn and weary. But his cousins' vacant stare and swollen eyes suggested something more than exhaustion from a long, uncomfortable journey. Perhaps the inspectors on Ellis Island had been rude to Angelina. Had they been less than gentle in detaining the children? Giovanni thought it best not to question them until they reached Brooklyn and had something to eat and a little rest.

Angelina managed to keep her composure until Filomena opened the door to the apartment she and Giovanni shared with three *paesani*. Eight months pregnant with her fifth child, Filomena had trouble embracing her young relative. Her welcoming laughter stopped when Angelina grabbed her arm and began wailing. Words came haltingly, perhaps because the speaker found them inadequate for explaining the horror of the girls' death. Yes, she would like to go to church in the morning and pray for their innocent souls. Yet it was hard to understand why Giovanni had cautioned them to speak about what had happened to Maria and Giuseppa only to their family and closest friends. The Irish neighbors in the building, he explained, must not hear about losing children to cholera.

"They see us as dirty, inferior beings to begin with, so we must not even let them know you just came off the ship from Naples." Giovanni explained that, when strangers asked, they must say they had been living with family outside Boston for almost a year.

"Tell them that, as a barber, you thought it will be easier to find work in New York. *Mi scusi,* but please, say nothing about disease and death. It will make things hard for all of us with the Irish and other Americani. They know us as John and Phyllis. We are trying hard not to make any trouble. Heaney upstairs, a drunkard if there ever was one, is cousin to my boss at the shoe factory. And well, these people look for any reason to get rid of us, even though we work for less than any German or Irishman."

New Yorkers in the 1890s regarded Italians with the same contempt Southerners harbored for Blacks, and that the Italian immigrants' descendants would bear for Puerto Ricans when they became the new immigrants in South Brooklyn two generations later. Fear of competition for jobs, and a belief in racial betters and lessers, led to prominent figures—including Charles Emory Smith, ex-United States Minister to Russia—to call for radical restrictions on immigration. In November 1892 he addressed a meeting of the Patria Club, an organization, which according to a socialist publication, included "leading fleecers of labor," who sought to maintain privilege by whipping up fear and patriotic devotion.

Smith pointed out that, while immigration was increasing, the quality of the people entering the country was deteriorating. At this meeting of elites held at a swanky Fifth Avenue address, Smith had a receptive audience for his historical perspective regarding how Anglo Saxons, the founders of this country, were being threatened by racial inferiors, significantly those from Italy. These aliens, this diseased population, were diminishing American greatness.

Moreover, unskilled, cheap labor was lowering standards and stealing the livelihood of others. Aware of news articles exposing *those people,* foreigners carrying cholera from filthy ports, the members of the Patria Club would have been a receptive audience.

Then in 1893, the *New York Times* published an article urging stiffer regulations on steamships to halt the transporting of infected passengers. The reporter asked readers to consider: "Does America really need any more scruffy Russians, Poles, and Italians?" Such outcries against Italians with inferior ways and contamination of the "American way of life" resulted in the 1924 Johnson-Reid Act. Now immigration had become nearly impossible.

So as they grieved the loss of their children, Angelina and Orazio worried that, if they showed any sign of illness, a noisy neighbor might report them to the authorities. "Keep healthy, and keep to yourself and Italians you know and trust" became their code during those early days. Being deported meant another journey at the bottom of a filthy ocean liner. For Angelina the trip would force her to relive the intimate details of the girls' suffering and death; for Orazio, returning to Italy was unthinkable.

Over the next two weeks, relatives and *paesani* visited the young couple to pay their respects at their temporary home with John and Phyllis. Then came the time to put the story, and their memories of their children, away. Orazio explained it was best for everyone. Angelina refused to believe she would ever feel happy again. This new life in America was far from what she had imagined. Her babies were gone and comfort from her Mama and sisters was an ocean away.

ALTHOUGH ANGELINA WAS GRATEFUL that the success of Compare Bartola's business required a new chair and an experienced barber, the long hours alone setting up the third floor apartment on 18th Street were the quietest, loneliest days she had ever known. When *paesani* or neighbors came by with their children, waves of chaos inside her head caused her to burn the coffee or spill the milk. One afternoon, Comare Rosina's little Antonia climbed on her lap and nestled her head between Angelina's breasts. Her kind nature compelled her to stroke the child's hair, but moments like these brought painful memories. They made the rest of the day almost unbearable.

"When they knock on the door, I will pretend I am not home. I won't answer it," she told Orazio. "Then they will go away and I can be alone with my memories of when I was with my babies in Italy. Alone I can have my tears."

Initially Orazio shared Angelina's mournfulness, but before long his ambition to secure himself in a life far removed from the sparseness and insecurity in Rutino gave him a new vitality. He grew impatient with what he regarded as her dwelling on the past. "You must stop always thinking about Rutino and the family as it was there. I miss our children and our town too, but we are in America now. Life here is better. Don't you like your new home? It is filled with things we could not have dreamed of back there. No? Look around this kitchen. In Rutino no one could imagine all the food and comforts we now have under our roof. Yes, we have had a terrible loss, but we must go on. You must try. Learn some English. Appreciate life in Brooklyn. After all, Angelina, there are people who are much worse off."

Angelina did not want to hear about women who had lost their entire family and had no one to take care of them. Feeling alone in her grief, and prone to depression since childhood, she'd close her eyes and imagine her babies sitting on her lap, the family gathered at Mama's table, Papa playing music. If they could all be together, sharing life in New York, then that would make things right. But they weren't. Maria and Giuseppa were dead. And her family was across that dreadful ocean, hungry and cramped but together. Frequently, she lost hours dwelling on the past. Orazio told her she was stubborn and ungrateful. Perhaps he was right. As the harsh reality of deprivation waned, her idealized memories of life in Rutino waxed larger than the American moon shining on the cobblestones in the streets of turn-of-the-century New York.

She did not know about survivor's guilt and lived before the advent of grief counseling, so she came to associate her loss with Brooklyn, the place with plenty that was not home. The idealization of things past rendered good fortune an enigmatic gift. This continued long past her arrival in this strange new world, for grief had wormed its way deep inside, attaching itself to the core of her being. It remained there for the rest of her life. Even during the years she was raising her American children and running a home as harmonious as well-played music, her voice, like her mandolin, bore a melancholic undertone. The merriest of moments were colored by its echo.

She did not have the awareness or vocabulary to talk about being displaced or shouldering great loss. So instead, she spoke about her headaches and the troubling things, her collection of phobias. "I get dizzy on a crowded street." "When someone brings news of a death,

I suffer because soon I will hear about two more." "Waiting for bad news makes my head hurt." Disaster was being invited if a piece of bread was discarded without being kissed up to Jesus, or if a "Thank God" failed to follow a compliment.

Sunday gatherings at John's, however, were a blessing. Sitting around the table with loved ones made the hours pass more easily. Phyllis needed extra hands to help with the cooking and table preparations. Angelina looked forward to setting out after mass at St. John the Evangelist, stopping at the bakery on 21st Street and walking alone to her cousins' apartment. This routine provided her with a sense of purpose. Sunday was the happiest day of her week.

Phyllis was busy with five little ones, so Angelina, with help from a cousin, *comare,* or *paesana,* prepared the dishes served along with the pasta and tomato sauce. It was clear she was in charge. "No, Peppina, that's not enough parsley," or "Giovanna, take the nuts out of the oven. You will burn them again." At dinner she'd nod appreciatively whenever the baked chicken or baby artichokes were praised. "God will provide," she'd say, but she had her doubts.

Angelina treasured the mandolin her Papa had surprised her with long before. Alone at home, she found delight in creating soothing sounds; it diminished the sadness, even if only for a while. The strings served as sprites whose magic lightened her mood. But it was too soon to play at gatherings. Her period of mourning was not yet over.

Standing as godmother to John and Phyllis' baby, Anita, started out as a painful event. Had it been a mistake to embroider the pink roses on the christening gown? While she sewed, her good intentions had competed with Anger and Envy. "My girls, they will never. . . ." Shame over her self-indulgence forced her to swallow her feelings. During the christening ceremony, Angelina passed the baby to Orazio. She felt faint. Why were Maria Michela and Giuseppa Anna buried in a watery grave while the child she was holding, and the other infants, had such color in their cheeks and finery on their bodies? The noise in her head stirred up the nausea she had been feeling off and on for the past few months.

Back at the apartment, Phyllis insisted Angelina lie down. She and her sister, Aida, would lay out the coffee and pastry. Never one to mince words, Aida asked when she had last been unwell. "It has been a while. My sorrow has turned my blood to stone."

"Angelina *mia*, that may be true, but if you have lately been with your husband, then you may be carrying a little angel." In the bathroom, she helped her undress. "Do your breasts look different?"

"I should have noticed they were swollen, and the nipples have turned as dark as when I carried my girls." She fought the urge to laugh out loud or bless her good fortune for fear that her happiness might be taken away. Like the ancient Greeks who feared the repercussions caused by *hubris*, the Rutinese believed boasting invited trouble. Later at home she would tell Orazio. Together they would offer thanks to St. Anna.

"Get up and have a canola—no, have two," Aida said as she pinched her cheek. But Angelina played it safe. She ate just one.

And it was only when her breasts and stomach grew full, and she felt her unborn child swim inside her, that she put away her widow's weeds and brought her mandolin to the Sunday table. It was then too that Orazio started calling her "Angie." "Because, after all" he explained, "you will soon be the mother of an Americana child."

"Not for me thissa name of Angie." Holding fast to her heritage, she remained Angelina.

DURING HER PREGNANCY, hope was sometimes swept away by waves of worrisome thoughts. But she rose above them when the midwife handed her a round, pink bundle. In honor of Orazio's mama, this child was also named Maria. Perhaps Orazio—now called "Ritchie" by everyone except his wife—nicknamed the baby "Mamie" to trick the Fates into granting his American daughter a life of mirth. Whatever the case, in 1894 both Mamie Longo and the fabled Mamie O'Rourke of the new hit song arrived in New York. A mixed blessing, Angelina thought. The child has eyes as blue as the Madonna's garment, and the baby's buried at sea with her bigger sister.

With the haunting of her losses now submerged in the borderlands of her consciousness, she enjoyed her new life. Yet like a banished demon determined to exact revenge, her sorrow always lay in wait. To appreciate this, it must be remembered that the Furies had angered the ancient gods revered in Southern Italy. Later, with the rise of Christianity, it was believed that the greatest threat was Satan, the fallen angel who challenged the order of things. Many Southern Italian immigrants, like Angelina Longo, lived in fear of these forces, although they knew little of their cultural history. And whether or not one regards this sort of belief as justified, magical thinking, blind faith, or some such blend, it cannot be denied that the Southern Italian experience of hardship, disempowerment, and displacement was understood as the work of some evil avenger.

Her happiness grew with the birth of the gray-eyed Michael, and continued to do so as Joseph, Anna, and finally Minnie came to fill out the house Orazio bought in 1902.

In later years, when the unthinkable happened again, Angelina wondered if her family's good fortune had offended some vengeful spirit that followed them from Rutino. Had she committed an act of defiance by giving her first four American children the names of their siblings whisked away at sea?

But for now, there was a growing family. Music and the laughter of children lit the Longo home. Misery, however, lay waiting in the alley leading to their garden, feeding on the figs from the tree that, like them, had been uprooted from Rutino.

Although she always spoke to Mamie in Italian, Angelina was glad that Donna Holman upstairs was teaching her English. "Listen, Mama, one, two, three, four, five, six, seven, eight, nine, and ten.

That's how many fingers I have. Toes, too. And four, that's how old I am."

Raising Mamie was a joy. And since she did not conceive another child for more than five years, until Mamie's first year at St. John the Evangelist Primary School, Angelina's days centered on attending to her daughter's care. Painful memories of losing Maria and Giuseppa now mainly caused havoc while she slept.

At first, like those of other newly arrived immigrants, Angelina's home was simply and sparsely furnished with items bought on the cheap or received from others whose good fortune had enabled them to decorate their South Brooklyn apartments with sofas, gas lamps, and tables far superior to what they had known in Italy. When Orazio began earning a decent salary, he encouraged her to shop for nice furnishings. For the next several years, with no babies vying for her attention and plenty of time to take Mamie walking in Prospect Park and shopping on Fifth Avenue, she enjoyed a routine of buying this or that for their home or the afternoon meal they ate with Orazio and whoever he might bring home from the shop.

Since Il Barbieria di Bartola was open until 7:15, and Orazio stayed around preparing for the next day and "learning the business," Angelina spent late afternoons making sick calls or paying a visit to someone in their growing circle in South Brooklyn. On other days, she'd teach Mamie the mandolin or a new Neapolitan song. Mothering her daughter gave her purpose, joy.

Five years after they settled in their new home, Compare Bartola died, leaving Orazio the thriving barbershop and a baby grand piano that had somehow come into his possession. Orazio turned "La Barbieria di Bartola" into "Ritchie Longo's South Brooklyn Barber Shop." He joined the Italian Barbers' Society, and although he rarely attended their meetings, he enjoyed the dinners they sponsored, where he made some lifelong friends.

Running a successful business came naturally to him. He liked to boast that his well-equipped shop was frequented by prosperous German and Irish customers. He kept a variety of cordials and a tray of *pignoli* cookies on a sideboard next to the cash register. He prided himself on treating his customers like old friends. And he recognized the importance of learning English. Initially, he had picked up a great deal from listening to John translate for Phyllis, and later he became an avid reader of the *Brooklyn Daily Eagle*. By the second visit to his shop, he knew a customer's name, his wife and children's names, and a little bit about his interests. Into a basic Italian sentence, he infused American phrases, delivering them with panache. Somehow he and these Americani understood each other.

"Richie, I hear your wife is in the family way. When do you expect the new arrival?"

"*Si*, Tom, *mia moglie* is, as you say, in the *famiglia* way. The baby it comes in *mezzo Novembre, dio* willing. And you family, *tutti bene*?" Proud of his English, Orazio encouraged Angelina to learn it too, for the children's sake and to show up those neighbors who treated them like greenhorns. Yet when they were together, he always spoke Italian. Just as she had refused to answer when he called her "Angie," she refused to call him "Ritchie." To her, it sounded as if he was bragging about his good fortune. "Richie, he calls himself, my Orazio. Bigga shot wants to sound rich, lika his bigga money."

The children started school knowing little English. Within months, they became proficient in their second language; still, at home they spoke their parents' Italian dialect. Angelina's English, however, did not develop much beyond the lyrics of the songs she sang with them. Shopping along Fifth Avenue was no problem. Many of the shops were owned by Italian immigrants or employed them. As for the Jewish or Polish peddlers who stopped outside their door, Mamie served as translator.

Neighbors smiled when she said "ullo *bella*." The peddler understood her "thanga you, *signore*" after he handed her change for an order Mamie placed. So Angelina told the family that her English was just fine. When Michael and Baby Joe sat on top the piano, and Mamie played "East Side, West Side," it did not faze her that she was repeating strange words. The melody and gaiety were enough.

> *East Side, West Side,*
> *All around the town,*
> *The tots sang "Ring-a-Rosie,*
> *London Bridge is Falling Down."*
> *Boys and girls together,*
> *Me and Mamie O'Rourke,*
> *Tripped the light fantastic,*
> *On the sidewalks of New York.*

She and Orazio built a home where family and *paesani* spent good times around the big mahogany table. Unlike some of the husbands in their circle, he never raised a hand to her or deprived her and the children of their comforts. Yet he made Angelina know that, as a man, he could come and go as he pleased without having to explain, and, when he wished, he would have a *puttana* who'd perform the acts that surpassed "a good woman's obligations." That too was his business. Denial helped her cope with the fault lines in her marriage.

VICARIOUS LIGHT. Angelina would not have known what that meant, but she did know that listening to her children's voices, especially when accompanied by music, and seeing the incandescent color of their eyes had a rainbow effect on her spirit. Blue, gray, chestnut brown, hazel, and green. Each of her children had his or her own eye color and a distinct personality that matched the color's aspect. It might not be too much to say that their auras were the configuration of the stars in her universe. And as those ancient Greeks in Cilento had believed, their movement created perfect, harmonious music.

Mamie's blue eyes matched her maternal nature. Born during a time when the deprivation that had driven her parents and unburied sisters from Rutino had been replaced by opportunity and security, Mamie was able to indulge her innate generosity. With the patience and tenderness of a Madonna, she helped her mother care for the four younger children.

Michael, Angelina's gray-eyed wild child, had the regal bearing reminiscent of the classical statues she had seen as a child when she, Barbara, and Marsiela accompanied their papa to Paestum. His determination and wanderlust often led him to places his parents had warned him away from.

Joe had Orazio's chestnut-brown eyes, but the light that shone from them was gentler, less burdened, more jolly, just like his nature. By age four, little Giuseppe, whom everyone except his mother called Joe, sat beside Mamie, "his teacher," at the piano, keeping the babies entertained. Before long, he initiated the music playing at the Sunday get-togethers, which grew larger each year as more relatives came over from Rutino and cousins were born whose births transformed their parents into natural citizens.

Anna's hazel eyes graced her quiet loveliness. And when they were clouded over with tears—for she, like her mother, had bouts of depression—the hurt they conveyed needed no words. After Mamie married in 1914, Anna became Angelina's second set of hands and in-house confidante. And then there was Filomena, baby Minnie, her last child. "The child made from our old bones." Minnie's big green eyes, laughing eyes, contained a magical power that made Angelina feel content despite all life's ups and downs. "Well, you just have to smile," she'd say, "when my Minnie is in the room, doing one of her dances or asking Michael to take her on his shoulders and spin her around."

The gifts bestowed by the old Greek gods are splendid. But these gods have eyes, and they are wont to become jealous and wrathful.

Beware their anger. Their hold is strong on Italians near and far from home. Without notice, they reach across the ocean and snatch their gifts away. This is their eternal curse.

Every evening, after Joe, Anna, and Minnie changed into their bedclothes, Angelina played her mandolin while Mamie practiced whatever song she was learning from Maestro Melfi. If Michael hadn't slipped out to join his friends, who, as Angelina did not yet know, were smoking cigarettes and flirting with women passing by the 4th Avenue pool hall, she'd have him dance with Minnie. Joe wanted to join his older sister at the piano, but he first had to dance with Anna. It did not matter if Orazio often missed these moments, having headed out to a Coney Island dance hall. This was where Angelina wanted to be.

TO CELEBRATE MICHAEL'S TENTH BIRTHDAY, Orazio announced that the family would ride the Fifth Avenue El train to the Sea Beach line for a day out at Coney Island's Dreamland Amusement Park. Coney Island, he told Angelina, was a place where the family could spend a beautiful day at a seaside resort without having to leave the city. "Hold off on baking a cake until the Sunday following Michael's birthday. This Sunday, the day our eldest son turns ten, we will have an American outing."

At first, Angelina was silent. Struggling with the memory of her first-born children, she resisted the urge to say that there hadn't been any amusement parks for them. Eighteen years ago, she and Orazio hadn't even had the resources for the ten-cent train ride. Moreover, she couldn't visualize such a place. "An amusement park? What means this amusement?" Since their arrival at Ellis Island, she had been back to Manhattan only once, and except for a few trips to downtown Brooklyn or Bay Ridge, she hadn't traveled more than a mile north, south, east, or west from their home on 18th Street. Rides? Attractions?

"*Che cosa,* Orazio?" was her usual response to modern conveniences, things of steel, rubber, and light that transformed life into a more colorful and rapid world than seemed safe or decent. To silence her when he thought she was being too critical or absorbed in what he had named the *miseria,* Orazio reminded her that he had adapted to American ways, modern ways. He had been able to make himself fit in, but she was stuck somewhere back in Rutino with the *miseria.*

Using his characteristic drama, he sought to entice her. "The beach, the hotels, they line the water's edge. And the rides," he added, "they are beautiful, each one like a little fantasy. Michael will soon be a young man. This birthday will leave memories he will share with his own children someday—the time his mama and papa took him and the family to Coney Island. All the children will have their fun. Ah, we will make *una bella figura.* And Angelina *mia,* there is music there everywhere you turn. The sound of mandolins day and night."

She smiled, thinking about the sound of music being carried by a salty breeze. He smiled, thinking about George Tilyou's Steeplechase dance halls, and Sophie Kowaleski, his dance partner and sometime lover. Angelina shrugged and gave the nod she'd give whenever she stepped further into American culture than she was comfortable with. It was as if she was saying, *I will go, but I am not entirely sure why.*

Angelina waved Minnie's hand when Orazio and the children called to them from their car atop the Ferris Wheel. And they waved again when they rode past on the Scenic Railway.

The children could not have imagined all the rides and sweets at Coney Island, but Michael was enthralled by the excitement. When he insisted on a second ride on the Loop the Loop, Angelina and Mamie began walking with Joe, Anna, and the baby towards the tiny carousel outside Bostock's Animal Arena. When he asked to go on the Loop the Loop ride a fourth time, Orazio told him he had had enough.

"Papa, please. This ride is like heaven. I feel my heart beat faster than ever before. Just once more, please."

"Okay, then *basta*. We are going to see the animals and then have some dinner at Gargiulo's before going home. Here's the money for one more ticket; your next ride will be on the subway."

Riding the Loop the Loop Michael was exhilarated moving through the air somewhere between his family and the clouds he would stay forever up where the air never smells of shaving cream and witch hazel remarks from mick customers who laugh behind his father's back while they drink his "annie set" and wink at each other when hand on heart he speaks about their country where they live like kings their wives might be nurses and school teachers but his Angelina keeps a kitchen that feeds a full Sunday table without blinking an eye could serve six more who might come visiting at the last minute yes sure macaroni and meatballs but more too and with her music sure Italian music well you laugh but you don't know Enrico Caruso and up in the air upside down with laughter and freedom to move about to become a man with dreams of dancing though the clouds two-tone shoes bought in Manhattan suit and hat too dancing beyond what tradition allows and no sorrow for ocean-buried sisters or a city controlled by men whose fathers own the bank or built the subway that will take him back to the house where his parents' love and the paesani's support and all the beliefs from the other side of the ocean will look to keep him from living like an American playboy grasping at good times up and around taking in the air larger than the life waiting for him below here he was ringmaster of his own show.

ON THE WAY HOME, Angelina noticed Michael was flushed. She worried he might have caught the influenza. "*Figlio mio*, put your head on my shoulder." But Michael relished the fire. Despite his mother's warnings and pleas, and his father's half-hearted scoldings, he spent much of his remaining twenty years having one escapade after another, seeking out excitement, excess, and danger.

At age twelve, the police brought him home. They'd found him drunk and wandering in Prospect Park. Home alone with the children, unaware Orazio was out dancing with Sophie, Angelina understood from the officers that her son was drunk, but her only response to their warning that he was headed for trouble was a simple, "Thanga you."

She put Michael to bed after washing his face and hands. His protests and excuses were countered by her motherly decree. "You make yourself sick with these friends. *Disgraziata* this staying out late. If you don't stop, you will wind up like some no-good Irish drunk. You will ruin your life and mine. Do you want to shame your family? No, you don't. Now go to sleep."

CHAPTER 4

Angelina's Story / Part Three 1911–1930: "The Diaspora Grows in Brooklyn"

Time moves faster here,
Tradition shunned, boundless need.
Strange new land called home.

NGELINA'S DAUGHTER DREAMED of attending The Normal College of the City of New York. Since she was a young child, Mamie had told everyone she was going to become a teacher. But Angelina could not allow this to happen. Teaching music privately in the neighborhood maybe, but working in a school, even one close to home, was unthinkable. Remembering her own bland school experiences back in Rutino, Angelina believed twelve years of schooling was more than enough, especially for a girl. "No Park Avenue school! Riding the subway alone is out of the question." Mamie asked her father. He would think it over. After he had, he told his wife it was her place to relay his decision.

She explained why they decided against her becoming a teacher. "For what you need a college education, Mamie? To raise babies and run a house for a husband? By time you are twenty, God willing, you will be someone's wife. And a wise husband does not want a wife smarter than him. A woman must not forget her place. No more of this teacher talk."

"But, Mama, that is not always so. There are neighbors' daughters studying to become nurses and teachers. They learn wonderful things about the world, and about music, too. This is 1911. What do you and Papa want me to do between my graduation from Manual Training and the time when I become someone's wife? I don't want to wind up working like a slave in a factory. Think about all those girls—many of them Italians—who died last week in that Greenwich Village shirt factory. What will you and Papa have for me?"

"*Basta*, Mamie, you are not going to any factory or some Normal College either. If you want to teach, you teach your little sisters to play the piano."

"You know I will, but there are other things girls can do, too. You know Mrs. Kelly, the teacher who lives up the street? Well, I heard her talking to another woman on the bus, and she said there are women—and some men, too—who are trying to get the vote for women. Can you imagine?"

"*Che disgraziata*! You see, Mamie *mia*, what happens when you send a woman to such a place as a normal school; she starts talking crazy. Where is her shame for sticking her nose into things that are none of her business?"

Angelina came to agree with Orazio that Mamie should take the job as a pianist at a movie theater near the Brooklyn Bridge. A customer told him that his cousin, Gino Bongiorno, the manager of the Columbia Theater, was looking for a pianist to play during the silent films. Allowing her daughter to play piano at the Columbia Theatre might place her in a strange environment, but it was not nearly as dangerous as allowing her to pursue an education.

"Don't worry. Your papa will go up to the high school and tell them you will not be coming back."

"But, Mama, I am supposed to graduate in three months. Can't Papa tell Mr. Bongiorno I can begin work then?"

"I do not understand you, ungrateful girl. You are going to be paid for playing music. Make yourself feel happy."

With the children dressed in their finest clothes, and accompanied by various relatives and *paesani*, the Longos listened to Mamie play "Over the Waves" and other tunes during the screening of *The Wizard of Oz*. Angelina cried when Mr. Bongiorno asked Mamie to stand up and the audience applauded. Excited by the experience to the point that Orazio kept telling him to sit still, Michael told his parents he was going to become an actor. "I am a natural. And I have the good looks." Orazio laughed.

Angelina made the sign of the cross and whispered, "God forbid."

Playing piano in the silent movies ended three years later when Mamie married Joe Naso. She enjoyed working and keeping the part of her earnings her parents allowed. The Colombia kept her repertoire limited to four songs, but Mamie never tired of playing them for the moviegoers. She told her mother she would miss pleasing her listeners.

"If you are lucky, before long Joe will buy you a piano. And with the big war going on in Europe, so many boys are gone from Brooklyn. Soon hardly anyone will be at the movies. Zi Enzo writes that in Rutino people fear the Germans will become their new masters. *Dio mio*. Count your blessings."

INDEED, WOMEN DID GET THE VOTE IN 1920. Angelina could not understand why each family needed more than one voter. Wasn't that a husband's place? The kitchen, not the voting booth, was a woman's domain. That fall was among the happiest times in her life. With Anna and Minnie at school during the day, she spent glorious hours with Mamie's children, Milo and little Clara, playing her mandolin and teaching them Italian songs. She and Viola Leopardi, the mother of Michael's fiancée, Rosie, were busy planning the wedding reception. And although he was only seventeen, Joe and his Nettie planned to announce their engagement at Christmas.

Angelina's family was growing, and all the shopping, preparing of dinners, and visiting enhanced the gayer side of her nature. With so many festivities taking place, she no longer kept her mandolin inside its case in the front hall closet. It hung on the wall over the piano that had been left to them by old Bartolo years before. The gift from her papa had come with her from the old world; now it was the centerpiece of her Brooklyn living room. It was the balm that helped soothe the loss of her first home, the family left behind, and her two babies.

As for Mamie, she did not register to vote for many years. Raising the children, and decorating the brownstone on 17th Street the industrious Joe had bought before they were married five years, she, like most second-generation Italian American women, lived a life that was a carbon copy of her mother's. Her routine was grounded in the old ways, and it was structured by her husband's expectations.

Keenly aware of her obligations, she helped her mother find a new dress and shoes and prepare the house for Michael's wedding festivities. Silvio Leopardi's 4th Avenue butcher shop had done well, so he could afford to host a wedding reception at Prospect Hall. Orazio thought the wedding plans were impressive, but the recently passed Prohibition Act forbade the serving of wine. Leopardi too was unhappy about the situation, but what could he do?

Orazio offered a solution. Since he opened the speakeasy on the ground floor of the family's new home, he had met a number of locals who rented spaces for large parties. They'd supply the beer and wine. Leopardi, he boasted, should leave the planning to him.

When Angelina heard what Rosie's parents were spending, she saw the wisdom in Orazio's idea, although her opinion had not been asked. In the end, Leopardi insisted on Prospect Hall. Orazio went along but convinced both Leopardi and the caterer to set up a table in the cloak room for the beer and wine he'd have delivered.

Barbara and Enzo were traveling from Rutino for the wedding. Papa's health had been failing since Mama died the previous spring, and he was too sick to make the long trip. Angelina's anxiety rose when Phyllis confided that a *comare* saw John and Orazio leaving a downtown restaurant with two women. Orazio had sworn he'd stopped seeing his latest Polish mistress, Wanda Wisneiwski; discovering that he had renewed the affair with "*la pulacka*" threatened to ruin her family's visit and the festivities. Would she be well enough to make her sister and brother-in-law feel comfortable? Would the coldness between her and Orazio make everyone around them feel awkward? What would they think if they only knew?

But there was something else: Anger churned in her stomach, overpowering the sadness that usually festered there. Perhaps she had become tired of ignoring Orazio's infidelities. Or she may have feared gossip or pity. Whatever the case, she decided one way or another she'd prevent her selfish husband and his *puttana* from destroying everything. Angelina decided to wait for the right moment; then she'd take action. She did not have to wait very long.

The night before Barbara and Enzo arrived, Orazio told Angelina he had promised a customer on 23rd Street he'd come by and cut his hair. Before returning home, he needed to stop by the speakeasy. The new bartender he'd hired wasn't working out. "No, you shouldn't wait up for me. I will probably stay all night, just to let him know I am watching." He kissed her when she handed him his hat.

There was still much to get ready for the family's arrival, so she enlisted Anna's help. "Fold the laundry I took in this afternoon. It's on the ironing board, and I want to press the living room curtains."

"I already have. I saved the laundry and put Papa's barber case on your dresser. I am surprised he didn't come back for it." Angelina mumbled a string of curses. "Mama, what's the matter? You look so upset."

That night, she waited by the window. Knowing his wife usually went to bed by 9:00, an hour later Orazio escorted Wanda and two of her friends to his club. He walked through the gate alone, having told the girls to stay a little behind him. He glanced up at the bedroom window and wondered why Angelina hadn't closed it before turning in. What was that shadow behind the curtain?

That was his last thought until he came to about twenty minutes later inside the club. Michael was standing beside him, one arm around the waist of a waitress, the other placing his cigarette in her mouth. The bartender, Giorgio, told him that a flower pot had come down on his head. He had lost consciousness, and they'd feared he might not wake up.

"Cheez, Pop, did you see what happened? Are you all right? You had us all worried."

That night Angelina dreamed she was in Naples waiting to leave for New York.

She and Orazio and their son, little Stefano Sforza, were spending the night in the fun house in Coney Island. Long rooms, low ceilings, haunting colors, a strange place not really fit for laughter.

The boy calling her "Mama" had bloodshot, droopy eyes. Surely he must be exhausted, so Angelina sang him a song until he drifted off. While he slept, she watched him flail his arms. She did not see him in the sea of wine or hear the music from the radio that drowned the promises he tried to hold on to. Angelina hoped that, by shaking him, he would wake up long enough to stop the flailing. Each movement of his body rendered him larger and larger until he was the size of a man. He woke with a familiar smile. "Come on, Mama. Put on something better than your black mourning clothes and dance with me." Frozen in front of the fun house mirror that distorted shapes, Angelina noticed she was half her size and twice her width, and she was trying to explain that her legs were frozen. While she looked in the mirror, she watched Orazio dance by with an American woman. Heads close together, they were laughing.

The man child with the bloodshot eyes would not listen. If she could speak, she would tell him he should only dance with the bride waiting for him at the boat. Fun house feelings. Fear, for what I cannot tell him, for what he will not know. Love for the son who is light itself. Terror for good that turns bad.

He was beautiful even with the red trickling from his ear. "Watch," she wanted to scream. "You will stain the pillowcase that was once the tablecloth Nonna Carmela made for the king. But he never came." Then water from the Bay of Naples rose into the room, and two baby dolls floated past her. Angelina realized her husband had lied about tossing the coins in the fountain with the statue of Neptune. She wanted to trick him into telling the truth, but she could not make words. Orazio told her and the man-child that the fun house would take them to America. Angelina wished she could find someone to take her and the boy back to Rutino, but when she tried, she could not move and she could not speak.

She woke with a headache that made her vision fuzzy. She pushed the dream out of her mind, down to the place where her fears and losses were buried. The place that was all Italian.

While she cooked Orazio's breakfast, she told him that he must forget about *la pulaka*, at least until the wedding was over and the relatives returned to Rutino. And you must talk to Michael about his disgraceful behavior. "*Che scorna!*"

"*Sta' zitto!* I know what I have to do and not do." He thought that for the time being he'd meet Wanda at his *compare's* club on 23rd Street. Yes, he would talk to Michael about his drinking and about sleeping downstairs "to keep an eye on the place." Orazio didn't need Angelina reminding him this was "bullasheet."

"Yes, Angelina, of course I know it is his excuse!"

A week before the wedding, Orazio spoke with his son about his outlandish behavior. Michael rocked anxiously from side to side, jingling the coins in his pants pocket while his father spoke.

"You think your mother and I don't hear the door opening in the morning and the sound of women's heels in the front yard? You want this to get back to Leopardi or his daughter? Isn't it bad enough that last year I had to send a waitress upstate when your indiscretion started to show? And, as if that wasn't bad enough, along comes that Irish *puttana* with her nonsense about how, when you tired of her, you insisted she watch while you seduced her daughter. Aren't you ashamed I had to pay her twenty dollars to keep her mouth shut?"

Michael began one of his defensive tirades. "But, Pop—"

"*Basta*, you are marrying a nice Italian girl from a good family. Stop your nonsense, and show some respect. You are a man, and, yes, you can have your way. After you are married, no one will fault you if you have a woman on the side. Even then you must keep low that flame of yours. And you will cut down on the drinking, too. That is making you worse. Listen to me, I'm your father!"

When he was upset, Orazio spoke Italian. Angelina heard raised voices. All the excitement, the good as well as the bad, was giving her headaches. Lying in bed, eyes closed, with raw potato slices inside a wet towel atop her forehead, she couldn't believe what she heard, couldn't understand why father and son were so drawn to women and to liquor. Who has done this to me? Some *sfachime* put the evil eye on me, *un malocchio*.

Angelina liked Rosie. She was a sensible girl, a good girl. Life with her might help Michael change his ways. He made friends easily, and the Leopardis were crazy for him. Nevertheless, her son did not like to work, and he spoke big. While he was growing up, she had laughed at his talk of becoming an actor or going out West to make a fortune in gold. Now his crazy ideas became tangled up with lies and excuses for broken promises. Still he could charm anyone into listening to him, because after all he was so handsome, the life of the party, especially after a few scotch-and-waters. But he was also reckless with his money—to the point where Orazio felt obligated to cover his debts.

"Getting married," she confided to Mamie, "will turn him into a settled man."

ANGELINA AND ORAZIO GAVE THEIR GIFT to their son and his fiancée the night before the wedding. "This key will open the door to your own grocery store. Yes, we are setting you up in business. Your father was able to rent one of the stores on the first floor of the new apartment complex on 24th Street and 4th Avenue. By time you and Rosie return from Niagara Falls, Papa and Joe will have it set up and ready to open."

His mother mistook Michael's faint smile and loss of color for surprise. She had been after Orazio to draw Michael away from the temptations of the speakeasy. "Too much liquor and women there for one like our Michael. He goes too far in having a good time."

Because his eldest son was charming and outgoing, Orazio had made him manager of the speakeasy. But the truth was, he spent more time drinking and womanizing than he did keeping the books and making sure everyone paid their bill. Some of the unscrupulous customers fed him drinks, knowing that, before long, he would call out, "Drinks on the house for everyone." So now, in addition to his piano playing at the speakeasy, Joe took on the role of manager.

Baby Doris Ann Longo, according to tradition, should have been Baby Angelina, or at least Baby Angela. An Italian man's first daughter is *always* named after his mama. Born pink-cheeked with deep dimples and chubby legs, Angelina said she was a miracle. Inwardly, she marveled that a baby could weigh almost nine pounds after a pregnancy that lasted only six and a half months. She believed Rosie's mother when she said her Michael had married a virgin. "So," she said while crossing herself, "Doris is one of God's wonders."

The birth had been difficult. Joe checked all the speakeasies and places where Michael's friends lived or spent their idle time. Still the new father didn't come home until two days after the baby's birth. When he arrived, he had a huge bouquet and a fantastic story that captivated his listeners.

The baby was not yet eight months old when Rosie stopped breast feeding. Michael insisted he needed her at the store a few days a week. Angelina agreed to help care for little Doris at Mamie's house. When Michael failed to set up the crib she bought, the job fell to Joe. Although she was unhappy with Michael's increasing irresponsibility, she reasoned that Doris would spend time in a "settled" home, growing up with her cousin Ted, the Nasos' fourth child.

Mamie warned Rosie that, once she stopped breast feeding, she ran the risk of getting pregnant. Angelina shook her head in agreement. But how could Rosie tell her in-laws that breast feeding did not always prevent pregnancy? What would they think if they knew she had already learned that lesson, and that Michael had fought with her until she consented to visit a doctor who fixed the mistake? For two weeks she had been in bed with cramps she explained away as a stomach virus.

Angelina never knew that, while Rosie balanced the books, stacked the shelves, and made sure the provisions were fresh, Michael slipped away for hours at a time. She relished watching Doris and Ted in their crocheted sweaters and polished shoes, so well fed and living in homes with enough heat and beds that were theirs alone. Being with them delighted her, even when she would forget and called Doris "Maria" or "Giuseppa" or remember how little. . . . It was best, she decided, not to dwell on the past. What a joy the family she and Orazio had made in New York! Five grown children, three of them married, living comfortably. Four grandchildren, more to look forward to.

INCOME FROM THE BARBER SHOP AND SPEAKEASY, and what remained from the grocery store's profits after Michael indulged his rich tastes and generous nature, allowed the Longos to purchase a three-story house on 4th Avenue. Renting out the renovated apartments was no problem; in 1926, work was booming on the South Brooklyn waterfront. Two tenants, Frederico and Leonardo, cousins from Bari, became close friends of Joe. Like him, they enjoyed music and baseball. And after Joe brought his buddies "Fred" and "Lenny" home to meet the rest of the family, Angelina invited them to their Sunday dinners.

She noticed how Anna and Minnie went out of their way making sure these guests were eating enough and were treated like family. Although she was two years older, Anna followed her sister's lead in some blend of conventional hospitality and blatant flirting. The most outgoing of the Longo girls, Minnie sparked the gaiety at these gatherings, leading sing-alongs and talking about listening to music and dancing the Charleston with Michael at his friend Ciro's club in Manhattan.

Since Fred and Lenny made it known they disliked working on the docks, and because Michael was spending more time in the local speakeasies than he was in the store, Angelina talked Orazio into hiring Fred to help Rosie. Then one Sunday, after Minnie and Lenny declared their intentions to her parents, Angelina suggested that Orazio avoid creating bad feelings between the cousins and take on Lenny as a barber's apprentice, teach him the business. Orazio did not need much convincing, since he had already decided these hard-working men would make good sons-in-law. Maybe their example would shame Michael into being more responsible.

Angelina had nothing near the grandeur of a Daisy Buchanan, but during the roaring twenties she and her family enjoyed the good life. Her daughters had their hair bobbed. (Something she would have never considered. Her long black hair had always been parted in the middle, pulled back, and tied in a bun; that is how it would remain.) Mamie, Anna, and Minnie bought chemise dresses and cloche hats at the new Abraham and Strauss downtown. Joe learned the latest piano tunes at the Harlem jazz clubs he went to on Saturday nights with his wife, Nettie, and their friends. And, as for Michael, he soaked in the city's roaring high life, as if he were a single man, the scion of a wealthy Americana family. So she regarded their prosperity as a mixed blessing: Her children were doing well, but the pace of their daily life made her feel out of step. When the elevated train sped by high above the shops along Fifth Avenue, she longed for the sweet quiet of Rutino.

It frustrated Michael that she questioned him over and over again about his plan to travel to Chicago with Ciro. "Ah, Mama, he's a great guy. You just need to know him better. Try talking to him when he comes by. You'll see."

"Talk to him? About what, his mafioso friends or the wife he divorced and three children he walked out on? He doesn't look anyone in the eye, always turning his head from side to side, as if he is making sure no one is coming to take him away. Too shifty. I see him, and my hand goes in my pocket to guard my change purse."

Her distrust turned into disgust when she learned they were traveling to the West Side of Chicago to do business with Ciro's bootlegging cousin. Michael explained his cousin was "looking for some good men to run an operation he was setting up in Manhattan. I could make a load of money off the booze and the night life. Before long, we could hire more help at the store. Then Rosie could stay home. How would you like more grandchildren, Ma?"

"Don't give me thata bullasheet! Why do you want to leave your wife and daughter alone and travel to who knows where and do who knows what with this gudda nudda and his cousin? Michele *mio*, where is your respect for your family? *Che scorna.*"

"Ma, come here. Let me could give you a hug. Trust me. It is 1927, and now, with Doris in school, Rosie, God bless her, can manage the store. Anyway, Fred is a big help, and Papa is two stores away. Someone my age has to travel the world to see how it works. Things like this make men bigger and better. Didn't you and Papa leave Rutino because you had a dream of a better life? Well, that's what I want too, maybe more."

As Fitzgerald's Gatsby had flown eastward to reinvent himself, the Longos' Michael flew westward with the same dream: becoming an American legend. Angelina didn't know about Fitzgerald's story, or other literary works, because she had never learned how to read much in Italian or anything in English. Yet she was intelligent and intuitive. And because of the various tragedies that had befallen *Cilentani* when they left home searching for more, she knew this would not end well.

Sure enough, when Michael returned to Brooklyn six months later, he brought home a "business associate," a red-headed, finger-waved singer, Louise Martin. He installed her in an apartment on St. Mark's Avenue. Before long, Michael spent most nights away from home, and when Rosie confronted him, he admitted he was in love with Louise. She signed Doris out of St. John's, and they moved in with her sister and her family somewhere near Atlantic City.

Angelina stayed in bed for a week overburdened by her headaches. A divorce! Divorce, she thought, did not exist; it was unheard of in Rutino and unthinkable for decent Italians in Brooklyn. And the church regarded this as a sin, an unpardonable sin. Michael would burn an eternity in hell.

What to tell the family and *paesani*? "That *puttana* broke up my son's marriage. Now my Doris is gone to New Jersey, and who knows when I will see her again." She blamed Louise and Ciro for Michael's taking money from the grocery store to cover expenses at his Greenwich Village club. She repeated it so often that she became convinced that "*la puttana* bewitched him with her painted face and phony red hair." Yet she would have thought much worse of her had she known the twenty-one-year-old Louise left her six-year-old daughter with her mother in Chicago and had no plans for returning or sending for the child.

It was understood that Angelina and Orazio would not welcome Louise into their home, but when there was a get-together at Joe's or one of his sisters' homes, and she did not have an engagement in some Manhattan club, he brought her along. On those occasions, when the music began, Angelina went into the kitchen and washed the dishes, or just stared out the window and worried, muttering, "Wives and mistresses, decency and drink, children here and children gone, loyalty and lying. My son, he confuses right and wrong."

HEADACHES BECAME DIZZY SPELLS, so Mamie and Anna took their mother to Dr. Blazer. He prescribed a sedative, Veronal, and recommended hot baths.

"Your mama needs a great deal of quiet and bed rest. Should the bad days increase and the headaches make her agitated," he said, "have your father call me to discuss a rest home. There's a facility in Queens, a nice quiet spot, on the site of a farm once owned by a family named Creed." While being confined and closely observed, he explained, the staff would keep an eye on her. He was hopeful that before long new treatments would be available. "Why, in Europe they are working on some surgery that brings relief by fiddling with the front part of the brain. And colleagues are talking about how, in the near future, electricity will be harnessed to control the impulses that cause such mischief."

Angelina understood none of what he said. The day's headache was getting worse. She was grateful when the doctor picked up her chart and opened the door. He held her hand as they were leaving. "You be a good girl now, Angelinie, understand? And get yourself some bed rest. Take your medicine, like you are told. You're gonna be okay."

"What must I do?" she asked the girls. They told her about the Veronal, and the baths, and the bed rest. And they reassured her that the headaches would eventually get better without there being any more visits to Dr. Blazer or any other doctor. Her family would take care of her, always. Disturbed that the Veronal kept her in a stupor and destroyed her already diminished appetite, Orazio called on Pavone the pharmacist. He came home with a bottle of Bayer aspirin and some chamomile leaves for making tea. Pavone gave assurances this was sufficient for calming his wife's nerves.

Angelina's children didn't understand the complexity of their mother's anguish. But they instinctively knew that it was rooted in the disconnect between Rutinese expectations and the lifestyle of one who saw himself as a modern man with big dreams and a passion for good times. Intent on not causing more trouble in the family, his brother, sisters, and their spouses acted civilly to Louise. But since they shared many of their parents' old world beliefs, they believed she was the source of his estrangement from Rosie and Doris, and mismanagement of the store. They also resented the anguish it was causing their parents.

Their extra visits to see Mama and Papa came with funny stories of what their children had said or done, a little gossip about some foolish *paesani*, and lots of knowing nods and comforting hugs. Still, Orazio felt he was doubly cursed, because Angelina went on and on about *la puttana*, the *infamia* to Rosie and her family, missing Doris, and how sick all this was making her. She dwelled on his excessive drinking, womanizing, and disdain for respectable work.

"Orazio, where will this disgrace end?" Distraught that Michael had abandoned his wife and daughter, Angelina—not yet sixty-three years old—had acquired the appearance of an octogenarian. Her once jet-black bun had gone gray, and long strands of hair lingered outside her bun, as if they had been too tired to make it in the round-up.

More disturbing was how frail she had become, walking with a shuffle, shoulders always slight but regal, now arched over. Then there was the tiredness and periodic confusion, but since it would be generations until doctors recognized how small strokes brought on signs of advanced aging, she and her family placed the blame on "the trouble with Michael."

TOO TIRED NOW TO HAVE A HOUSE full of company, even if her daughters took over much of the work, Sunday dinner and large gatherings shifted to the Naso's 17th Street brownstone. Angelina was uplifted by her children's doting. She told comara Sestina, her childhood confident from Rutino, that her family had the power to quiet the chatter in her head and ease the cold feeling of loss in her stomach. After dinner, Joe would bring out her mandolin. While he played Mamie's piano, she strummed along, her little American grandchildren singing Italian songs intoned with American accents. But she felt as if her shame stood waiting outside the front door.

Preparing for Minnie and Lenny's wedding helped lift her spirits. She and Orazio brought the couple to Michael's Furniture on Fifth Avenue to select a bedroom set. The gifts that came in the mail lit up the house. When Lenny's family arrived from Bari, there were dinners and parties at her children's homes to welcome them into the family. Mamie and Anna took their mother downtown to Abraham and Strauss for sheets and a bedspread, so Minnie would have something from her mama to open along with her other shower gifts.

Her daughters convinced her that it was not a sign of disrespect to shed the mourning clothes she'd been wearing since word came from Rutino the previous year that her brother, Angelo, had died. Brown, she agreed, was subdued and appropriate. They also begged her not to dwell on Angelo's death and the new hard times that prohibited her sisters from making the trip.

THE LONGOS WERE FORTUNATE that Orazio's businesses survived despite the IOUs and bad checks that had been mounting since the stock market crash of the previous October. Angelina was pleased that Orazio bargained for a good price at Prospect Hall. The gaiety at the April 1930 wedding of Minnie Longo to Lenny Venturi reflected nothing of the Depression's hard times, which darkened other weddings— that is, until a brawl abruptly ended the affair an hour earlier than was expected.

Two weeks earlier, Louise's uncle, Benny Horan, had arrived unannounced from Chicago. Benny was a fast-talking investor traveling from city to city, backing private clubs. He was in New York, looking at some properties near Times Square. He dressed a little too flashily, even for Michael's taste, and was the personification of trouble. Not wanting to set Louise off, Michael kept his suspicions to himself, although he had never heard about an Uncle Benny, or any of Louise's other relatives for that matter. She'd told him when they met that she had no family. There had been a house fire in Evanston, where her two older sisters and parents had perished. Since the age of three, she explained, she had lived in one orphanage or another.

By pointing out that he was family, Michael convinced his father to invite Benny to the wedding. "Thanks, Papa. You're tops. Now speak to Mama. And make sure she doesn't stare at him with raised eyebrows."

Benny showed up wearing a tuxedo and his trademark gold-and-red suspenders. At first, the band leader said it was fine for him to come up and sing "Ain't Misbehavin." But one song turned into six. Finally, someone yelled out, "Enough is enough!" Then, without any accompaniment, Benny started singing "Making Whoopie." Taking him by the elbow, the band leader ushered him off stage. When Benny called him "a talentless wop," fists started flying. The owner of Prospect Hall ordered the waiters to remove Benny, the musicians, and some guests who had joined in the fray. The brawl continued outside on Prospect Avenue until police from the 35th Precinct arrived. In the midst of the chaos, Benny Horan, with the ease of the card sharp he was, slipped out of sight.

Angelina never learned the details of Benny's return to Brooklyn a month after he'd ruined Lenny and Minnie's wedding reception. And if she had, the story would have been incomprehensible to her Southern Italian sensibility. A man treats his host's woman with respect, even if she is no good.

One night before the couple sat down to dinner, Benny knocked on the apartment door, announcing he was "passing through New York" on his way to Philadelphia. He wanted to visit his favorite niece. Shaking Michael's hand heartily but, as usual, not looking him in the eye, he mumbled something about regretting what happened at the wedding. He gave Louise two kisses on the lips and one on the neck that left teeth marks. "I am meeting with some other big-money people about a club we'll be backing in North Philly."

But one week became two, and by early June Benny was still there complaining of some back problems that made him reluctant to travel "just yet." He needed nursing. "Who better to take care of me than my little tootsie of a niece?"

Michael was annoyed that Benny had returned. He touched, and talked to, Louise in a way most strange between an uncle and his niece. Her not-all-that-funny stories made Benny laugh a little too loud. Patting his niece's behind, Michael rationalized, was the way modern American uncles showed affection.

Talking it over with Louise always ended in her laughing it off. Michael's suspicion, she said, "Is exactly what I'd expect from a dago mama's boy whose family warps him with Eyetalian nonsense about how a woman should live."

Then Louise would break him down, telling him she had seen him flirting with some starlet at the club. "It is a shame that one woman is not enough for you." There would be screams and threats. Michael would make intimidating gestures, and Louise would give him the superior look and scornful smile that Americans gave greenhorns trying to act like their equals. After they had exhausted all their posturing, accusations, and lies, they'd pledge devotion while satisfying each other's sexual fetishes. Empowered by having kept hidden her true relationship with Benny, Louise turned Siren.

Keenly aware that Michael was the patsy who'd pay her way while she established a singing career in the New York, she'd indulge his sexual fantasies. His desires were kaleidoscopic. Every opening on her body was at his command. He had her in ways he believed were unthinkable with some nice Italian girl. The dramatic performance was mutually beneficial. Louise needed financial support; Michael needed to prove he was much more than some dago mama's boy.

Orazio told his wife he was tired of arguing with Michael. She must remind him about his responsibilities to the family business. Angelina called the apartment, and when *la puttana* realized it was her, she repeated Michael's name until he came to the phone.

"It is a disgrace that you leave Fred alone in the store six days a week. Where do you go every day?" She did not care that he was running a speakeasy in lower Manhattan with Ciro; he must fulfill his obligation to the family business and work in the store at least twice a week. When Angelina pressed her daughters for details about their brother's ways, they told her to stop worrying. He was living a different kind of life, a more American type of life. Minnie, regarded by the family as the most "modern-minded" of the three Longo girls, tried to allay her mother's unrelenting complaints.

"Yes, Mama, we know she is a *puttana*, but Michael is a grown man. This is his business. We have to accept that his time away from the store is taken up with work at his club and helping Louise establish her singing career. Yes, he is visiting everyone less and looks as if he has worries and secrets, but that's the way it is when you are 'a man about town.'"

All agreed it was a shame he hadn't brought Doris to the wedding; they reassured Angelina that, as soon as school was out, Fred would drive to New Jersey and pick her up, so she could spend a few weeks with the family.

Angelina occupied herself with plans for the visit. She'd teach Doris more songs on the mandolin. Together they would sit in the backyard, eating figs and picking green beans. Doris loved the subway. She'd ask Mamie to take them downtown, so she could buy identical dresses for Clara, Gloria, and Doris. "Ah, *bene mia*, two children blue-eyed like their mother, the other gray-eyed like her father, everyone looking something like my little ones from long ago."

And she was comforted that her grand-daughters' laughter and chatter always made her enjoy the moment. Once again, she could say, "Come, *figlie mie*, we eat a little bit, then we go outside, and we play music and sing some songs by the fig tree. Yes, you come now. We go have a good time." With Doris there, she was sure she would have more energy and fewer headaches and dizzy spells.

NO ONE COULD HAVE IMAGINED the horror of that June day in 1930. The morning of the 10th was uncomfortably hot. By 7:30, the temperature was 81 degrees. Michael had been conflicted about Doris' visit. There was no end in sight to Benny's stay, and Louise showed little interest in getting close to his child. But he loved and missed the girl, and he longed to see her. Yet it was also true that, in spite of the stock market crash and so much unemployment, business at the club was booming. He really didn't have much time to spend with Doris either.

Over breakfast, he and Louise argued again about her spending time with Doris. She was adamant that the child must not sleep over at the apartment. "To be honest," she told Michael, "I don't know how long it will be before Uncle Benny is well enough to travel. He needs my care. Anyway, it was your family's idea to invite her. They are responsible for her." She would like to bring Doris to Prospect Park or Coney Island one afternoon, but she did not have all that much free time. Her act needed some revamping, and she had to put that first.

Tired of the arguing, Michael finally told her not to give it any further thought. Muttering something about him taking so long to understand, Louise stood up and reached across the table for her makeup case. Michael took a frying pan from the counter top and brought it down hard on her buttocks. "Guess I was pretty quick now, Louise." Smoothing out the robe he had lifted before he struck her a third time, she smiled and told him to be quiet or he'd wake Uncle Benny. Michael exploded, "Tell him, when he wakes up, that it's time he leaves for Philadelphia or Chicago, or hell. I just want him out."

Michael decided to visit his mother on his way to the store. Angelina said she was surprised to see him. Ignoring the remark, he handed her a Macy's shopping bag containing a baby doll and a child's pajama and robe set. Since Doris would be sleeping there—a point Louise encouraged him to emphasize when he handed the items to his mother—he wanted to drop off these things and some money for what she'd need.

He sat at the kitchen table and asked for a cup of coffee. His mother looked at him as if to say, "*Now* you know your mother. After all this time you finally come."

"Mama, I am sorry I haven't been around for Sunday dinner these past few weeks, but with Louise's uncle visiting again, I need to help entertain him." The shaking of his legs beneath the table made it wobble. Angelina's stomach absorbed the tension in the room. "I could bring them around on Sunday, but Papa and Benny...well, after what happened at the wedding...it's best not to invite any trouble. You know what I'm saying, Ma?"

Angelina shrugged and raised her eyebrows, the way she always did when she wanted to convey indignant resignation. She told her son he should come by often while Doris was in Brooklyn, even if it meant taking Louise with him. "What do you think, we don't plan on spending time with her? Louise is looking forward to their getting to know each other, to becoming pals. Ah, what's the use of explaining?"

She closed her eyes and shook her head. "*Figlio mio*, my gray-eyed beauty, you are my heart, and I wish you every happiness. But to have this happiness, you need to put your family first and know your obligations. *Capisce?*"

"Yeah, Mama, I know. Trust me, you and Papa made sure all my life that I knew." He rose and put on the new straw hat Zi Enzo sent from Rutino. "Look I'd love to stay longer, but Fred is waiting for me at the store. I gotta run before he starts bellyaching. They'll be plenty of time to visit soon with Doris here and all. Now, come on, let me spin you around once and steal a kiss."

From the front gate, Angelina Longo waved goodbye to her eldest son until his "fancy" red car turned left on 4th Avenue. Next time he came by, she'd tell him she wanted to welcome Louise into the family. "No," she told herself, "I will ask no questions about her past or plans for a life with my Michael. The word *puttana* will not slip past my lips."

Since their bookkeeper, Murray, phoned to say he'd be in around 11:30, Fred was glad Michael got to the store early. Orazio had hired Murray Bernstein when he opened his first shop in 1903, and the accountant knew the Longos' business and property assets better than they did. Michael had taken the account books home to see which customers were failing to pay down their outstanding credit. The Longos had been generous, but with more people out of work or going broke, the amount of debt was becoming a growing matter of concern. Orazio wanted Michael to go over who owed what and how the store's income was being affected. Knowing this would prepare him for Murray's warning that they were being generous to a fault.

Michael told Fred he would return with the books in an hour. "Don't worry—I'll be back before Murray gets here." On his way to the St. Mark's Avenue apartment, he stopped for a dozen roses at Weir's Florist. He'd apologize for striking Louise and tell her again that she was everything to him.

The heat was stifling. So many neighbors were sitting on the front stoop, trying to get a little air, that Michael laughed to himself thinking the building must be half empty. He parked the Chrysler across from the apartment and rolled down the roof. Hot under the collar, he'd get a little breeze on the drive back. As he walked towards his building, he hoped Benny had gone out; he and Louise needed to patch things up.

He had a plan. After he gave her the roses, he would lay her on their bed and massage her in the way that never failed to arouse her. He would tell her what a big star she was going to be. He'd get her to admit that he was the love of her life. Then he'd make love to the exquisite buttocks he had battered before he left. Lost in his reverie, Michael entered the apartment fully aroused.

Murray would just have to wait around the store until he returned. He closed the apartment door ever so gently and tiptoed inside. He wanted to surprise Louise. But it was he who was met by surprise—the devastating kind that comes at you so quickly you do not see it until you recover from the initial shock.

Breakfast dishes were still on the table. There was noise, people's voices, in the rear of the apartment. Was the radio on? It couldn't be, because if it were the sound would be coming from the other direction. And the man's voice was familiar. Michael crept towards the unmistakable sound of sexual passion. The door to the room where Benny had been staying was open, but he wasn't there. Outside the back bedroom, Michael saw Louise's robe and undergarments lying on the floor next to a man's trousers with red and gold suspenders.

Rage and confusion pounded in his brain while he took his pistol out from the bottom of the hamper. The image in the bathroom mirror staring back at him had the look of a madman carrying a gun in one hand and a dozen roses in the other.

No one knows what Michael said when he interrupted Louise and Benny's lovemaking. Later, his mother repressed the urge to think about the details, but the unanswered questions haunted her. Three deaths caused by the son she had seen drive away less than two hours before. Her mind failed to grasp the immensity of the tragedy. If only I had warned him better, she thought; if only he would listen. It was pointless. Eternal silence stood between them.

The family made sure Angelina Longo never learned that the crime scene had been filled with red: red rose petals falling from their stems as they were hurled in the air, red drapes tied back, and, in the background, a red-hot sun shedding light on the blood-splattered room. On the bed lay two lifeless, naked bodies, their faces frozen with a look of horror. And a few feet away, the blood of her gray-eyed son, who stopped the pounding in his brain by putting a bullet through it.

WHO IS TO BLAME FOR SUCH A TRAGEDY? Is it the curse of the immortals for old wounds? Think of Neptune and the storms he sent to challenge those ancient mariners. Or of Ceres, blamed for turning Salerno into a wasteland after malaria drove the Greeks from its fields. Perhaps abandonment was the one act the goddess could not tolerate. Think about the suffering she encountered when her only child was taken by a demon lover to the underworld. Ceres had bargained with a higher power for her daughter's return and been granted a short season of reunion. But could this meager compensation satisfy a mother's loss of a child? And because she is immortal, Ceres' grief will not end. Perhaps she draws bitter comfort knowing she is not alone in her pain.

Generations of Southern Italians have suffered for ancient acts of abandonment, whether it was their identity as a people, ownership of their fields, or loss of their homeland. Historically, they have been thwarted in their attempts to hold on to what they believe is theirs. But when it comes to losing a child, the loss is most devastating. And way too often a family's personal tragedy snakes its way into the future.

Unanswered questions are plentiful: How exactly does the past impact the lives of future generations? What enables those who experience grief and loss to carry on? And how will one who mapped her grief by writing her family's story, withstand the relapses so characteristic of the addictions *her* own child battles?

The answer is no one knows for sure. Or as they say in the Mezzogiorno, "*Chi sa?*"

CHAPTER 5
Back Over The Pond

Courage warms crystal
Wall, ice shielding battered soul.
River, run with words.

London, Wednesday, 6 July 2005

EVERY FIVE MINUTES Beethoven's *Ode to Joy* bounded from my cell phone; 6:00 a.m., a splash of water on my face, and back to proofreading. The next day my manuscript, *Angelina's Story*, would be on its way to my editor and friend, Jed Zabar. Ah, the completion of three years work!

I should have felt a sense of total satisfaction. But not all was well.

Christopher, my only child, the light that brightened my difficult marriage, suffers from what therapists diagnosed as a complex blend of personality disorders, anxiety, and depression. Dismissive of therapy and pharmacology, Chris self-medicates. During his sophomore year of high school, it was as if some Fury had snatched away his happiness before thrusting him down a slippery slope of reckless behavior.

Gone was his passion for sports, art, and music. He distanced himself from the cousins he'd grown up with, much to the relief of their parents, who feared the bad influence he'd exert over them. His new friends told him I was overbearing, too preoccupied with his schoolwork and his comings and goings. He agreed. It's been two years since I've seen or heard from him; my phone calls are not returned.

WHILE HE WAS GROWING UP, we spent our Saturdays in Manhattan at the movies, at the Children's Museum, and at least once a month at Roxy's, the art supply store across from the Students' Art League. The next morning, I'd find an illustrated thank you note with *I love you, Mom* sitting above his signature. I loved raising him.

The first change in Chris came when he was twelve. Always chatty and quick to show affection, he hardly spoke to me, and when he did, it was usually in anger. Such behavior is not unusual for an adolescent boy living with a single mother. But there is a back story. He repeatedly heard from his father and his father's family that I had broken up his family. After we separated, his dad, Caspar, became the beleaguered hero of our personal tragedy. Chris' idealized view of him stood in stark contrast to my reality of breaking free from an abusive alcoholic.

Two weeks before I asked him to leave, Cas became violent when we passed each other on the staircase leading to our bedroom. Our respective resentments and threats to leave each other had escalated. We hardly spoke except to exchange sarcastic remarks. That afternoon, I took advantage of Cas' poor hearing and let out a sigh of disgust. By time I drew my next breath, he'd turned around, pushed me against the wall, and wrapped his hand around my throat. The attack was short but frightening. This time there were no insults about my weight (I was starving myself at the time) or my failure to appreciate him and all he had given me, just a menacing look and a hand around my throat. Was it the sigh, or had he been listening while I left the message for a divorce lawyer?

The night before, I had decided to confront my worst character flaw: being a slow learner who wallows in denial and self-pity. Maybe it was lying there reading Ovid's *Metamorphoses* that activated me. I realized that I had two choices: stay with Cas and, like Ovid's mortals, whine about my fate and anger the gods; or start a new life and transform our home into a safer place for Chris and me. Fortunately, I was in too much pain to be held back by my insecurities.

As a child, Chris embraced life. There wasn't an after-school activity he didn't join; there wasn't a week when he didn't place a hefty Scholastic paperback book order. "Mom, can I just order one more? You know I love these books." And love them he did, devouring them with a hunger to learn that warmed my motherly, teacherly heart. "Mom, I know I'm playing baseball and soccer, but I want to try out for Brooklyn Academy's basketball team too. Okay?"

"Sure, Chris, I think it's great, but soon you and I will be living in the car, going from practice to practice," I'd joke. No activity was too much for him.

But our home was filled with his father's alcoholic outbursts and my growing anxiety and obsession with my work. There were early signs that Chris was in trouble: acting out at school, talking rudely to his teachers, making awful remarks to his classmates about women.

Cas never laid a hand on Chris. But he abused him emotionally, talking to him and treating him inappropriately. One morning, I overheard Cas ranting, "These bitches will walk all over you if you let them." What resentment had overtaken his sanity? Had someone stopped by, or was he on the phone? I ran up from the basement and asked him to keep it down before Chris heard him. But there was Chris sitting at the kitchen table, eating his breakfast. I felt anger swelling while I watched him talk to our ten-year-old son. It was as if he was intentionally trying to warp him.

For Chris' first Christmas I bought a copy of *A Child's Book of Poetry*. On the frontispiece I wrote what I hoped would become a reminder of the happiness he brought to our lives. Sipping his second Rob Roy of the evening, Cas said he wanted to write something, too. I was stunned by his inscription and told him so. Believing it was my responsibility to squelch his inappropriateness, I stuck a smiling Santa sticker over his words: *Dear pal, I want you to know how happy you make me. Love from your Dad, Maurice.* By time Chris entered nursery school he had begun mimicking his father's edgy, sarcastic humor.

No doubt, Cas was proud of Chris, routinely telling him how smart he was, how handsome he was, and how much he loved him. But he seemed happiest when he was joking around with our son as if he were one of his bar buddies. Without any apparent reservation, he'd tell Chris stories of his booze-fueled antics, or about putting down people whom he found ridiculous in some way or other, and those were usually women, especially me.

"Once, pal, my friends and I were asked to leave the Catskill Dude Ranch, because we showed up for dinner with water-filled balloons under our tee shirts. Water bubbies." Chris thought his father was hilarious. When I gave Cas a look, he'd raise his eyebrows and tell our son, "We'd better stop. The English teacher is giving me the stink eye."

Cas' mother and brother often joined in, believing that, unlike me, they were showing this little boy the lighter side of life. When he was in the sixth grade, a dean at the Brooklyn Academy overheard Chris tell classmates, "Mothers who spend a lot of time at college are lesbians." When she asked him what that meant, he answered, "I have to ask my Grandma Tessie."

In 1992, his father and I separated. His face in photographs from that time has a pale, deadpan look. Eyes downcast, he has turned away from something too hard to look at. He was angry with me because, as his father explained it to him, my "nagging" was driving him crazy. "Now she wants me out of the house. So, you'll have to put up with her alone, pal."

Despite the dysfunction, Chris earned high grades and three graduation awards, but he grew quieter and quicker to anger, there and at home. Things will get better, I reasoned, if I keep him busy, show him love. He'll survive. Through the mountains of snow that lasted from January through March in 1993, we trudged to the drama coach's studio, where he prepared for an audition at the High School of Performing Arts. More like two kids than mother and son, we'd run along 18th Avenue to Hansen's Ice Cream Parlor. Melted marshmallow dripping from the hot cocoa lining his sprouting moustache, Chris would recite a monologue.

BUT HE WASN'T ACCEPTED to the High School of Performing Arts, a chancy ambition unless you have parents in the philharmonic or on Broadway. Not making the football team at Bishop O'Hara High School was another disappointment, but not making the cut for the baseball team devastated him. During his years at the Brooklyn Academy, where tryouts resulted in placement, not rejection, Chris had been one of the guys, a team player. Now, he'd complain, "This place sucks. All these priests are good for is giving out detentions."

Maybe Monsignor didn't hear me when I introduced myself as Dr. Naso. Hands folded atop a large oak desk that eerily brought me back to my years at St. Mark's Elementary school, he pontificated. "Mrs. Simonelli, all Bishop O'Hara boys are special, but there are rules and regulations. Chris has trouble following them. Homeroom," he explained, "begins at 8:20, not 8:23. Hair gel is forbidden, and shirts must be tucked in at all times."

The buzz was that the priests were especially impatient with boys of divorced parents. After telling Monsignor Kelly how I spent my days, I clearly felt like an apostate and an absentee mother. Raised eyebrows and a mocking smile were his response when I mentioned I taught literature and women's studies. Fr. Kelly took on a tone I suspect he reserved for the spiritually AWOL.

"Father, Christopher needs to feel more accepted, better about what he does well, which is playing sports. His father and I always encouraged him to ask questions and speak his mind. Maybe there's a program here or a guidance counselor he can talk to. He needs positive feedback. . . . Oh, I see—you have three sets of parents waiting outside. Sure. But I'd like to reschedule another meeting, perhaps for when you're not so busy? . . . Yes, then I will wait until I hear from the school secretary."

By the end of sophomore year, Chris was expelled from Bishop O'Hara. The small infractions had turned into larger ones. He seemed unable to stop cutting class after class and smoking marijuana in the toilet. Expulsion from the next high school came a year later. By then he had moved from marijuana to LSD and God knows what else. He refused to admit his drug use or even talk about it. After that it was one experimental program or another for at-risk students.

One of the many guidance counselors who tried to help him told me, "It would be better if Chris came into the building and attended class, instead of sitting in the schoolyard smoking pot and reading Nietzsche." I sought out a number of therapists, but Chris either jumped out of the car on the way to an appointment or sat there silent, with his arms crossed, for the entire session. These interventions—a solitary project, since his father said this was all part of growing up and my family let me know that they didn't want to get involved—proved fruitless.

Now, a month away from his twenty-fifth birthday, he still hasn't functioned as an adult. He hasn't completed college; he has no resources of his own. Bright, well-read, and sympathetic to the plight of the poor and oppressed, like others with untreated emotional problems and a history of drug abuse, his affect is unpredictable. One moment he is shut down, and the next he is talking non-stop. At times his rapid speech is incoherent.

Chris aspires to becoming a comedian/comedy writer, a nihilist version of Lenny Bruce. Yet as he tries to make it in a field both highly competitive and risky for those with addictions, he refuses to work a day job. To cover expenses, he depends on loved ones who enable him, primarily his father and his girlfriend, Brandi.

Financially dependent on own her parents, the jobs Brandi takes come and go. Although she and Chris are together day and night, she's convinced her parents they've split up. Her father told me she sees him occasionally to lend emotional support, because his family has abandoned him.

Receiving a voicemail message from Brandi is the prelude to an anxiety attack, binge eating, migraine headache, or all of the above. "Arianna, you need to show Chris you care. He isn't an addict. He just needs more financial support from you. If you helped Caspar pay Chris' rent, he'd give him more spending money. Your son needs you to take responsibility, and you really shouldn't harp on his getting involved with NA. He sees through these ridiculous twelve-step programs."

Confident that she is wise beyond her years, she is long on advice. "Maybe if you help support him, he'll show you some respect." I've wondered if that's the story Brandi tells herself to justify supplying him with the anti-depressants doctors tell me will only serve to worsen his condition.

But I've played my destructive part in this family tragedy. My reaction to Chris' behavior became obsessive. I'd rummage through his book bag and bureau drawers, looking for drugs. I'd call his friends' parents, trying to enlist their support. I'd insist on driving and picking him up from places instead of giving him the freedom he was craving. And then there was the self-pity. "How could you do this, knowing I am still getting over pneumonia?" I hated myself for passing on to him the guilt-tripping techniques I had encountered, and resented, as a girl in my own parents' home.

At age fifteen, Chris began staying out all night. The first two times he did so, I called the police. Then he'd return home more defiant than ever. I became fearful and resentful.

"Where were you last night?"

"That's none of your business. Stop nagging me."

"Who were you with? Didn't you think I'd be worried out of my mind?"

"That's impossible. You're already out of your mind."

One weekend, a shattered window told the tale of where he'd been. With Caspar away at his cousin's beach house, Chris and his friend, Davey, broke into his apartment and spent the night drinking and drugging. Davey's mother told me she'd found a note in her son's room about a suicide pact he'd made with Chris. Through it all, I didn't see clearly enough that he was acting out his pain. Nor did I seek out a support network to help me help him. Things went on this way far too long.

Eventually he told me that he wanted no contact with me. And although I am not presently in his life, he pervades every inch of mine. Two years and an ocean away, it is as if he's right here with me, back turned, walking down the hall, refusing to look at me when I call out his name.

Of course, being less than central in a twenty-five-year-old son's life is not unusual.

Most people in my circle have children living in other states. Their relationships are long distance, geographically, and, in some cases, emotionally. But they *have* a relationship: time together, and a parent–child bond that will last a lifetime. I'd gladly have settled for that.

Chris acts as if I am some old enemy who won't go away. More often than I should have, I pleaded with him to address his emotional and substance abuse problems.

Conversations became verbal minefields. Each time I phoned, I felt sick when he said: "Yeah, Mom, what do you want?" Hearing this never failed to stun me. Anxiously anticipating a nasty comeback, I lost my ability to carry on a decent conversation with him, offering success stories about rehab and twelve-step programs until we were both sick of hearing me.

On some level I believed I deserved the rejection. Hadn't it been my responsibility to prevent him from ruining his health and well-being? The last time I spoke to him was early in May 2003. Chris sounded extremely agitated, and while I was careful not to bring up his need for treatment, I couldn't say a word that didn't set him off.

Like other Mother's Days since his troubles began, that year he did not visit or call. But the next day my spirits rose when I received a card with his return address. "I can't believe my eyes," I murmured. "Maybe there's hope. Maybe he still feels the bond." But the harsh words written in the rear of the recycled "I Miss You" card I had recently sent him ended hope for even minimal contact: *Don't call; don't write.* A double spondee, four arrows aimed straight at my heart.

How severe was my damage?

My pain sought refuge in social isolation and wild consumption, primarily spending and food. Had I ever stopped to notice how many milligrams of sodium I consumed after Chris lashed out at me? I'd turn to the comfort of salted chips, lying to myself that the vegetable-flavored ones weren't as unhealthy. Some melted cheese to dip them in, because, damn, I *had* been a good mother. Lots of Diet Coke to wash it down. To hell with the warning about the phenylalanine. "So what if I have an anxiety disorder and should stay away from it?" Some cold cuts added an Atkinseque mask of an attempt at weight control. Should I ring him back and try again? I'd wonder, standing before the microwave, not-too-unconsciously hoping that, between all the cheese, additives, and radiation, something would kill me.

The credit card debt I racked up was an ironic blessing. Paying it down with money from overload teaching kept me solvent and busy.

BEFORE RETURNING TO MY MANUSCRIPT, I thought about how Christopher's story would be an essential part of a new project, a memoir. Over the years, I had kept a journal of what was happening with him and my efforts to recover my life from the wreck it had become. I realized that I didn't have the courage to begin writing it in the first person. Too close; too painful. At least for the moment, I needed the emotional distance of he, she, and they. I and we must come later. And the telling required something beyond conventional narrative and the staid dignity of Times New Roman. Was there a chilling font whose form complemented the severity of the words lamenting how this had come to be? This post-modern family tragedy coursed through my mind like a stream of consciousness cascading in waves.

"Once a brilliant student passionate about drawing and writing stories he'd later bind into books. . .Chris began taking drugs by age fourteen. . .he went from one high school to the next. . .expelled from each because he disregarded rules including bringing drugs onto school property. . .Ari's father told her she should be tougher on Chris . . .demand more from him. . .Chris' father didn't see the point of confrontation or therapy. . .his grandmother was horrified at the thought of telling strangers family business. . .Ari's sisters changed the subject when she brought it up which was probably too often. . . she felt overwhelmed . . .at age sixteen Chris decided to live with his father. . .he did not ask. . .he just packed a bag. . .and demanded Ari drive him there. . .the next year he was hospitalized for a drug overdose. . .by age eighteen he had accrued several DWIs and a drug arrest. . .but his illnesses were ignored because Caspar frowned upon medication and did not really see the point of psychotherapy or support groups. . . even when they were being used to help Chris after Ari placed him in a psychiatric hospital for observation. . .the principal of the second high school he attended had found written plans he and another student were making to mail drugs to a friend at boarding school. . .at the hospital Chris was diagnosed with depression and personality issues. . .he was given medication counseling and behavior modification exercises. . .Caspar laughed along with Chris mocking the social workers' suggestions. . .he yelled at Ari when she tried to stop him. . .Chris agreed with his father that it was Ari who should be committed. . .when Chris went to live with him Caspar took him off his medication. . .he said Chris was doing better. . .Ari was not told about the arrests that followed. . .nor was she told of the visits from a girlfriend's parents after he had become abusive. . . Casper later explained that it was none of Ari's business and Chris' girlfriend had probably deserved it anyway. . . she was another bitch. . .Chris made excuses why he could not spend time with Ari. . .and when he did there invariably would be an argument that cut things short. . .his mother did not know how troubled Chris was. . .there was much she later learned that had been kept from her. . .and the diagnosis of a mood disorder had not yet been made. . . anyway Caspar and his live-in girlfriend did not want Ari calling or coming to the house to pick up Chris. . .they said they knew how to handle it. . .they found Ari's phone calls irritating. . .she had been told that she must sit in her car at the corner and Chris would walk down to meet her. . .many times he decided not to. . .so Ari would wait and wait because she was not welcome at their front door . . .she was frustrated by the lies cover ups and dismissal of her efforts to seek out help for her son. . .a supportive family would have been a blessing to her but none was there. . .her dad Ted and his wife Sadie told her to forget about Chris and move on with her life. . .Ari's eating habits resulted in bizarre weight fluctuations. . .she went from size 6 to size 16 up and down again depending where she was with her eating disorder. . .she sublimated her grief and anxiety. . .work became her safe place. . .Chris often told his mother that his father and his father's entire family knew she was crazy and all she cared about was dragging Chris off to fancy schools expensive vacations too many after school activities and then they reasoned that all this led to therapists and doctors and how many times had she said that medication might help Chris calm down . . .the Simonellis said Chris was old enough to make his own decisions about how he wanted to live his life and that included whether or not he wanted to go to school. . .Chris thought it best to virtually stop attending school once he moved in with his dad. . .Ari did manage to get him a high school diploma after hounding and manipulating the director of the alternative program Chris had been transferred to. . .fortunately there were times when Chris sought her out. . .for example the night he was arrested in Queens for jumping the subway turnstile. . .and again the night when his heart raced because he drank and drugged for hours at home where he had been left in the care of Cas' girlfriend's brother. . .they had needed a weekend at their beach house. . .at the hospital Ari asked the doctors to phone Child Services. . .the case worker was sympathetic but except for eight mandated visits to a daytime drug program nothing changed. . .after that Chris asked to see less of Ari. . .but he did tell her once in a moment she likes to recall that she must never move far away because she knows where to find help and someday he would need it. . .so in July 2005 in London Ari was still waiting for that request. . .it had been almost four years since Chris walked out of a California state rehabilitation facility he had been sent to following two arrests for possession of cocaine and driving with a suspended license. . .Ari flew to California to visit him but when she arrived the director of the facility said Chris did not want to see her. . .she was told that they were not at liberty to answer any further questions. . .after he left rehab Chris failed to meet his parole officer and keep a court date. . .his probation officer had forewarned Ari. . . but there was Caspar sending cab fare for Chris to travel from the San Diego rehab to Los Angeles. . .he was annoyed because Ari refused to participate as he called it in paying for the cab fare or in helping out when he wired money to the motel where Chris sat in his room or by the pool high on drugs. . .alone and on the run. . .he told his parents he did not want to see them because he was working everything out. . .later on Caspar paid off the bounty hunters from California just as he had done two years before when Chris was arrested in Colorado. . .he also paid for the lawyers. . .Somehow or other Chris made it back to Brooklyn. . .and like Melville's Bartleby he became the unmovable resident of the office from which Caspar ran his

demolition business. . .there was no shower stove or refrigerator. . .but there were several bottles of liquor left over
from some function. . .Caspar told Ari she was crazy when
she asked him to remove the alcohol from the office where
their son was living. . .Chris did manage to feed himself
however by ordering whatever he wanted on Caspar's credit
card. . .Caspar did not complain too much over any of this
. . .because he did not want to make Chris angry. . .Any-
way he was a man and he believes a man must be left
alone to make his own decisions. . .Ari knew how her ex-
husband felt since she herself had been fearful of violent
outbursts much of the time during their courtship and
later during their marriage. . .these days Caspar had to
watch his anger. . .the girlfriend who became his new wife
had both health insurance and a good credit rating . . .she
demanded that talk of Chris' problems not enter the home
she had leased for herself and the financially addled but
more subdued Caspar. . .when the story worsened and Ari
realized that all her efforts to help Chris were not helping
him and that they were filing her with thoughts about
driving off the pier on Dock Road in southern New Jersey
. . .and asking Chris to get help only made him angrier. . .
she listened to a colleague's suggestion that she attend an
Al Anon meeting. . .she decided to try the twelve-step program and later was happy to find a meeting she loved and
yet another in London. . .eventually she stopped trying to
fix the situation. . .and though she stopped thinking about
driving off the pier. . .every day she grieves for Chris. . .
misses him. . .loves him. . .and waits. . .as she does today
in London where she is having a hard time focusing on
finalizing her manuscript because she not only misses

Chris but she is exploring her own story and where she came from and how her past provides context for the misery. . .and how it has affected every aspect of her. . .of my life."

REMEMBERING THE COURSE OF THE TRAGEDY left me anxious. During my recovery, I learned I could soothe myself by meditating on the positive realities of my life. *I am Arianna Naso, a cultural critic and literature professor at the College of New York City. I am passionate about my work. My students are amazing. I have friends who love me. My health is good. I am finishing a book that has a contract. And from the window before me I see Fleet Street and the wedding cake shaped tower of St. Bride's Church.* A hot shower and repeating "The Serenity Prayer" centered me. I was grateful, especially since the manuscript was due at my publisher's office by August 25th.

INITIALLY IN FITS AND STARTS, and then with the obsessive devotion that propels my academic work, I'd been researching and writing a biography, Angelina's Story, based on Angelina Longo, one of my parental great-grandmothers. Born in 1870 in Rutino, a small Italian town near the Amalfi Coast, her story has all the elements of a good biography: a magical homeland plagued by troubles that result in the protagonist's emigration, the love of a charming but difficult man, the building of a new life in a comfortable yet strange place. And there is something else, the loss of an adult child. A shameful memory shrouded in silence and buried in the family plot in Green-Wood Cemetery.

I grew up listening to family stories and witnessed haunting silences. I knew that Angelina and my great- grandfather, Orazio, came to America in 1892, and that, two years later, my Grandma Mamie was born, the first American in her family. My father had a vague memory of hearing about two children dying before Grandma was born. And although I knew my grandmother's sister, Minnie, died while my mother was pregnant with me, no one spoke about my great-uncle, Michael. Everyone acted as if Uncle Joe was Grandma's only brother.

For almost sixty years, no one spoke about or answered questions about *Michele* Longo, the name chiseled on the grave marker in Green-Wood. Except for a cold gray stone, the memory of the Longos' eldest son, whose mental illness and addiction to excess ended in 1930 when he committed murder-suicide, had been erased.

EARLY IN MY ACADEMIC CAREER, I spoke at a conference, "Growing up Ethnic in New York." As part of my preparation, I interviewed family members, gathering information about their experiences and particulars about our neighborhood, Bensonhurst, Brooklyn. Talking into my tape recorder, my father and his sister, my Aunt Clara, gave an account of the family's coming to America. They were expansive about people and places I was too young to remember. From the get-go, they nudged the interview in the direction of how our family achieved the American dream.

But when I asked the forbidden question, the interview was over. Who wants to talk about *him?* Why are you bringing *that* up when there's so much good to remember? Confronting silence in response to a loved one's shameful acts was all too familiar.

SOME YEARS LATER, I was stunned when one of my father's cousins provided me with what later research revealed was the family's spin on Michael's murder-suicide. I became consumed with my great-grandmother's losses, although I was careful not to confuse them with mine. But it didn't stop questions about post-traumatic memory and genetic predisposition to addiction and mental illness. And there were other questions too: How did my great-grandmother cope? Was anyone willing to listen? How did she feel when her son disappeared from the family circle, when deafening silence erased the memory of flesh and blood that was so much more than the disease that challenged it?

My father and aunt enjoyed telling cheerful stories about how their father and their grandparents loved American life, and how America had welcomed them. "Your grandfather was proud to be an American. He came here with nothing and, within ten years, he'd opened a business and bought a house, a brownstone no less." Aunt Clara added, "None of that was possible in Italy. Of course, there is still no place in the world as beautiful as Italy."

I'm not sure how she knew this, since she had never visited Italy, let alone Grandpa Joe's village or Rutino.

But they were uncomfortable with my questions about the hardship that forced the family to leave Italy and the hostility they confronted as immigrants. Their generalizations and awkward pauses yielded a whitewashed version of the shameful memories that haunt the immigrant experience. Such are the ways of denial.

I was careful not to situate Angelina's story in the context of the poverty and exploitation sociologist Edward Banfield indicted in his 1958 *The Moral Basis of a Backward Society*. Wielding cultural bias and an attitude of Anglo superiority, Banfield identified "amoral familism"—the rigid focus on family matters that excludes participation in community affairs—as the core of the Southern Italian sensibility. Because of their distrust of outsiders, he argued, Southern Italians' participation in community projects is limited to extended family networks. Laden with primitive behaviors, they put little stock in law and order.

Banfield's view placed guilt and shame on the peasants, the impoverished *terroni*, without taking into account their long history of being colonized. Both inside and outside the classroom, I was passionate about the inherent bias in Banfield's complicated point of view.

I tracked down available records concerning my Longo great-grandparents and their offspring. At the same time, I delved into the immigration experience of Italian Americans whose ancestors came from the area south of Rome. When these dark-skinned peasants began to arrive in the late 1800s, the Anglo American ruling class saw them as inferiors who were polluting American society. Their gregarious, sometimes boisterous ways frequently subjected them to ridicule and suspicion. In the twentieth century, Italian Americans were allowed into the professions, the academy, and politics later than other new Americans. When they were, they were frequently made to feel like interlopers by their peers. Well into the twentieth century, the establishment kept them at arm's distance.

Seeking refuge in the traditions of the past, transplanted Southern Italians worked diligently to achieve success. Dubious of higher education, Italian American immigrants typically chose work as the road to success. They told their sons, "You don't want to become smarter than your father—do you?" If their daughters knew their place, they needed no reminder. If a woman went off on her own, there would be many a "God forbid." If she ventured towards a life different from the one that had been scripted for her, she ran the risk of being likened to a *puttana*, a whore.

Most Italian immigrants spent the little leisure time that remained after work with family and *paesani*, enjoying food, wine, and song. The wine that drowned out the pain of poverty and displacement was abundant. At times, it flowed like an oil leak that threatens to destroy the oceans and the balance of nature.

I'M ONE OF THOSE REINVENTED WOMEN, a *puttana* who strayed into academic life. I admit I feel safest when I am alone with my work, and perhaps this has been the deciding factor in taking on one long term project after another. So it seemed right to wed my professional skills and family stories and write an imaginative biography. These days, the genre of creative non-fiction allows writers to invent details and events in biography and memoir that enhance the emotional impact. Since details were scarce, and because I wanted to imagine how my ancestors were impacted by the *Risorgimento*, the struggle that unified Italy in 1861, fictionalizing Angelina's story was the logical choice.

I hoped that grappling with Angelina's losses might help me deal with my own. And if not, here was a story of valiant coping that deserved telling.

While I proofread my completed manuscript, I was conscious that I was missing typos and unnecessary repetitions. Time for a mid-morning cappuccino. Crossing the Strand to the Caffé Nero, I reminded myself I needed to stay focused on the proofreading. This morning there would be no walking over Waterloo Bridge or along the South Bank, taking in the scenery and stopping here and there. That must come later.

CHAPTER 6

Re-Membering By The Strand

Night passed, sky pinked day.
Then I espied outstretched hands
And rose basked in light.

ARMED WITH A SKIM CAPPUCCINO, I continued proofreading the section in which, on a hot June day in 1930, my great-uncle, Michael Longo, arrives home unexpectedly, shoots his lover, the man in their bed, and then himself. Until I unearthed it, Michael's story had been buried in the dark recesses of the family's memory.

But the stream of consciousness about Chris' situation rendered me scattered. Ashamed as I'm to admit it, I'm easily distracted by worrisome thoughts and haunting memories. Too often my concentration is held hostage by my psyche. Inadvertently, I drifted into the mind-numbing writing project I was completing for Luis Aviles, the dean of my division at the college. Personal and financial independence, I learned, is heavenly. But it is costly, very costly. Consequently, at every given opportunity, I take on extra work. So as my internal chatter disrupted my concentration, I turned over a page of the Angelina manuscript and began the introduction to the Ethnic Studies brochure the dean needed by the end of August.

The College of New York City is committed to preparing students to expand their historical knowledge, critical and comparative skills, and examination of America's rich cultural diversity. The College's Ethnic Studies program offers a variety of interdisciplinary courses that. . . .

"Damn, I've turned to the brochure for Luis when I should be proofing the last chapter." (Deep breath.) "But my book is moving forward!" (Breathe out.) "Tomorrow this time, the manuscript will be on its way to Jed." (Breathe in.)

Jed Zabar, chair of the English Department and my dearest friend, has offered to edit the manuscript. Despite our closeness, he'll be brutally honest. During endless conversations about writing, we've discussed the ups and downs of the writing process, or "writing processes" as I say, owning my quirky way of approaching and completing a writing project. When I was hired as an assistant professor in 1985, Jed had been there for over a decade teaching creative writing and Walt Whitman's poetry.

Back then, the English Department was housed in a large room with faculty work stations that resembled insurance company cubicles. Students lined up for Jed's help with their writing, for counsel about coming out of the closet and coping with homophobia, and for advice about how to navigate the Scylla and Charybdis that threaten first-generation college students. Many times they were there for all of the above. Colleagues also gathered around Jed's desk, relishing the sparkling wit that complemented his bejeweled ears and red-tinted eyeglasses.

These days they line up outside the office he occupies as department chair to confer on academic matters. But he regales each one, often with me, his deputy, sitting nearby, laughing at his quips, knowing how weird he feels performing a service no one else had the heart to sign up for after the previous chair made a quick exit. In horn-rimmed glasses and color-coordinated Banana Republic outfits, he has scraped the glitter but maintained the wit.

The behemoth size of the English Department has necessitated long hours of working together and traveling to Modern Language Association conferences to interview prospective colleagues.

Since he is non-judgmental, I quickly began feeling safe enough to confide things about Chris and my marriage I hadn't told anyone other than my therapist. Without asking a million questions, he listens. What a relief. How many times had I opened up to someone only to confront moronic comments like, "Thank God ours are good kids," or to hear questions, one after another, that stomped upon my emotional minefield. "How long has he been doing this to you?" "Why do you take it?" "Why don't you just put him in a program?" With Jed there is quiet, gentle compassion. His phone calls to check up on me, his reminders about the good things in my life, have taken me through many crises.

I've become friends with his partner, Gary, and he's included me in his circle of friends. My eggplant parmigiana reminds him of the dishes he enjoyed as a teenager when his mother defied Jewish tradition and married a Sicilian *goy*. We've bonded as a team, as foodies, as souls who too often have felt like outsiders. And although our colleagues call us "the odd couple," this oddness took me out of the deep freeze of isolation.

Two workaholics devoted to our craft, we've accomplished a tremendous amount of work. Laughing about things others might find ridiculous punctuates our long days at the college and hours on the phone. Beneath Jed's casual exterior and history of civil disobedience lives a strict adherence to following rules and regulations. In contrast, some combination of life experiences and internal wiring has rendered me flexible and prone to taking short cuts.

I tease him for being too neat; he raises his eyebrows when he stands at my office door, arm braced on the door frame, as if he's surveying a train wreck. The office I've occupied at the college for the past twenty years is cluttered. Students walk in gingerly, lest they trip over a mountain of books and papers. In contrast, Jed's office looks like the Gubbio Studiolo at the Metropolitan Museum of Art. When things get too intense and I'm craving a little comic relief, I move his rock collection out of order. His Jack Benny look and *faux* chiding bring me back to earth. Over the years, we've built a cache of vintage stories.

"But do you know me?" is the way we sometimes greet each other. That began after we were stuck once in traffic on Canal Street during rush hour. Engrossed in what Jed was saying, I waved back to the traffic cop signaling me to go. She pulled me over, pointing as if her finger were a gun, and asked why I had waved. I was speechless. Then, while she decided whether or not to write a summons, she asked twice, "But do you know me?" I didn't get it. Jed sidled over to my right ear and whispered, "Don't argue with her. Be pleasant." Of course he was right, but I remembered how, as a founding member of the Gay Activist Alliance, he had been jailed after the Stonewall riots kicked off what he affectionately refers to as "the movement." Driving down Canal Street, ticket free, we laughed about the incident. "But do you know me?" has become our code for negotiating trouble.

The trust and friendship I've felt with Jed have helped me form relationships with men: straight, gay, or elsewhere on the gender spectrum. I now see a date as an opportunity to get out there and enjoy life, without thinking about some future we may or may not have together. I've learned enough about myself to recognize that I suffocate easily. Commitment and exclusivity have yet to make their way past the three-headed dog my memory keeps around to protect my damage. But that's okay. I've come to regard questions like, "Is he the one?" as ridiculous as someone asking, "But do you know me?"

Still there are times when I am warm and engaging at one moment and distant the next. I've left great social gatherings when, somehow or other, the gaiety rubbed against my feelings of loss. After years of living in an abusive marriage, I've learned to hide things from the world. People comment that I am always smiling. I am grateful that I don't give away the pain that grafted itself onto my consciousness.

Most of my family never asks if I have heard from Chris, if I have any news, let alone how I am managing. The chilly silence disturbs me. Shakespeare knew the danger this silence creates. In the Scottish play, Malcolm, following the loss of Macduff's wife and children, forewarns his kinsman, "The grief that does not speak whispers the o'er-fraught heart and bids it break."

Those blessed few who voice their concern, and do so with mindful regard for my feelings, allow me to feel more connected, more whole. The rest of my family acts as if Chris never existed.

Why can't they honor my wish to include him in their memories of the times we enjoyed together? Perhaps they feel awkward, or maybe they have given into the urge to erase the memory of a troublesome relation. There is no mention of him when they recall things kids in the family did while growing up. I've stopped asking them to include him in our conversations. Instead I've mimicked their hurtful behavior and detached from them emotionally. As of yet, I haven't been able to respond in a healthier way.

COMBING THROUGH MY DRESSER before my trip, I came across a felt floral corsage Chris made when he was seven. He woke me that morning, tugging my hand and urging me to see what "someone left on the kitchen table." There I found a note written in a childish hand beside a tiny bundle wrapped in tissue paper: *I love you Mom. Hope you like the gift I made for you to wear.* Fingering the faded corsage and remembering the joy of watching him grow, I felt the way I did the day after my mother was buried: cried out, numb. Ever mindful of my losses—past and present—I work hard to control my emotions. "Standoffish" is how some people describe me. The up-side of this vigilance is that I never give in to the urge to scream, "I have lost my family, and I am alone." Beneath my flattened demeanor, Anger competes with Shame.

When Chris moved in with his father, I shut down. Living in a state of animated suspense, I medicated myself with work, food, and spending. Eating binges alternated with days in which I lived on seltzer and pretzels. Exercise? Digging out my credit card to pay for some binge purchase. Then there were the shameful phone calls. "Dr. Naso, this is American Express. We want to alert you that someone has charged over four thousand dollars on your card this month. Is the card in your possession, or has it been stolen?"

"Yes, I have it—everything is fine," I'd lie. I couldn't even admit to myself that I was out of control. Yet there were signs.

Friends suggested I try Al Anon. Jed's partner, Gary, a doctor and an addiction specialist, explained it helps people whose loved ones suffer from the disease. And although I agreed to take some literature and a meeting list, I slipped them unread into a drawer. "I'm not the one with the problem," I told myself. "I'm already obsessed with Chris' addiction. Al Anon will only make me feel guiltier."

My friend Elaine started going to Al Anon in her early twenties when she realized her anger issues had been shaped by growing-up in an alcoholic home. Her father had been fired from one job after another because he'd fail to show up or return from lunch too drunk to function. Back in high school, I remember her refrain: "My screwed-up family is bringing me down." Her parents argued over money, and after the bank repossessed their house, they divorced.

When I complained about Cas or Chris, she'd remind me she'd been in Al Anon for years before recognizing that her addiction to marijuana and pills was part of the family disease. I dreaded what was coming next, what I called her cult babble: "Why don't you give it a try? Maybe it'll take you to the feelings hiding under that calm exterior. Want to come with me on Tuesday night?"

My answer: "You've got to be kidding."

Was this the same Elaine, I wondered, my groovy high school friend who'd drive our rowdy crew—high on the diet pills we abused to keep our energy up and our weight down—from club to club, where we'd dance the night away? What did she mean that maybe I needed to take a look at myself?

But I remembered the summer night when we skidded down an exit ramp on the Garden State Parkway. Cas had spun a story about some friends spending the weekend in the Catskills. In actuality, he and his friend, Harry Romano, had invited a few girls up to a cabin they rented in the Poconos. Since my own friends were heading for the Jersey shore, I didn't raise the usual fuss. I made my own plans and had my own lie to tell.

"Dad, Marnie's family invited me to their house in Spring Lake for the weekend. I promise I'll be back early Sunday night. Okay?" I was twenty years old and about to begin my junior year of college, but since I was living under my father's roof, I needed permission if I wasn't coming home to sleep.

Late Friday night, my friends and I left the East Village and headed for the Garden State Parkway and Seaside Heights. High on amphetamines, radio blasting, we rocked the car, gyrating as if we were still on the dance floor at the Electric Circus. Elaine, Marnie, and I were bellowing out some tune, laughing over who knows what. The smoke from Elaine's joint was sharpening my buzz. I felt great: high enough to think I was some version of Gracie Slick. Exit 82 came up quicker than my addled mind expected. I didn't slow down. I was still rocking as we swerved towards the railing. When the car behind us stopped inches from the rear door, Elaine screamed, "What the fuck, Arianna! Better watch where you're going!" A near miss, back to reality, but not far enough into reality to realize how I was careening towards trouble.

I still wasn't ready to face my own addictions, not the diet pills of the past or the eating and spending I alternately used to medicate my pain and punish myself. And my family history with alcohol, I thought, was something I needed to forget. My father's binge drinking was hardest for me to admit, even to myself.

Dad was fastidious about the responsibilities he apparently resented. It took a serious bout of flu, or recuperation from back surgery, to keep him home from work. My parents felt the same pride over scraping together the tuition for St. Mark's Grammar School that my friends feel when their children get accepted into one of the highly competitive private schools on the Upper East Side.

Dad, or I should say Daddy, for that is what my sisters and I called him until he died last year, never refused to drive us kids to a friend's house or explain why something worked the way it did. He'd delight in telling riddles and watching us work out the answers. It was he who taught me to be a fearless swimmer, tossing me into the air above the waves at Coney Island and yelling, "Kick your legs, move your arms, and you'll stay afloat." In later years he bragged about his oldest daughter learning to swim before she learned to tie her shoelaces.

To all appearances, he and Mom had a loving marriage. Gifted dancers, at parties their friends cheered when "Ginger and Fred" took the floor. They always walked off the dance floor hand-in-hand, as if they were newlyweds. Drinking helped Dad float above his depressed moods, leaving behind, if only for a while, whatever disappointments and responsibilities plagued him.

When we were young children, Mom sometimes sent me and Julie to the Rustic Tavern to bring him home for supper. "Don't leave him there. Make sure Daddy comes back with you. Do you understand?"

Julie usually returned crying, "I couldn't get him to leave. Now Arianna wants to stay there, too." Drawn to the chaos, the music blaring from the jukebox, the potato salad and cold cuts Dad and his cronies were feeding me, I'd sit atop a barstool, ignoring my mother's wishes. Party Dad was funny; he was never too tired to give me a hug.

On Mondays through Thursdays, his dry days, sober impatience hung over the house like the sword of Damocles. He was irritable, short-fused, and long-handed with Julie, Nina, and me. Well into my teens, I looked forward to Dad's drinking, because I had a better chance of getting my way. If he refused to give me money for new sneakers or a haircut, I didn't ask again until scotch and soda returned the sparkle to his eyes. It was as if the drinking provided a veneer of normalcy in our home. But of course the dependency and mood swings of alcoholism just increased the tension and unpredictability.

And the excess was covered with lies. Coming in wasted from the Amalfi Social Club every Friday night was explained away as having had "one too many." Large family gatherings, where wine drinking went on from mid-morning until late at night, were explained away as being Italian on Sunday, being with your family. These were the good times, the fun times, of my childhood. Warm as most of these memories are, they too often replaced sober nurturing and fostering of my discovery of the world.

Saturday evenings, when Dad joined us for supper at Grandma Lena's, he was either still buzzed from Friday night or had resumed drinking at the Club. Uncle Ralphie worked a second job on Saturday night, so Dad always drove Aunt Mel and my three cousins home. Nine people in a car without seatbelts, and Dad in no shape to drive.

"Ted, stop that, or you'll cause an accident!" Mom screamed after he veered back into lane and slowed down.

Then, to tease her, he'd swerve to the left and over the line into oncoming traffic again. Armed with the twisted shield of alcohol, he was trying to be funny. "Come on, Bella, what's the matter?" he'd laugh, arm around her shoulder, head turned toward the back seat, where my sisters, cousins, and I were laughing hysterically. Too giddy to wonder why Mom and Aunt Mel kept asking him to pay attention to his driving, and unaware that a '59 Chevy Impala wasn't equipped for nine passengers, I enjoyed that Saturday night ritual the way other girls enjoyed ice skating at Rockefeller Center or going to the ballet.

One night, Dad's mood turned dark when we rammed into a car in front of us stopped for a red light. Acting as if he had been wronged, he stormed out and into the face of the other driver. "For Christ's sake, you're driving like an old woman!"

Just as outraged, the other driver got out of the car. He mumbled something I couldn't hear, but I watched Dad clench his fists and shout, "*What*, what was that about my being drunk? If my wife wasn't in the car, buddy, I'd teach you a lesson about opening your trap and minding other people's business."

A few years later, Mom unexpectedly suffered a fatal heart attack. She had been the love of my forty-two-year-old father's life. He began drinking more frequently, often passing out after a bout of crying. The habit of drinking his blues away remained, but the jollity, weird as it may have been, was gone.

Then there is my youngest sister. Nina was only twelve when our mother died. Her troubling behavior and anger issues however pre-date a loss from which it seems she never recovered. When she was eighteen, Dad ordered her out of the house because she made Sadie, his second wife, nervous. Years later I learned she intentionally drowned the roots of Sadie's plants, things like that, to make her miserable. For a long time, I was Nina's fiercest defender.

My sister hides her drinking and drugging behind a firewall of isolation. Although she is passionate about social justice, she seems to be in a constant state of war. She moves from one apartment to the next always because of noise upstairs or someone who gets on her nerves. Except for me, she has never invited anyone in the family to her home. She also moves from one accounting job to the next.

Nina's bosses somehow always turn out to be "morons." Simple translation: She challenged company policy or menaced a manager or coworker.

We have vacationed together, shopped together for Christmas gifts, and traveled together to family functions, yet we have also gone long periods without talking after she rants about some real or imagined way I've wronged her. I hate myself for the times I teased her or pulled rank as older sister; maybe that's why she's gone off on me.

The raging typically begins after I leave a restaurant or shopping mall because I figure she isn't going to show. Not showing up, or arriving an hour and a half late, doesn't seem to faze her. The problem, as she sees it, is my calling her on it or asking for an explanation.

Chris told me that, whenever he complained about me to Aunt Nina, she hijacked the conversation to assassinate my character. Nina's motto is "Revenge is best served cold." Once I told her that a student I'd failed for plagiarism was hounding me; she suggested we slash her tires. She wasn't joking.

Yet all the young children in the family light up when Nina walks into the room. She romps with them on the floor, and they laugh hysterically at her tirade of goofy, off-color remarks. If she catches my hyper-vigilant gaze, she turns up the heat until the parents call for a time out. I look forward to the day when I can break through the cement blocks of resentment I have allowed to accumulate. I will also need to lower my expectations. When I do, I hope I can reach out with love while maintaining self-respect.

Substance abuse is a family disease, intergenerational more times than not. And my family has all the symptoms.

How could my preoccupation with food, my compulsive overspending, obsessive worrying, and fear of relationships be helped in Al Anon? I imagined the meetings to be cult-like gatherings of whiny fundamentalists. Since I was in therapy, wasn't I was already addressing my problems? If there was anyone who needed a twelve-step program, it was Chris. He was the one in trouble.

One night, Max, a young colleague, phoned while I was trying to compose myself after Chris screamed at me. He was being held in an LA County jail awaiting trial for possession of cocaine. He was in hyper-manic state, speaking rapidly, repeating that he could not understand why I wasn't doing anything to get him out. Nothing I said calmed him down. The irritation may well have been set off by the drugs I learned flow like water among the inmates.

I tried to reason with him. "Honey, I understand that you can't take it, but you have to wait for your court date. No doubt they will send you to rehab, not prison." Each word set him off. Now I realize that I was only feeding his anger.

Chris had been at his friend Jamie's Ventura Boulevard condo when the narcotics police showed up. He had met Jamie in a North Hollywood club that gives ten minutes of stage time to comics who bring in customers with money for drinks and drugs for sale in a back room. The search of the condo turned up an arsenal of drugs. When they found four ounces of cocaine in Chris' backpack, they arrested him. Chris said that if I flew out to LA, he'd refuse to see me. I could only be helpful to him by getting him out on bail. "If you weren't so stupid, you would know that."

Thankfully, I had the self-control not to bring up Colorado. Two years earlier, he had been arrested outside Denver for possession of cocaine and marijuana. Released on the bail Caspar paid, Chris boarded a Trailways headed for New York City. Colorado listed him as a fugitive; now that he was under arrest in California, he faced time in both states.

After several screaming phone calls a day, I became ever so grateful for caller ID. Given the circumstances, I was barely able to function. Recurring bronchial infections turned into pneumonia and zapped my energy. My doctors feared the stress had compromised my immune system. Prescribed one antibiotic after another, the infections became harder to treat.

Any more calls and, well, I don't know what I might have done. So, I told myself it was alright to abandon my child, because I had to preserve myself.

Max told me his brother-in-law was finding help in Al Anon with problems intensified by his daughter's addiction to heroin. His wife, Natalie, got on the phone and, in her exuberant way, urged me to try a meeting at St. Vincent's Hospital in Greenwich Village. She explained how, in response to her father's alcoholic outbursts, she had attended Al Anon meetings there, worked the steps to recover her serenity, and found support from the caring and talented people she met. "Try it," she said."All you have to lose is the noise that these problems fill your head with." I was too worn out to argue, so I agreed to call her after I went. She told me this was "bookending," following up on your own self-care.

TEN MONTHS LATER, I moved from Brooklyn to lower Manhattan. I was only beginning to understand how substance abuse affects family members, but I already knew that I could have a better life than the one I had been living for so long. The embrace of friends who listen with unconditional love and acceptance helped me rebuild my shattered trust and sense of self. We speak the same language, share similar dysfunctional experiences, and suffer from the damage they created. In this environment, I've begun to see myself more clearly.

Following one Friday night meeting, I sat in the Village Den going on and on about Chris' refusal to seek help and the denial I had encountered from him and his father. My voice bordering on the obsessive, I was unaware that my grief was enmeshed with my own unresolved feelings about abusing diet pills.

After let's say my sixth vignette about how Chris was trapped by the cocaine's euphoria, Lee asked what had been my drug of choice during my wilder years. Slipping French fries into my mouth and anticipating the ping of salt about to hit my tongue, I reluctantly spoke about the rush that kept me popping prescribed uppers long after there was any reason to lose weight. I admitted that medical problems began accumulating. Starving myself resulted in rectal bleeding and fissures, and my heart and thoughts raced in tandem. Although I'd become erratic in keeping up with school or work responsibilities, I was punctual for every appointment with the doctor who supplied me with diet pills.

"So maybe you're not that much different from Chris," Lee said.

I noticed Samantha and Cindy looking at me, waiting for an answer. The internal rumble began. *How dare Lee accuse me of this while she digs into my fries? Is she trying to embarrass me, diminish me?* For sure my ego had been tapped, but my defenses, recently tempered by the awareness that the addict and the addiction are not the same thing, rendered me ready to listen, and to bow before the truth. True, Chris was an addict, but I realized that I shared, and possibly had passed on, the addict gene. As I was talking about dancing non-stop in clubs or staying up all night partying, I smiled the smile of the addict, the one who wishes for the next rush, that next moment when she no longer has to be herself. But I also had a moment of truth about how difficult it is to stop using something that lifts you up and away, placing you in a daze that stops the pain, the insecurity, whatever the source may be.

Lee knew I needed to look past Chris' dilemma and come to terms with my own. Gradually, in meetings and socializing afterwards—what I've come to appreciate as the appropriate audience of fellow sufferers—I started sharing more honestly about the self I was trying to make healthier and happier. Because members of this support network listen without reacting or giving advice, I opened up, started to let it out, and heard what I needed to change, slowly, imperfectly, but steadily. The emotional excavation work before me is massive but inevitable. After all, I may have been an enthusiastic student turned professor, but I did my most rigorous and sustained work hiding my fears and flaws from everyone, especially myself.

Becoming more aware of the interior monologue of self-deprecation that played like my private sadomasochistic melodrama, I began seeing myself more realistically. Working the steps and attending meetings often filled with young men recently committed to sobriety, I became hopeful that, in his own time, Chris would find his way. The unexpected bonus that helped me rebuild my life was the friendships I made in "the rooms." Endless phone calls, and time out with new friends, indulging our shared passions and interests, moved me further past the isolation my friendship with Jed had broken. On Friday nights, Samantha, Cindy, and I are regulars at French Roast in the Village, just as Barry and I indulge our passion for modern dance, and Paul and I for talking about growing up in Brooklyn.

I've also found community in Battery Park City. Living across West Street—one block south of Ground Zero—provides me with a daily example of how renewal follows devastation. Healing is palpable in my neighborhood. Memorial services and newly built spaces honoring the loss abound, while locals who lived through the 9/11 attack share their stories with newcomers like me.

"That night Angel and the super stayed behind and went through each apartment, making sure everyone had gotten out. Danny and a few of the dog walkers rounded up all the animals not yet retrieved. They brought each one to the ASPCA for temporary housing and care until their people came."

"I was coming home after walking Sara to 234. She was in the third grade then. My heart was racing as I ran back to get her."

"The manager of J&J Produce brought all the cold drinks outside. He handed them out to everyone who came down Albany Street."

In my building, part of a complex just off South End Avenue, most of those forced to evacuate came back to rebuild their lives. Now, children scamper around area parks and skateboard on the Hudson River promenade. The youngest ones, students at the local nursery school, roll by in multi-seat buggies. Like a symbol of the vibrant renewal of lower Manhattan, these toddlers can be seen sitting side by side, enjoying some event or other in the Winter Garden being staged for them.

Walking through local parks, or along the Hudson River promenade, never fails to delight my senses: sight, smell, and sound. The maze of flowers, the dusky smell of the sea beating against the brick embankment, counter the obsessive thoughts that obstruct my happiness. My neighbors stop to talk to me; shopkeepers wave when I pass by. Before the first year was out, I'd walk beside the river, amazed that people were remembering me and bits about my life: "Hi, Professor, how you doin' today?" or "Will I see you at the pool later on?"

In the end, goodness can't be destroyed by trauma. It has been therapeutic for me to witness this.

Time at the gym and in the pool have renewed my relationship with my body. My recovery has enabled me to rethink who and what are healthy for me. I've renewed some old friendships, being careful to keep reasonable boundaries and show compassion. The change has been slow but ongoing. Now when someone grabs me by the wrist or holds my arm while we speak, I am less likely to back away. Running and swimming, and sharing my feelings without fear of a hurtful response, continue to melt the icy wall of isolation into which I had retreated.

I began to derive joy from small moments, the instances that make up my day: a morning Starbucks, stopping to savor the river view, exploring Manhattan streets new to me, taking time to study the architecture. More present in the moment, pleasure entered my body, my spirit, and my mind. Without planning for it to happen, I became confident enough for sexual intimacy without thinking: *What if?* and *How could I?* I had always been anxious and rigid about sexual intimacy.

Before I met Caspar, most of my sexual encounters had resulted from recklessness or neediness, not a desire for intimacy. Even during the brief period when my behavior was promiscuous, I'd tell myself, "We have to be 'a couple.'" My residual Catholicism necessitated plans and promises. But my anxiety drove me to poor choices, away from caring, available people. Like my relationship with food, my sex life went from feast to famine, until I became a full blown sexual anorexic. That happened during my marriage to Cas and for years after our divorce. Loving a depressed father who was quick to anger and uncomfortable showing affection to his children, I instinctively was drawn to unavailable men.

John was still married, yet always promising he was about to call it quits. After two years, I got tired of waiting. Next there was Henry, whose beeper rang during the most inopportune moments, beckoning him back to the emergency room. And Jeff, who told me up front that he had intimacy problems. Great, I thought, we can work on intimacy together. But Jeff just couldn't seem to commit, that is until he met Leo.

In a circle of friends, I always saw myself as the outsider. Friendships with few expectations and no pressure, I told myself, was my comfort zone. By age thirty-seven I had been living the life of a seventy-year-old social recluse. Most women become adept at dating in late adolescence. For me, someone who'd rather admit to committing mass murder than being a slow learner, feeling relaxed on a date, being myself, and enjoying the moment took much longer. To be exact, I didn't reach home until I was well into midlife.

Opening up about the substance abusers I had lived with and the physical abuse in my marriage made it safe to face my eating disorder and see myself more realistically. Consequently, I began to dismantle the accumulated self-hated. Now and then I still get lost in a reverie of worry, self-pity, or anger, but they are catnaps compared to the long sleep that had followed my way of dealing with mine and my loved ones' problems.

So the Ethnic Studies project slipping into the workspace intended for my manuscript offered testimony that, despite my progress, the wounds were still open. Once again, I'd lapsed into a state of mental disconnect.

But, as it turns out, disconnect is not pointless or stingy: it endows the afflicted with the ability to multitask, especially when it comes to creative pursuits. With Angelina's story nearly completed, I decided it was time for me to write my own story. Who would publish it, and who'd read it, mattered less than the realization that I knew I needed to write it.

While my left hand circled a date on my academic calendar for beginning my memoir, my right hand picked up my nearly completed manuscript. My mind kept time repeating two lines from Petrarch's "*Italia Mia*," first in English and then in Italian.

> *I speak to tell the truth,*
>> *Not in hatred of anyone, nor scorn.*
> (*Io parlo per ver dire,*
>> *Non per odio d'altrui, nè per disprezzo.*)

Maybe the two stories are actually episodes from a long history of trauma. After all, the subjects are bound by blood and buried memories. I wasn't certain how Angelina's story and mine connected, but it did not matter. I had a plan: I was going to find out.

SHOUTING VOICES FROM THE ADJOINING ROOM brought me back to the moment.

"If you don't shut up now, you're going to be sorry. Do you hear me, you hell-bent bitch?"

I'm not quite sure if it is my work with language, or years of living in a violent marriage, that causes my stomach to clench whenever I hear someone—man or woman—say "you bitch."

The second voice was a woman's. "For once, for just once, listen to what I have to say without preparing some self-centered response. What I need to say is about me, and it's about us, if we're going to stay together. Or is that what you are trying to do, get me disgusted enough that I bolt out this marriage? Huh? Are you listening? Why won't you turn around and talk to me like you're at least half interested?"

Listening to the woman's plea, I knew what would come next. Through the wall I heard a high-pitched scream and what sounded like shattering glass. Having once lived on the other side of the wall, I recognized the sounds of a man trying to intimidate his woman into silence. Then came the sound of a slammed door, the palpable barrier between the woman left crying in the room and the man mumbling down the corridor about how he'd "teach the bitch not to push him, if he had to kill her doing so."

In the mirror above the desk I saw my face: It had turned red. My eyes looked like they had seen a ghost, which of course they had. Practicing self-control, I didn't coil up in bed or order a ton of room service. I might have allowed bad memories to rattle me or let loose with language more fitting for the London docks than a hotel room on the Strand. Instead, I offered up gratitude for having gotten away.

Still, a pounding headache testified to the years when I had alternately been loved and battered by Caspar Simonelli. All that began in August 1967, what folks remember as "the summer of love."

CHAPTER 7
Brooklyn Roads

Mother whisked away,
Keeper of our household gods.
Family life undone.

BELLA, MY MOTHER, ASSIGNED CHORES to Julie, Nina, and me, but compared to what was expected from many of our Italian American friends, we had light duty. Other than clearing the dinner table, loading the dishwasher, and sorting out clean laundry, we were free to indulge our interests and spend time with friends. During her own childhood, Mom was "the extra set of hands" that helped run a large household. Growing up, she swore her children wouldn't spend their days dusting woodwork or scrubbing floors. She never encouraged us to become professionals, had no context for academic guidance, yet her faith in us, and her disdain for the type of overbearing parental interference many of our friends experienced, created a professor, a musician, and a CPA.

A toddler when the stock market crashed in October 1929, my mother had a less privileged childhood. Her own mother, Grandma Lena, couldn't give her children or herself the things my sisters and I took for granted.

During the Depression, money was scarce in the Leone home, but Grandma Lena knew how to stretch a dollar. Throughout her life, priority number one was making sure her family ate well. As for the finer things she may have craved, she went without. Three nights a week, after finishing work as a carpenter and washing off any trace of a laboring life, Grandpa Jack donned his tuxedo and spiffy shoes and headed to the Manhattan club, where he worked as a singing waiter. He may have been a gifted tenor, but each week he brought home little pay, especially if he had a bad run at the racetrack.

The family regaled us kids with memories of Grandpa's taste for gourmet food and fashionable clothing. "Grandpa had class" was the refrain that colored their telling. It was less frequently told, however, that, during the Depression, Grandma was left alone to deal with the New York City Relief inspector, who periodically reviewed the family's need. My father shared a less romantic view, recalling how the money Grandma received to manage the household fluctuated between meagre and scarce.

Grandma became pregnant with Aunt Mel a few months after the crash. With four children to feed and Jack laid off from his day job, the family could not exist on the token salary from the Manhattan night club. Brothers and brothers-in-law were now unemployed or earning less as well, so my grandparents had no safety net. Every now and then, Grandma told the story of the Relief Inspector offering to help by taking beautiful little Bella "off her hands." The inspector, recently married but too old to bear a child, wanted to raise her. "She might have asked for your Aunt Mel," Uncle Vito would add, "but every time the inspector came by she was either crying or had a cold. Your mother was so adorable, always polite, real lady-like, even as a little girl."

Listening to this story, I'd imagine how Grandma Lena resisted the urge to push this woman down all three flights of the tenement's stairs. But she would have been wise enough to smile, act as if the insult was a compliment, and astutely change the subject.

Shortly before Mom's sixteenth birthday, Grandma signed her out of Manual Training High School. Before the war, Uncle Vito handed over most of his Brooklyn Navy Yard salary to Grandma. But the army sent him first to Georgia and then to the battlefields in Europe. And after the army declared Uncle Louis 4F, he moved to Manhattan, where he worked during the day and studied pre-law at City College at night.

Grandpa broke the sad news to Bella: "Your mother needs you to help out with the bills." Surprised by her tears and plea to stay in school long enough to get her diploma, Jack explained that he wasn't happy about it either, but that her mother had decided. Except for the wish inscribed inside her yearbook, she buried her desire to study textile design at Pratt Institute. Comare Santina introduced young Bella to her floor lady at the Richelieu Pearl Factory. Her education ended the next day.

"Green-Wood Cemetery up the block," Mom confided to her sister Mel, "is a fitting backdrop to this deadening work. The strands of pearls I inspect are sent off to who knows where." In later years, she recalled feeling trapped at Richelieu until Dad, her Ted, proposed marriage.

Grandma Mamie and Grandpa Joe paid for the wedding at Prospect Hall. Mom spent the few dollars her parents returned from weekly earnings on her trousseau. A few weeks before their wedding, Dad ran a bridal shower at the Italian jewel of Coney Island, Gargiulo's Restaurant. When he arrived at the end of the party, he fessed up to buying the blond wood hope chest, but insisted the shower had been given by Mom's family. Remembering my parents' openness with each other, I imagine this was among the few lies he ever told her.

SHE'D CUT CORNERS WHEN SHE SHOPPED FOR HERSELF, but my mother made sure her little girls had pretty outfits, as well as money in their pockets for candy, records, dance lessons, or school trips. My sisters and I were not shy about asking for nice things. Until I was seventeen and about to begin college, I took all this for granted.

Mom and I spent a lot of time in July 1967 planning for our first airplane vacation. The whole family was traveling to San Francisco for my Uncle Louis' installation as district attorney. My sisters and I had been let in on the plans for the surprise party Uncle Louis and Aunt Kelly were planning in honor of Mom and Dad's twentieth anniversary. Five years before, Grandpa Jack had died of a massive heart attack, so the family was upset he would not be there to hug his son and sing at the celebrations, but the rest was sheer excitement. Grandma Lena, Uncle Vito and Aunt Lettie, Aunt Mel and Uncle Ralphie, my cousins Butchie, Camille, and Christine, and the five of us had tickets for the same flight. Butchie and I planned on throwing a Nerf ball between us and the younger kids. Half the fun would be watching our fathers restrain themselves when we got raucous.

As if his success wasn't enough to create envy, Louis Leone had a world-class sense of humor and knack for winning the love of everyone he met. Initially, Uncle Vito and Aunt Lettie refused to "travel out all that ways." "Louis is gonna need an extra set of shoulders to hold up the largest head on the damned west coast. Cheeze, the last thing my brother needed was for some cockeyed politician to puff him up some more. God, I love the guy, but it is amazing how playing lawyer turned him into such a big shot." While he spoke, Aunt Lettie nodded, repeating and validating what he was saying.

"Gotta admire a guy who's always gotten by with a line of bull and a winning smile. Ah, I guess I am just getting old and cranky. He's my kid brother, and God I love the stupid bastard. Count us in. Cheeze, Lettie, don't let me forget to tell Zeke I will be away the second week of August. Sanitation isn't going to be happy about another request for time off at the height of the vacation season. Damn that Louis!"

We were like two kids that hot July day when Mom and I took the subway downtown.

"Let's go to Nedick's first for lunch. Can we? This way we won't get hungry while we're shopping. Anyways, a nice orange drink will cool us off. Boy, it is hot, isn't it? Mom, you don't look so well. Do you feel alright?" My mother smiled the way she would when she was trying to hide something worrisome from us, but I did not put that together for many motherless years to come.

"I'm fine—the heat has me down a bit, just like it has everyone else. Ari, stop looking me over that way! Please honey, if you worry like this at seventeen, what are you going to do when you're my age and have a husband and children?"

I shrugged in my wiry, sulky way and put my head down on her shoulder, waiting to feel her arm around mine and her lips kissing my hair with the familiar tenderness. We had our squabbles—some of them rabidly judgmental—but they never lasted long. Our arguments routinely ended with us sitting at the kitchen table, talking and laughing over cups of tea about this or that.

We got off the Fourth Avenue local at the Lawrence Street station and headed in the direction of Abraham and Strauss and Nedick's.

"Now that I've lost more weight, I see myself in a lime green bikini that ties below my waist. What do you think, Mom? Won't that be hip?"

"Sure, Arianna, get one if you want your father to kill you."

"But, Mom, all my friends—"

"All your friends don't have Ted Naso for their father. Please, Ari, for once listen to me. Don't ruin the trip by making your father crazy over your defiance. It ruins things for everybody when he gets into one of his moods. Didn't you get what you wanted today already? Like you asked, we left your sisters home with Daddy. We are doing what you wanted—just you and me shopping, because you are the oldest and you need a few extra things. Your classes at Hunter begin soon after we return home from San Francisco. So just pick out clothes that won't make you look older than you are or like some *strega*. And I want you to eat a decent lunch. Don't think I didn't notice you sliding your eggs and toast onto Julie's dish this morning."

I thought about how I might convince her to buy me a bikini. Why were the women in my family so preoccupied with the men's wishes and moods? "Not me," I vowed to myself. "I will never be so concerned about them. Never."

"Here, you go in first, Ari. Get two seats at the counter, near the fan. I'm so warm all of a sudden. I'm not hungry. Just order me an orange drink, and make sure you order a sandwich for yourself. I'm going to the bathroom to put some cold water on my face."

I nodded and turned toward her. Sweat dripping down her face, she walked towards the bathroom as if she were inside someone else's body, someone much older than her forty-one years. She turned around, as if to make note of where I was sitting. I thought to tell her, when she came back, that the sun must have been bouncing off her navy paisley shirtwaist. Somehow it reflected a blue tint onto her lips. But as it happened, I never got the chance to tell her that or anything else. After the door was opened by the manager, and Dad and Uncle Milo arrived before the ambulance, and during the three days in the Valley Funeral Home and that rainy morning at Green-Wood Cemetery, I could only speak to her in my mind and in my dreams.

Far too often I still feel like a girl sitting alone at some counter, waiting for my mother to come by and kiss my hair.

The loss of a life alters a family's future. Shaken to its core, robbed of that core, a vacuum was created. Tears were cried in private; next came dumb-found grief. A family splintered, each alone dealing with the loss and grief. Too much silence, decisions made in haste to make things normal, to make life better.

Each of Bella's children ran in her own direction without holding hands to form a lifeline. A family can not exist this way. Each of her children adrift searching for love.

Relationships and friendships formed in haste during the period of mourning caused future mourning. Ari couldn't fill the void: tried with diet pills, tried with therapy, but didn't know how to get at or get out the truth. Dad in his loneliness brought home a Fury; her arrival destroyed what was left of Bella's family.

In years to come, family and friends said that Ted had been brainwashed. In years to come, the family believed Ted had been out of his mind when he distanced himself from his daughters and acted more like a father to Sadie's fatherless children. His grandchildren remember how their parents were discouraged from visiting the home their grandfather shared with Grandma Sadie. The cousins were stunned by the pervasive negativity and sarcasm from the woman they referred to among themselves as Step-Aunt Sadie. They had witnessed the loss and abandonment.

So absorbed with her search for love, Ari was unaware how the destruction of her family and the tragic choice she was about to make would impact her future and the life of an unborn child. During the summer of 1967, Arianna Naso was very young, very naïve, and very devastated over her mother's death.

LABOR DAY WEEKEND WAS DIFFICULT for our family. Every year, Mom had invited the tribe over for an end-of-the-summer barbeque. She'd cook and clean and bake, making sure everything met her high standards. Julie, Nina, and I helped set up the yard after Dad hosed it down. Our excitement typically resulted in joking and teasing—put downs of each other's looks and little quirks—that bordered on the unhealthy. Then we'd escalate to shoving and tears. It was not my father's style to gently break things up or provide a mild rebuke. Maybe we'd been so raucous that we didn't hear his initial intervention.

Like the 16th-century Florentine writer Niccolo Machiavelli, Dad believed the ends justify the means. Growing up, I both loved and feared him. Still, his threats never stopped our rambunctiousness, because his explosions, especially when company was coming, were often colored with humor. I believe part of him still held on to memories of his own childish antics.

"Bella, I am going to murder one of them, so the other two will learn a lesson." Or, "Arianna, it is some example you are setting for your sisters." On one occasion, he even threatened to withhold our allowances for the rest of our lives, if we wound up doing damage to anything on the card table that served as the entertainment center playing the music of Jimmy Roselli and the other "boring old Italians," as my sisters and I called them.

From beginning to end of the annual get together, the air on 75th Street between 14th and 15th Avenues was filled with the melancholy sound of Roselli, Jerry Vale, and Connie Francis. Their voices declared love for their mothers, the objects of their affection, for wine, and for an imagined, idealized Italy that bore little resemblance to the impoverished southern villages. Dad's music entertained the neighbors he'd invited to "Come over and have a drink." He'd boast how Bella "cooked enough food to feed an army." Flashing his handsome smile and hugging our guests as they walked up the driveway into the backyard, he bore no resemblance to the stern disciplinarian. This guy was all about love and affection.

Into the night, the men repeated old stories, shaking their heads and laughing as if they were being told for the first time. They floated their plans for the future—a piece of property in the Poconos, a small place near Palm Beach.

The children they alternately plied with food, kisses, and dirty looks served as bartenders. The tips became more generous as the hours passed, but the real perk was the occasional swig we chugged down when no one was looking. By the end of the night all the men, and a few of the women, would be "feeling good" and had the stories and headaches to prove it the next day.

That year, following a mass to remember Mom on the two-month anniversary of her death, Aunt Mel invited everyone to her house for a barbeque. "This isn't a party," she said, "but a chance for everyone to be together in our grief and wish Arianna well with the classes she'll begin next Tuesday at Hunter College."

I was the first woman in the family who had made her own decision regarding college. Unlike many other Italian American men of his generation, Dad actually encouraged his daughters to pursue an education. I may have been a thorn in his side, but he recognized my intelligence and at times commented that my big mouth was that of a lawyer in the making. "Because, God knows, Ari, your mouth will drive a husband crazy, so maybe you should learn how to use it in a courtroom instead of in a kitchen."

Yet Dad made it clear that I must not quit my part time job as a file clerk at B. Altman & Co. Stability was something he took seriously, and to him stability meant always having a job.

In his youth he had passed up the opportunity to study at City College to play for the Brooklyn Dodger's farm team, the Johnstown Johnnies. He might have moved up to the major league, but just when the right people began noticing him, he married. Mom was lonely while he was on the road but didn't want to travel. So he left the team soon after I was born and bought a pool room that yielded a weekly salary of about fifteen dollars. After Julie was born, he enrolled in the New York School of Printing. Great-grandpa Orazio managed the pool room in his absence. Eventually he found a buyer, which enabled Dad to start the job he landed at *The Journal American* with a clear head.

During the lean times, my Naso grandparents helped pay the rent and keep Julie and me in nice clothes, and the Leones helped out with food. The ghost of these years haunted my father. And although he eventually became the chief compositor for the *New York Times*, earning what he called "a decent living," he never achieved the financial success of his immigrant father or older brother. Nor did he ever show any sign of being passionate about his work. He was first in his department to sign the early retirement agreement when his job became automated.

Through the years, talking about his baseball days brought light, and sometimes tears, to his eyes. And I don't know what I overheard, or who planted the thought in my mind, but I will always believe I ruined my father's promising baseball career. Whenever I'd ask him about this or how he felt about giving up his passion, he'd dodge the question.

ALTHOUGH I WAS FIFTH from the youngest girl in a family of eleven nieces, I was the first to enroll in a four-year liberal arts college. Only one other cousin had received any schooling beyond high school: my cousin Jenny, who'd recently finished her first year at Kingsborough Community College.

Cousin Jenny had been a solid "A" student at New Utrecht High School. During her senior year, her guidance counselor, Valeria Russo, encouraged her to apply for college. She offered to help with the applications, and suggested Jenny's parents come in for a conference. Uncle Henry agreed that Aunt Gloria would meet with Miss Russo, but he warned her away from "making any promises or signin' anything." While they walked down 80th Street, Jenny instinctively knew her plans were about to be derailed. Aunt Gloria kept reminding her not to say too much.

The daughter of Italian communists, Valeria's mother, Claudia, had been among the first women to graduate from City College. Her career as a social worker for a city agency had exposed her to scores of Italian children whose families regarded educated women as a threat to family harmony. Valeria Russo's parents were well known advocates for women's rights in Astoria's Italian American community. Their daughter made educating Italian Americans about personal and professional choices available to women her passion, too. Confronting the old-world thinking she encountered in Aunt Gloria was her crusade.

While Miss Russo explained how Jenny's math skills and ability to talk about the problem-solving process were signs of "a potentially gifted teacher," Aunt Gloria hid her disdain for female authority figures beyond a tight smile and haughty look. When the counselor brought up the relevance of the Scholastic Aptitude Test, Aunt Gloria cut her off, explaining, "With all due respect, I must tell you I know what it is."

Valeria Russo rolled her eyes. She asked why Jenny's father refused to give her time off from the family bakery to attend the SAT prep course. "Surely, Mrs. Orlando, your husband wants to nurture his daughter's gifts. We're only talking about six Saturdays, and, with a score of around 1400, Jenny could be accepted to a wonderful private college. Personally I think she would flourish at Haverford or Swarthmore. Since they are less than a three-hour trip from Brooklyn, she could come home frequently and the family could visit. If money is an issue, there's no doubt that Buffalo, New Paltz, or even Stony Brook would—"

Jenny blushed when her mother asked, "What about a junior college? Wouldn't a good student do well no matter where she went to school?" Gloria Orlando wanted to say something too about Jenny being a girl and needing to hand over money each week to help cover expenses and for the things she would need when it was time to marry. She wanted to ask what kind of mother could sleep knowing her beautiful daughter was living in some dormitory where only God knew what happened. Her conviction was bolstered by the memory of the story about Nonno Orazio refusing to allow her mother to attend a normal school and become a teacher. Aunt Gloria kept this and much more inside.

"Well, yes, Mrs. Orlando, there is, of course, some truth in that, but you cannot compare attending a community college, say Nassau Community College or Kingsborough, with the experience of going away to school, or of competing in a challenging environment. There are financial aid packages for families that can't—"

Gloria Orlando, who had heard enough, stood up, motioning for Jenny to do the same. "Miss Russo, I don't think you understand. My husband and I appreciate your interest in Jenny, but really in a few years she'll marry Danny Hudec. We, that is my husband and I, hope you'll help her with the Kingsborough paperwork. Or if she insists on spreading her wings a bit, with the Nassau Community application, though she knows she must come home every night, like we discussed. She'll study business, so she could help her father with the books. Then we won't have to depend on. . .a stranger." Jenny was relieved her mother had refrained from saying 'that Jew accountant.'

Once she began Kingsborough's accounting program, Jenny buried her resentment beneath the pleasure she received from the presents her father and boyfriend showered upon "their little student." That September, it was Jenny who baked the cake for the off-to-college barbeque. And as she set it down next to a stack of Jimmy Roselli records for all to see, she made a point of letting me know how lucky I was.

ALL AFTERNOON, TWELVE-YEAR-OLD NINA had been pouring rum into her Coca-Cola. Her devious behavior stemmed from what the family called "a bad case of nerves." Hyperactive since birth, her earliest sentences had been peppered with swear words. My parents' laughter when she uttered what sounded like "my toy fruck" set Nina down the path of saying whatever, to whomever, whenever she felt like it.

Numbed by my own grief, I failed to notice my rambunctious sister growing silent in the weeks after Mom's death. She'd spend hours in her room, writing at her desk. When Dad asked what she'd been doing or looked through her things, he found nothing. Always a picky eater, she sat motionless at the table, refusing to taste the meals he put together for his girls. It was my job to make sure Nina finished what was on her plate. But night after night, I scraped most of my youngest sister's meal into the garbage Julie took outside. The family never discussed how distant Nina had become since Mom's death. And no one noticed that she had started drinking.

Although Nina was academically gifted, she was easily distracted, usually on a different page from the rest of the class. When the teacher asked her a question, students laughed, not realizing that, despite her confusion, she was probably the best reader and writer in the class. Since kindergarten, Nina's angry responses and disruptive behavior had resulted in Mom being called in by the principal.

After her death, I became the one who made the excuses for Nina's behavior. I talked a neighbor out of telling Dad how Nina cursed out her children, then snuck back when she thought no one was looking and slashed their bike tires. When Nina was caught smoking in St. Bernadette's schoolyard, I asked the monsignor not to call our house. "It's best if I break the news to my grieving father."

Dad tried holding the family together, but, as I realized in later years, he lacked the ability to do so. When Mom was alive, she often explained away his failure to hug us or show signs of fatherly affection, reminding us how much he loved us. I had always been the rebel who took Dad to task for his excessive use of parental authority. On my tenth birthday, I had been devastated by his wrath. He'd caught me digging into the ground with a spoon, making a mound of dirt by Grandpa's fig tree.

"What the hell are you doing making such a mess, digging up the yard like that?"

"I'm planting a garden, Daddy, with seeds I picked out of leftover green beans. My teacher said it's fun to grow your own vegetables."

"That's not how you do it, you little imbecile. You don't know—"

"Dick and Jane's mother never call their children imbeciles!" I had exclaimed, sobbing. Why—"

Before I could finish my sentence, my mother stopped hanging out laundry and yelled down, "Ted, why not try wishing her a happy birthday?" To make amends, Dad took us to dinner at Spumoni Gardens. He knew the road back to my heart ran through my pudgy belly.

Years of such encounters made me distrustful of my father's love. Yet Julie, with her innate sense of entitlement, took his love for granted. She was crushed when he began treating us more like nieces than daughters after he remarried. But it was Nina who suffered most. The baby with kick-ass ways became an adolescent with a dead mother and a father lost to depression, alcoholism, and what felt like indifference.

After Mom's death, Dad drank more heavily, more frequently. The grief, and unprecedented domestic responsibilities, intensified his dark moods. He'd often drink until it made him sick. The morning after, Julie would warn us, "Careful, Grumpy is approaching the breakfast table."

Later in life, he'd say, "I can't believe how much I used to drink. For Chrissake, I could have killed myself."

He had deathbed regrets. The last time my sisters visited him, he told them, "I'm sorry I wasn't there for you kids when you needed me." I'd had my golden moment a few years earlier. Sadly, it came after my father acquired the altered personality that accompanies the onset of dementia. I'd recently won a teaching award and was functioning as the general contractor coordinating the craftspeople renovating my house. Dad went on and on about how proud he was of my accomplishments and independence.

"Arianna, you've done so much with your life, always on your own. I know, if Mommy were alive, she'd be as proud of you as I am. Things are getting tougher for me, but whenever I turn around, there you are. You are the light in my life."

My life has been filled with stunning surprises, but that topped them all. I was deeply moved, and I let my father know it. Yet a part of me, the keeper of memory, wanted to ask, "Who are you, and where were you on my tenth birthday?

BY EARLY EVENING, TWELVE-YEAR-OLD NINA was visibly drunk. No one at the barbeque seemed to mind much, though. If one of us kids reached for the bottle, it was sometimes seen as a rite of passage. As if I'd been some sort of prodigy, it was frequently told how, at four years old, I'd gone from table to table, stealing sips of champagne at Aunt Mel and Uncle Ralphie's wedding.

Drinking was a way of life. When words failed to bond the brood of brothers-in-law, cousins, and *paesani* with their diverse interests and personalities, alcohol served as the great socializer. It was their reward for working feverishly, while earning just enough to live what they saw as a respectable middle class life.

UNCLE ENZO OWNED a *salumeria*. Working twelve to fourteen hours a day, six days a week, he made a decent living. The competition was steep along 10th Avenue, but the street skills he had acquired as a Sicilian immigrant on Mott Street created a successful businessman. Everyone at work, in the family, and in their large network of friends knew he was extremely difficult. But everyone loved him.

At home he was demanding and vigilant, always ready to pounce on what he deemed irritating or inconvenient. His family, however, did not live in fear of his outbursts, for his impish smile and brusque sense of humor were never far away.

His loud voice set the tone at his *salumeria*. He barked orders from 6 a.m. until 6 p.m. The same customers he had berated because, as he put it, "They're too damn stupid to read the 'In God we trust, everyone else pays cash,' sign," were likely to find a bag of groceries outside their door. His edginess had the appearance of a chronic case of heartburn. Drinking always uplifted his spirits, so people half believed his glass of red wine with a dash of seltzer was something of an elixir. Eating, drinking, and kibitzing at social functions transformed the curmudgeon into the life of the party. Scattered throughout the backyard were Aunt Clara and their children, each wondering when insults or terms of endearment might come their way.

Uncle Ralphie might have lived happily as an artist in Greenwich Village, if his father hadn't left his mother widowed at age thirty-seven. Fourteen-year-old Ralphie became responsible for supporting the seven siblings rendered hungry and fatherless on the eve of the Great Depression. Dreamy eyed and inclined to spending long afternoons on the fire escape, sketching scenes that captured the hustle and bustle of lower Manhattan, he became "the man of the house," against both his will and his temperament. Tessina Corso's brother, Salvatore, took young Ralphie to the Brooklyn Navy Yard, where a couple of dollars under the table landed him work as a laborer's assistant. There he helped carry cargo to and from the ships, performing the same work as the men, but earning a much lower salary. At their whim, Ralphie ran for cigarettes or coffee, only to encounter the wrath of the bosses for not doing enough work.

Having schooled himself in the language of his beloved books that were now accumulating dust on the windowsill by the fire escape, he approached the foreman in an articulate and direct manner concerning the unfairness of his situation. Doing his best to mock Ralphie's "fancy-talkin' manner," the foreman reminded him that people like him and his mother were starving and throwing themselves from windows. He should be grateful for the opportunity he'd been given. His rejoinder to Ralphie's response was harsh and humiliating. "What will your mother say if you lost this job?"

Inside his young mind, Anger danced with Shame, while Intelligence and Sensitivity looked on in horror. Today, as an adult with a family of his own to support, Uncle Ralphie is the assistant manager of the shipping department at the Murray Hill Lithograph Company. After a few scotch-and-sodas, he grabs the closest ear and goes on and on about how management enjoys screwing labor and always has and always will.

While Vito was the patriarch of my maternal uncles, Uncle Milo was the eldest Naso brother, more than ten years older than my dad, whom he always called "Pally."

During his high school years, Milo had been what decades later became known as an "athlete-scholar." Mamie and Joe Naso were told he was gifted in mathematics and science, but they did not need a high school teacher to tell them that their son was the best basketball player ever at Manual Training High School.

When his father's tuberculosis resulted in rehabilitation at an upstate facility, Milo traded a scholarship at City College for work in the family bakery. He began spending less time on the court and more at the Rustic Tavern, always with a shot of scotch and a chaser of beer by his side. After the Japanese bombed Pearl Harbor, he left Brooklyn for the South Pacific, returning five years later with a wife, child, and hope of finding a city job that offered security.

And there were other stories that could be told about the men and women who spoke—drink in hand—over the sounds of Rosemary Clooney singing "Mambo Italiano." They had drunk themselves into jollity. Above them, in a frenzied dance, floated the Hours, the *Horai*, goddesses of the seasons. They have the power to quell dreams and aspirations. Like the ancient Italians, whose fates were decided by such immortals, my future was rising towards the full moon that lit up Aunt Mel and Uncle Ralphie's above-ground swimming pool. But I failed to see the signs, for the air was filled with the cigar smoke from the men's liquor-tipped Coronas and the vaporous remains of the sausages Uncle Enzo brought from his store.

In this buzzed, ethereal state of denial, everyone found it rather cute when little Nina was caught more than once slipping rum into her Coke. At first, Dad was amused by her slurred speech and hazy eyes. But he stopped laughing when she stumbled against the makeshift mini bar set atop a card table, causing a bottle of vodka and half a bottle of Johnny Walker Black to spill onto the lawn.

"Damn you, Nina, don't you ever watch what the hell you're doing? Just sit down now and stop it. You have had enough. Don't let me see you with another drink in your hand unless it is coffee. Just watch out—do you *hear* me?"

As he shook his head in exasperation, Nina turned to him, saying loud enough for everyone to hear, "Maybe it's you, Dad, who should 'watch out.' I tell you that fat Petrocelli woman is after you. She called the house three times this week. I know that because, when she called the fourth time, this morning, she told me so herself. What nerve! Mom's not even dead two months and—whew."

Julie asked, "Who is she? What does she want?"

Dad began to answer, but Nina cut him off. "Don't you remember her from the Saint Anna Society's picnics? She's the one Cousin Butchie says looks like Fred Flintstone."

"Shut your mouth, Nina! Sadie Petrocelli is a very nice woman. Her husband, Carlo, was Grandpa Joe's godson. Grandpa came to America with his father from San Nicola. Carlo died three months before Mommy, and I'm sure Sadie wants us all to—"

"Become a family?" Nina asked sarcastically.

With that, Dad slapped her so hard her top lip began to bleed. My grandmothers and aunts, applying the skills and wisdom that come with years of exposure to angry alcoholic outbursts, quickly calmed things down. Even more quickly, I went inside and called my friend Elaine. She told me she was meeting Maura and Angie at the Sandbar Lounge, and would pick me up along the way. "I'll be gone from this craziness in less than an hour," I confided to Julie.

Walking down my aunt's driveway, I had no way of knowing how my life was about to change. If I had, I would have turned around and rejoined the party.

CHAPTER 8

Postcards From A Violent Relationship

Dancing in the dark,
Wanton need ignores lies, worse.
Stepping up for more.

CASPAR WAS A LOOKER THEN. And sweet, too. At least that's what I initially saw. Driving to the Sandbar Lounge, Elaine was in high spirits, but I was still fuming over the incident between Dad and Nina. What bothered me most was how everyone had treated what happened like a normal parent-child interaction. Is it Dad's grief over Mom's death, the drinking, or is it just *him*? I wondered. The inexpressible "it" was the violence I took for granted.

Turning up the radio, I thought out loud, "Shit, this is my last weekend before school starts. You could count on my family to ruin it. As if things aren't bad enough, they have to act crazy. I'm not going home until I'm sure they're all asleep, even if I catch hell for it tomorrow." Elaine nodded in agreement.

Gracie Slick rocked on about finding someone to love, the question that colored 1967, the summer of love.

"Oh, Lord, let Jimmy T. be there tonight!"

"Isn't he going out with Alice Certo?" I asked.

"Not anymore. He found out she was sleeping with one of his cousins. So goody for me."

The Sandbar Lounge had been a bar and grill where couples groped each other in dark corners on semi-circular velveteen couches. It was the sort of place Uncle Ralphie called "an upholstered cesspool." Local boozers, bored housewives, and the occasional couple out for a few drinks had been the clientele before the owner, Lou Basso, died and his son, Junior, removed the stained couches and converted the kitchen and lounge area into a stage and dance floor. A few strobe lights, bands lined up every Wednesday through Sunday, and Brooklyn's 86th Street had its first disco.

"Hey, Babe, I hoped you were coming," Jimmy T. said, kissing Elaine on her cheek, his right hand playfully interlocking with hers.

"Hey, Arianna, I didn't see you. How ya been? Your family doin' okay? It's just such a shame about your mom and all."

"Thanks, Jimmy. Yeah, things are. . . . Well, I don't even know how they are. Pretty weird, I guess."

"Ah, come here Ari. Give me a kiss and say hello to my cousin, Caspar Simonelli. This blond Romeo did himself a favor tonight, driving all the ways from Union Street to hang out with some cool people." Dressed in straight-leg jeans and a button-down shirt, Cas stood out among the bell-bottom, tie-dyed regulars.

Him to me: "Hi, it's Cas. That's what everyone calls me. And, please don't hold it against me that I'm related to this crumb."

Me to him: "Hello, Cas. I'm Ari."

The night ended with us laughing over coffee and cheesecake at the Tiffany Diner, then walking along the Narrows. Cas noticed an ocean liner making its way under the Verrazano and wove a story about lovers slipping away from demanding spouses. While he spoke, he sipped on a beer from the cooler I later discovered was a fixture in his car. He was easy to talk to, a good listener, nodding and responding with gentle humor. I felt safe and happy.

The moon and stars above the lights of the hilly borough across the bay resembled a huge landscape painting. Clearly, I was star-struck. Had I found that someone whose love would help ease the feelings of pain and loss? *(Remember, reader: I said I was very young, very naïve, etc., etc.)* As we kissed good night in front of my house, Cousin Bruce Morrow was dedicating his next song, Jay and the Americans' "Some Enchanted Evening," to all his "groovy cousins out there with that special someone."

I took it as a good sign. Bali Ha'i or 75th Street, the South Pacific or Brooklyn. It made no difference. I just might have found the love of my life. Having had a long history of convincing myself that black was white and an apple was really an orange, I walked through the front door happily deluded.

Somewhere in the mythical distance, the Sirens plotted and the Nereids cried because a vulnerable girl was about to make a terrible mistake. Past tragedies in her family rendered her easy prey. For she had grown up hearing and seeing that where there is love there is alcohol, sometimes violence, and always loss. But now, with her hormones raging, and ignoring the beer filled cooler in the backseat and the smell of liquor on Cas' breath, Ari's emotions raged unchecked.

If only the immortals who stood watching had foretold the abuse about to begin.

And that the worst of it would be the destruction of the child born into this sometimes happy, but always troubled relationship.

The next day, Dad reluctantly agreed I could drive to Jones Beach with "the guy you just met who kept you out half the night." I smiled and didn't argue that 12:30 wasn't half the night. When the front bell rang, I kissed my father. "Daddy, I am so excited; I know you are going to like him."

Dad did like Cas. Over the years, I noticed how easily they conversed with each other. Cas admired my father's practical wisdom and wry humor, qualities he recognized in himself. Each one appreciated that the other knew how "to enjoy a drink." Both men were generous with their friends and loved their families, especially their mothers, good wives to hard-working, hard-drinking men born in the old country. They were alike too in that a quiet, genial manner masked a hot temper and narcissistic behavior.

Maybe this familiarity is the reason why it took me some twenty years to leave Caspar Simonelli. It will take even longer to fully understand the damage our relationship created. I don't know how long it will take our son to figure out the mess into which he was born.

Brooklyn, New York, February 1968

I lay there motionless while Caspar held his hand over my throat. Several times Cas told me the relationship was over. He was tired of my "nagging." "You push me away, Arianna. Now you act surprised because I'm seeing other girls." I'd get hysterical, crying and pleading as if I were desperate. Feeling as if I was about to fall into an endless chasm of loneliness, I'd beg, "Don't leave me." A freshman in college, I was studying the liberal arts with a radical faculty that included second-wave feminists dedicated to activism and consciousness raising, but I held fast to this abusive relationship that was breaking down my self-image.

Since we both still lived at home, Caspar and I conducted much of our lovemaking in the backseat of his Chevy Impala, and as opportunity made available, in one or the other's bedroom when no one was home. At least once a week, however, we'd would rent a room at the Howard Johnson's in Sheepshead Bay, and share a bottle of wine and take-out food from Lundy's. Then we'd make love until, satisfied and exhausted, we fell asleep. That night, Cas drank more than usual, and the more he drank, the more agitated he became.

My first impulse was to laugh. But then I saw the dead look in his eyes. The tension in his fingers made me realize screaming or moving away could prove fatal. Moments before, he had been stroking my cheek while he arched his body and slid out of mine. As always, he looked reassured, proud of his manhood.

Was this the same man who had just made love to me, or the animal that had once again possessed his body? He looked so cold while he held my throat. There had been other times when Caspar's frightening behavior made me cry. Times when he shoved me or flew into a rage over nothing.

A little more than a month after we met, he'd grabbed my arm so tight it left marks in the shape of his fingers. My father asked why the hell I was wearing a long-sleeved shirt on a sweltering day. Cas had told me if he ever caught me "fooling around," or telling anyone what went on between us in private, I would be "one sorry bitch." Dad was confused when I started to cry but asked no further questions. He figured I was grown up now and would probably marry before long. My craziness would become Caspar's problem.

Initially, the violence was intermittent. He'd insist I was at fault. Ashamed to admit to myself that I was being abused, I'd agree when he followed injury with insult, telling me, "You sure know how to push my buttons, Arianna." Although I had a wide circle of friends when I met him and was making more friends during my first year of college, I was terrified of losing him. I'd promise to stop what he had convinced me was nagging him about his drinking and showing up late. If I had been more attuned to what was going on, I would have asked more questions: "Why does talking about your drinking infuriate you?" "What makes you think you can talk to me and treat me the way you do?" "Where did you learn this sort of behavior?"

Had I asked these questions, and if the effects of growing up in an alcoholic home had been as widely known then as they are now, I would have understood I was dating the son of an active alcoholic. His father, Marco Simonelli, began the day with three shots of scotch and ended it checking the results at Aqueduct and lotto tickets he bought with his carpenter's salary, an empty bottle of wine at his side.

Often, young Cas watched his father throw the dinner on the floor after being called home from the Tip Top Tavern by his grandmother. While Tessie, his wife, cleaned up the mess, Marco told his sons their grandmother had no business "doin' what she done. You don't treat a man that way, especially in front of his friends."

Like many children of alcoholics, Cas was fiercely defensive of his father. Marco compensated for his outbursts, often treating him and his younger brother, Charles, to hot dogs at Nathan's and rides at Coney Island using money Tessie was holding for the rent. A compassionate listener, a warm man who, given a different set of circumstances, might have become a community activist, Marco was the only one in Cas' family who'd hug me or ask how my family was doing without Mom.

But when he was twelve, his father had gone back to Sicily for a visit and never returned, leaving his five children with an embittered wife who turned their Red Hook tenement into a seedy boarding house. Marco escaped to the battlefields of France, where he earned medals for his bravery as part of a reconnaissance brigade. After a German bullet pierced his shoulder, he began an alcohol-induced downward spiral. Tessie Giordano was waiting to care for him back in Brooklyn. They married in 1945, soon after he returned.

Despite his large heart and gregarious manner, Marco's unyielding determination to have things his way kept his family from reacting to his "bouts of illness," their code for his serious addiction to drinking and gambling. Cas resented the poverty and chaos, burying his anger and shame under a veneer of cheerful behavior. As an adult he'd recall his steely determination to work his way to financial success. "I knew before I left eighth grade that I'd become my own boss, own my own business." His resolve to answer to no one but himself became my misfortune.

Whenever Cas became violent, I wouldn't respond, but I'd ask myself a number of conflicting questions.

"How dare he strike me like that just because I had disagreed with him in front of his friends?"

"If I ask why he did this, will he give me an answer, an apology, or become violent again?"

"Why do I take this?"

"Does this mean he is tired of me and trying to break things off?"

"Could I live without him?"

Cas' apologies were seductive; he'd go out of his way to please me. I convinced myself things would get better. And I played the game. I was manipulative myself, so I'd hold out for a weekend in the Hamptons or Catskills, his treat. If I hadn't allowed this relationship to destroy the self-confidence I'd grown up with, or if I'd been aware of the controlling behavior associated with alcoholism and abusive relationships, I might have broken it off. Instead, I handed over my power.

I should have left Cas the first time he abused me, but I didn't. That happened much later.

Brooklyn, New York, 1970

"You're too fat."

"You look terrible. Yellow is definitely not your color."

"Why don't you wear more make up, like the other guys' girlfriends?"

"You're too opinionated."

"You mustn't think much of this relationship the way you disagree with me in front of other people."

"You've gotten too thin."

"I don't want to see you anymore."

As typically happens in abusive relationships, Cas began alienating me from my friends. The ones he was sleeping with, or had tried to, were the first ones he put down. He'd greet them with a smile and kiss, but in private he'd assassinate their character. Eventually, he targeted my best friend. "Elaine is too mouthy," he said. "What makes her think she knows more than everyone else?" It was clear he didn't like outspoken women, but Elaine had been my buddy, my confidante, since sophomore year of high school. "Start acting like her, Arianna, and we're through."

Elaine said that, since I met Cas, I had been constantly worried about what he might or might not say or do. "And you've become so quiet." I actually believed she was jealous. When she laughed at my explanation that Cas cared enough to watch out for me, I figured he'd been right about her, and I told her so. Eventually, she stopped returning my calls.

I began spending more time with the girls dating Cas' friends. Like me, they were eager to become wives and mothers, but there was a difference. Following their Italian American mothers' footsteps, they were content to have ended their education at graduation from high school. They thought highly of my love of reading and ambition to have a career, but such things never became a shared interest. Beyond talking about the guys, clothes, and what was in the movies, we had little in common.

Cas and I became close with Erin, my friend from B. Altman's, and her boyfriend Steve. They were more conservative than my old friends and the new ones I was meeting at Hunter. Treating Cas as if he were the life of the party, Erin and Steve played along when he teased me about abandoning make-up and high heels "for your hippie *espadrilles* and political babble." We'd spend weekends together in the Hamptons on Steve's boat, partying late into the night. But we did this less frequently as I became more preoccupied with my schoolwork.

He had a lot to say about my family, too. And it still haunts me that I didn't realize that he was trying to undermine my already-troubled relationships. Charming and attentive in their company, he'd turn snitch before the door closed behind them.

"Nina showed me one of your 7th-grade class pictures. Where'd you get the kinky perm?"

"Have you noticed how your sisters look at each other when you begin one of your anti-war or women's lib rants?"

"Julie said she doesn't know how I put up with you."

"He's just trying to be there for me," I'd lie to myself whenever he complained about Nina speaking to me so disrespectfully. His warnings rang true, but his interventions were mean spirited. For years he told me, "You shouldn't be so nice to her. She doesn't deserve everything you do for her." I needed to admit to myself that my family was often sarcastic and judgmental, disapproving of the new me that was absorbing—if not yet participating in—the wider, more inclusive world view I was discovering in college. Still it wasn't Cas' business to meddle with our family dynamic. Years later, when Cas was gone from my life, I confronted their toxicity and showed up for myself.

Was I totally naïve? In denial? Somewhere inside, a healthy part of myself was yearning to come clean with one of my friends, talk about it, and figure out if the relationship was "normal" or not. But the shame of Cas' put-downs kept me silent. Only after years of therapy, and the give and take in my support group, have I learned that you need to respond to violence and abuse as if you are swimming near a shark: You need to get out of the water, quickly.

In my late teens, I believed my sexuality was a betrayal of what I had been taught by my traditional Italian American family and the nuns at St. Mark's. Sex should exist only between husband and wife.

And there are books a good Catholic should not read; they are the idolatry condemned in the Bible. How far I strayed from the lessons in the the *Baltimore Catechism*! For eight years, my classmates and I had repeated the answers to questions one virginal teacher after another called out from our little book.

Question 370. *What are we commanded by the sixth Commandment?*
Answer: *We are commanded by the sixth Commandment to be pure in thought and modest in all our looks, words, and actions.*

Question 371. *What is forbidden by the sixth Commandment?*
Answer: *The sixth commandment forbids all unchaste freedom with another's wife or husband; also all immodesty with ourselves or others in looks, dress, words, or actions.*

Question 372. *Does the sixth Commandment forbid the reading of bad and immodest books and newspapers?*
Answer: *The sixth Commandment does forbid the reading of bad and immodest books and newspapers.*

I had been sexually active since my early teens; deep down I believed that marriage would redeem the spiritual damage caused by my sinful behavior. With my family life in turmoil after my mother's death, I was determined to find my soul mate. The irony here is that I found someone but sold my soul in the bargain. Although I was not attracted to any of the household duties I'd watched my mother and grandmothers perform so meticulously, I was bent on becoming Mrs. Caspar Simonelli. I was proud that I was insanely in love. Looking back, I see that I was very confused and needy. One afternoon, I acted out my obsession in the Hunter College library, using my nail file to carve *AN and CS 4 ever* while I was supposed to be studying.

Which pages in Wollstonecraft, Woolf, or De Beauvoir should I have been reading more closely when I drifted into this destructive (to both the table and to myself) reverie? A while back I sought absolution by making a generous donation to their library fund.

During our breakups, I'd shut down sexually and starve myself. Intensely focused on the relationship, and emotionally immature, I sought to control the only thing I could: my body. In my warped logic, where shame played havoc, shedding pounds made me less inferior. Thinner than I imagined I could make myself, I took to dressing up in Carnaby Street-style leather mini-skirts with tight-fitting epaulette jackets. But despite the voraciously provocative look, I was sexually anorexic. The guys I dated during our breakups barely got a good night kiss.

Our breakups ended on a night when Cas parked under a lamp-post and waited for me to come home. He'd tell me how he'd been miserable without me, and I'd believe him. Relieved that we were reconciled, I'd mistake his narcissism for caring when he questioned me about what I'd been up to, where I'd been and whom I dated while we were apart. I was silent because I had nothing much to tell; he mistook my silence for holding back.

Our make-up rides always ended at the Narrows, where, without asking, he'd resume his place inside my body and my life. Kissing me while slipping his hand under my skirt, he sometimes boasted that, during our breakup, he'd been with someone more sexually sophisticated than me. "How good it would be for our relationship if you were more adventurous." When I didn't respond, that was the end of any gentle foreplay.

I should have left him many times during the years we dated, but I didn't. That happened much later.

Brooklyn, New York, 1973–1976

I was a graduate student when we became engaged in 1973. Cas placed the ring on my finger that Valentine's Day, then drove me, my father, Sadie, and my sisters to the Aida's Villa on Montague Street. With Mom gone, I didn't want an engagement party, and Dad was relieved. But Sadie Petrocelli, the former neighbor he'd been dating for some time, insisted on a family outing. It was obvious that she was insinuating herself into the role of mother-of-the-bride, telling me that "we" must shop for my gown at Kleinfeld's and urging Cas to call her friend Tommy for a good deal at the Golden Terrace. Julie told me there was quite a commotion during the car ride back to Bensonhurst when Nina asked Sadie if she was certain I planned to invite her to the wedding.

The next week, we had tickets for *Jesus Christ Superstar*. I was stewing when he picked me up an hour and a half late. He was drunk, very drunk. When he was an hour late, I had called the Tip Top Tavern. The second time I called, I thought I'd heard Cas talking in the background, but the owner had said, "No honey, he left over an hour ago."

As soon as we got into the car, he reminded me that he didn't like me calling the bar. I asked him how he knew I had called if he was already gone. He flew into a rage, striking my face so hard my head hit the side window. Waiting for the light to turn green at 28th Street, Cas looked as if he was about to strike me again. I jumped out of the car.

Walking and crying at the same time, I felt frantic. What would happen when we began living together? Was this what I had waited for almost six years? Having spent that time hoping for what I foolishly believed was the logical conclusion to our relationship, I failed to understand that my expectations were illogical and I was sabotaging my future.

I stopped in front of my cousin Stefano's beauty salon. Years before, it had been Great-Grandpa Orazio's barber shop. Inside, a night-light cast a shadow beneath the empty chairs where women I loved had once sat. Feeling comforted by the familiar territory but saddened by the reminder of loss that had wracked my family, I was absorbed by memories. I didn't notice Cas parked by the curb. He walked over, put his arm around me, and began crying. He told me that, as long as he lived, he would never touch me again. If I forgave him, he'd make a good husband.

At the time, I was more than a year into my graduate work, and I had taken a few courses cross-listed with the new Women's Studies Program. In one course my professor, Judith Stephens, had us read the greats. In *A Room of One's Own,* Virginia Woolf comments, "Wife-beating was a recognized right of man, and was practiced without shame by high as well as low." Yet somehow I didn't connect what was happening to the long and tragic history of misogyny. This is Cas, I rationalized, the guy everybody likes and who always makes it up to me. He isn't some old-fashioned brute, is he?

I gave him a hug and got in the car.

Although we were almost two hours late for our reservation at Mama Leone's, we were seated immediately after Cas slipped a fifty-dollar bill to the head waiter. We missed the play, but, as Cas explained, the important thing was that we were together. I agreed, denying the truth when one waiter, then another, asked if I needed some ice for the swelling on my face.

It was becoming increasingly dangerous for me in this relationship. But I didn't think about leaving him. That happened much later.

I remember the months before and after our May 1976 wedding as a peaceful, happy time. Frequently, couples argue over expenses, the guest list, and who will sit next to whom, but we behaved like two old-time partners who knew how to give and take. One afternoon, we spent almost an hour in Macy's, deciding which shoes would go best with Cas' rented tuxedo. And I called him during my bridal shower, inviting him to come join in the fun as soon as he was ready. His need to be in control seemed to evaporate as the wedding day drew near. My days were filled with wedding plans and writing term papers. I had never been happier. I believed the feeling would last forever.

There was a moment of foreboding, however, on the way to the Golden Terrace. Nina walked so closely behind me when we left the church that she wound up sitting between us in the limousine. Lifting her over him while he slid next to me, Cas' cigarette brushed against my veil.

"Cas, watch your cigarette. It would probably be best if you put it out."

He gave me the sort of look Sicilian bridegrooms once gave their spouse on their wedding day just before launching the traditional slap that established power. Hoping that no one had noticed, I pretended nothing was wrong. Like a Sicilian bride of yore, I had been put in my place. As always, I ignored the fault lines.

Not long after we returned from our honeymoon in Paris, Uncle Enzo told us about a small one-family fix-me-up on Benson Avenue that was what he called "a steal." The owner, a long-time customer in his *salumeria*, had asked my uncle if he knew of anyone who had a large down payment and willingness to take over a mortgage facing foreclosure. The generous cash wedding gifts from our family and friends more than covered the down payment.

Cas and I spent nights painting our new home, ripping up the dirty rugs covering parquet floors, while eating pizza straight from the box and listening to music. And we talked about our dreams. Cas wanted to start his own demolition business, and I hoped that before long I'd finish my Ph.D. and become a professor. We were dreaming of two vastly different lifestyles, one rugged and physical, the other staunchly cerebral.

Still we shared the dream of creating a beautiful home. On Saturdays, we'd stop for breakfast somewhere on a country road, *en route* to estate sales, and later drive home with a trove of vintage treasures. When friends visited, Cas enjoyed cooking and tending bar. I ignored that it was okay if I invited Erin and Steve and my cousin, Butchie, and her husband, Jeff. But if I suggested, inviting some of my old friends, he'd usually object. As for my new friends from graduate school or the College of New York City, where I was tutoring, he'd complain he felt uncomfortable listening to the women voice their ideas and their men chime in with them.

Early on there were signs our marriage was in trouble, but, as always, I chose to ignore them. Although I was unaware of the term *mammismo* at the time, I recognized my husband and his mother were enmeshed. Cas stopped to see his mother every day after work. On payday he'd spend hours at the Tip Top Tavern. Yet I turned my head and pursued my own agenda. With Cas preoccupied, I had plenty of time for my coursework and time out with my college friends. He liked the idea that I was part of a study group preparing for exams. Sometimes my graduate school friends and I were actually meeting; other times it was a convenient cover for fun in Manhattan. There was no other man, but there was another *life*, the academic life, and it was seducing me.

THAT OCTOBER MARCO SIMONELLI died of cirrhosis of the liver. His family was bereft by the loss of the man who had made their home both a heaven and a hell. Cas used alcohol to medicate himself over it, drinking more at home and at the bar. He resented my suggestion that he talk out his feelings with a therapist. "Christ, Arianna, is therapy your answer to *everything*? Wasn't it me who helped you through your mother's death? Is some money-grubbing shrink going to bring my father back or tell me what to feel?"

It would have been best if I had a therapist I could tell my secrets to and open up about my anger and sadness. But I was preoccupied with my work and accustomed to stuffing down my feelings. So I convinced myself that, after Cas and I learned how to live with each other, and I had my Ph.D. and a teaching job, everything would fall into place. While I may have complained about his drinking, I took no action. I just accepted it.

But I couldn't look the other way when Cas got drunk the morning of our first Thanksgiving as husband and wife. After breakfast, he said he was going to his friend George's house to talk about a prospective construction project. He'd be home in time for us to leave for Grandma Lena's. He came back an hour after we should have been there. Ashamed to tell my family the truth, I ignored the messages they were leaving on our answering machine.

In my Italian American family, no one ever showed up for a holiday without their spouse. Ever. So I could not imagine going to my grandmother's alone. How would I answer their questions and react to their pity and disbelief?

When Cas came back drunk, I decided to shame him. "Is this how we are going to spend Thanksgiving, with you drunk and in no shape to go anywhere? Haven't you learned *anything* from what happened to your father? How long will it be before your liver begins to—"

Before I could finish, Cas started kicking and punching me, continuing even after my head hit the wall and I fell down to the hardwood floor.

He went to bed in a drunken stupor. That night I called my grandmother and lied about a stomach virus we had.

"Why didn't you call us?"

"We were just too sick to talk."

Grandma knew I was lying, but she allowed me to save face. In our family that was privileged over confronting the truth.

I should have filed a police report, come clean with myself and everyone else, telling what happened on Thanksgiving and the times before. I began to shut down, responded more coolly to Cas, and became less available in bed. But I stayed. Leaving him happened much later.

Brooklyn, New York, December 1979

Until recently, my periods had been twenty-six days apart. So when six weeks passed and there was no sign of one, I scheduled an appointment with my obstetrician. The exam showed signs of pregnancy, but Dr. Graves suggested I postpone celebrating until the test results were in. I decided I'd tell Cas when I was certain. Earlier that year, I'd had a miscarriage, and we had been devastated. I'd hoped to get pregnant right away, but my history with uterine polyps that resulted in one surgery after another scared me into thinking I might go through the rest of my life both motherless and childless, a generationally disconnected wretch.

If the test results show I'm pregnant, it will make this Christmas special, I thought. *The night before, I'll hide a teddy bear dressed as Santa under the tree. In its hands, I'll place a transcript of the doctor's report rolled up like a royal scroll.*

But there was a good chance that I felt tired and achy because I had been busier than usual. In addition to tutoring and now teaching as an adjunct at the college, I was studying for exams. There was another possible explanation, too: After my last D&C, my periods had become less regular.

Christmas was less than two weeks away, so there was shopping and wrapping and decorating left to do. The day before my results came in, I felt exhausted after a day at work followed by the two-hour Renaissance seminar taught by the professor I hoped would someday supervise my dissertation. After the seminar, I stopped at

Century 21 to pick up a few presents. The store was so crowded I hardly noticed Cousin Butchie waving from a few feet away.

"Hey, Ari, how ya doin'? Do you believe this crowd? I still have to pick up a few things on 5th Avenue, and I'm wiped out."

"Yes, I can't wait to get home and take off my shoes. I've been in them since seven this morning. My feet are starting to swell."

"Are you feeling alright, Ari? You look a little pale and tired. You almost ready to go home?"

"Not yet. Caspar asked me to pick up his brother's gift at Chuck and Jack's. He's not big on doing his own shopping."

"Well, whatever you do, get some rest. You really look worn out. Maybe you're coming down with something."

"No worries, Butchie. It's nothing a hot cup of tea and legs up on the couch can't cure. Anyways, see you at Grandma's next week. I can't believe it's almost Christmas Eve."

"Take care. Say hi to Cas."

It was almost 8:30 before I got home. After I changed into my bathrobe, I phoned for Chinese food. Cas wanted to finish reading his newspaper and have another Rob Roy, so I asked them to deliver. No sooner had I hung up and walked into the pantry than the phone rang. "Cas, will you get it? I'm getting things ready to set the table." He mumbled something I did not quite hear, but I thought it best not to ask him to repeat it. He stopped mixing his drink and picked up the call from Aunt Mel.

"Butchie ran into Ari in Century's and is worried about her. Is everything alright, Cas? She says that Ari looks pale and exhausted. She does too much running around with school, and work, and keeping up the house. You should get her to slow down."

"Yeah, but you know how she is, Aunt Mel, a real, er. . . fireball. Wants to keep on top of everything. Makes her happy."

After I finished speaking to my aunt and finished setting the dinner table, Cas called me into the living room. Did he suspect that I was pregnant? He was sitting in the recliner, drink in one hand and a rolled up newspaper in the other.

"What the hell have you been telling your family? Always looking for pity, aren't you, Arianna? Got it so hard, do you? Give me a break."

"Hey, Cas, I'm exhausted. I haven't stopped all day. And after dinner, I have to work on a paper. If anyone needs a break, it's me."

As I thought about his dark moods and how pregnancy and motherhood might soon make me a lot more tired than I already was, I began to sob. I hadn't noticed he was holding the rolled up newspaper like a bat until he raised his arm and pummeled my left leg.

Devastated by his cruelty, I blurted out that perhaps I looked so tired because I might be pregnant. I relished telling him about the blood test and nausea. Crying, I lay in bed, petting our dog, who gave me the warmth I craved.

When Dr. Graves' nurse called with the positive results and to set up an appointment, it was Caspar who cried, leaving me feeling smug in my self-righteous indignation but uncertain about the future. I never forgave him for what had happened that night. Worse still, I haven't forgiven myself for not fighting back, saying something like, "You've crossed the line one last time. I won't tolerate any more abuse. It's over—we're through."

Bringing a child into this relationship, was reckless on my part. Not leaving then, and allowing the child to grow up in this chaos, proved disastrous. I should have left Cas, but I didn't. That happened much later.

CHAPTER 9
Missing The Exit Signs

Gaze at a new life
Child, escape the ancient curse.
Come, step out of line.

Brooklyn, New York, July 3, 1980

MY DUE DATE WAS STILL nine weeks away. I had only gained twenty-five pounds, all in my mid-section. If Mom were alive, she would have predicted I was carrying a boy. One early July morning, when I looked down, my feet were gone. They were hidden by what looked like a rippling balloon. Often, I'd slip off my clothes, lie on my back, and relish the waves of life coming from the unborn child I already loved.

But since my miscarriage, I was taking nothing for granted. Dr. Graves said it probably had been an ectopic pregnancy, which, as he explained, always results in miscarriage. If the embryo continued to grow, my fallopian tubes might have ruptured. I obsessively looked for signs of vaginal bleeding. The anxiety about miscarriage stayed with me even after this baby began to grow and move with the strength of a little kick boxer. Several times, I woke up in a sweat following a nightmare about delivering a dead infant. When I did, I wouldn't shut my eyes until I felt the baby moving inside me.

During that special time, Cas was not always emotionally available. If he had been drinking, or if he was in one of his dark moods, he'd turn unreasonable or violent in a flash. Not wanting to admit the truth about my marriage, deeply ashamed of the way I was being mistreated one moment and bought off with presents or a night out the next, I told no one. My outwardly ordered life was masking unimaginable danger and internal chaos.

When anxiety or sadness became overwhelming, I'd sooth myself with a piece of cheesecake while filling out a Spiegel catalog order form, not stopping until I reached the last line. Sometimes I'd pause just long enough the get a second piece of cheesecake. No one would have suspected such reckless behavior, since I talked the talk of the responsibly prudent.

That year, July 3 fell on a Thursday. Cas finished work at 3:30, but said he couldn't meet me at the A&P until 6 p.m. Since it was payday, his routine made anything earlier impossible: He needed to cash his check, and make his daily stop at his mother's house, before having a few drinks with the guys at the bar. Eight months pregnant, and grateful I felt well enough to continue working, it would have been best if I had eaten by 6:00 and gone to bed early. But Cas always insisted we eat out after we shopped. Late in the afternoon, I took a nap before meeting him and woke up to the rhythms of my dancing belly.

I was waiting for him outside the A&P when he showed up, forty-five minutes late, reeking of liquor. I turned away as he reached to kiss me. I was annoyed but only in that vague way characteristic of an alcoholic's wife whose denial prevents her from seeing the full tragedy in which she is playing a major role.

We had enough hot dogs and hamburgers in the freezer for our

July 4 barbecue to feed our fourteen guests, but I wanted steaks for the evening meal. Cas headed for the beer and drinks section. I filled the cart with barbecue staples and three large packages of filet mignon. For a few dollars more we'll have a feast, I thought. Anyway, this will be the last gathering at our house before the baby is born.

At the checkout counter, I noticed Cas opening a beer. Maybe he'll put it away if I shake my head and give him a critical look, I thought. Once again, I was wrong. Becoming angrier when he saw the totaled bill, he took the cart rather brusquely from my hands and motioned for me to walk ahead. I ignored his tirade about spending money as if it were water, until the loaded shopping cart jabbed me three times in my lower back, almost causing me to topple over.

A woman walking a few steps behind us had been watching. She asked whether I was alright, whether I needed to sit for a minute. Loud enough for the woman to hear, Cas said, "Ari, take your time walking. I'll load the groceries into the car."

I sat with the woman on the bench out front, denying what she had witnessed. "He's a ruffian and a joker who sometimes takes things too far. And me, I need to move more carefully."

"Yes," said the woman, "you need to be more careful indeed. Here, let me give you my card." At home that night, I read it: *Lisa Miller, CSW, Take Back the Night Foundation.* I threw it in the garbage.

Shame had turned my denial and insecurity into a block of emotional cement. I should have called the social worker's number and left him then. But I didn't. That happened much later.

Brooklyn, New York, 1980–1988

In August 1980, Christopher was born into a tense, violent home. He was a happy, outgoing toddler who loved playing sports and drawing. By age three he was reading and forming his letters. I never had to toilet-train him. A keen observer since he first opened his blue eyes, he trained himself by mimicking what he saw.

But during his early years, Cas and I battled and grew apart. Chris became the hostage in our war. To counter the chaos, I made sure he had a routine, but I overcompensated by bringing him to one artistic or sports activity after another. I swore he would have the foundation that neither his father nor I had received. These experiences, I believed, would keep him grounded and safe from idle distractions, like hanging out in a bar.

When I was hired as an Assistant Professor of Renaissance Literature in 1985 by the College of New York City, Cas became fearful our son wouldn't identify with him, wouldn't become part of his world. So he more frequently played the reckless older brother. He routinely gave in to Chris' every demand and sent one signal after another that there was nothing wrong with breaking the rules. Cas ignored the warning signs our son's teachers routinely called us in to discuss once he began school.

His kindergarten teacher noticed how often he acted out. "It seems," she said, "that he just can't get enough attention." Chris always earned good grades, but each year we were called in because of his disruptive behavior and disrespect for his teachers. At home I tried to reinforce his teachers' efforts, created activities aimed at making him aware of the importance of cooperation and reminding him that we all had to respect boundaries. But when I tried to involve Cas in helping to socialize our son, he'd make rude comments and facial gestures. He'd remind him they were buddies; no one had a more special bond.

My anger with Cas became palpable. I'd stomp around the house like a Fury whenever he brought Chris along to the Tip Top Tavern. On more than one occasion, he had our six-year-old call to tell me they were having such a good time, they'd be late for dinner.

I'd go on and on about how Cas was setting a bad example for Chris and becoming more unreliable. I seemed to be lying in wait for his next wrong move, so I could pounce on him. Knowing he had a short fuse, I kept my most severe criticism to myself. Or I'd go down into the basement where, alone with a rumbling washing machine, I'd let out a tirade of what I thought and felt about him. The passion I once felt for Cas was slipping away. And I was beginning to fall out of love with him.

One evening, Chris heard us arguing because I suggested we give him a time out for being disruptive during a class trip to the Brooklyn Botanical Gardens. He had disregarded the safety precautions the teachers set. When it was time to return to school, Chris and two classmates had walked out a back entrance and sat on the curb. Their teachers had been terrified until a park attendant made an announcement over the loudspeaker that the missing boys had been found. The children all agreed it had been Chris' idea.

I should have known better when I smelled liquor on Cas' breath that it wasn't the time to suggest that we work as a team to teach our son appropriate behavior. His voice grew louder and more threatening. When I asked him to lower it, he walked out. The next day Chris told me that, on the way to school, his dad had explained, "I know you have a hard time following the rules, because you're a lot like me. Ignore your mother. She makes a big deal out of everything."

Many times I overheard Cas say, "Don't worry, pal. Soon I'll be leaving your crazy mother—you'll be coming with me. I already looked at an apartment with a great room for you and a pool in the backyard." When our marriage ended four years later, Cas did indeed have an apartment where Chris had his own room, a piano, and a lake out back. It also had an adjoining door to an apartment where some married Mafioso had set up his girlfriend and their baby. Every time I picked Chris up, the door between the apartments was open.

My therapist told me to insist that Chris only visit his father at his grandmother's. Cas ignored my suggestion, and I did not push the point, knowing that, short of taking my son and leaving New York, there was little I could do, unless I wanted to get a knock on my door or maybe worse. As I look back, I believe that, if I hadn't been so fearful, I would have found a way.

Chris' life might have turned out for the better; he might have avoided the expulsions and drug abuse that plagued his adolescent years if I had left Cas when I first realized the damage his alcoholic behavior and my frayed nerves were creating. But I didn't. At least not soon enough. And to this day, I regret not having taken action. The biggest tragedy? I forfeited the chance to become the calm and centered parent who could teach my child by providing him with an example.

Cas' parenting style was beyond belief. And Chris saw his father's reckless behavior as an escape from my hovering over him in a state of frantic concern. My friends, my father, and my therapist often told me I should leave; they assured me I could make it on my own. But I didn't take action. That happened much later.

Brooklyn, New York, June 1989

After Cas opened his business, he refused to take time off for vacation. Most weeks he worked seven days, and sometimes well into the night. When I called him to come home for dinner, to say goodnight to Chris, or to say goodnight myself, his secretary, Wendy, was always there. He began insisting we refuse invitations from family and friends, not that there were many friends left.

One weekend, Erin and Steve invited the three of us to spend the weekend at their upstate cabin. Cas had me phone them to explain we couldn't get up there Friday night; we'd be there early Saturday morning. But late Friday night he got a call from Wendy saying a client needed to see him in the morning. We finally got on the road at 1:30 and got stuck in traffic. We didn't arrive until almost 5 p.m.

Our friends let us know they were disappointed. The next morning, Cas told them, and me, that he wanted to be on the road by 3:00, so he could return phone calls and get things ready for the morning. After that weekend, we saw much less of these old friends, and when we did, they complained how obsessive we'd become with our work.

When I was hired by the College of New York City, I was still writing my dissertation. My department chair advised me to publish at least one article before my second-year reappointment. And each time I saw the Provost on campus, he reminded me, "The tenure clock is ticking."

Tired and stressed from the pressure at work and at home, I gained twenty-five pounds during the first year I taught. Cas became more critical of my appearance, and I transferred what was left of my passion to my work. We agreed that maybe it was time to talk to a counselor. I needed to explore why I was obsessed with my work, and Cas admitted he was drinking too much. But after two appointments, he decided he didn't need any help, just less grief from me. I decided to stay in treatment with Davis Paulson to find out what I wanted. What I did not find was a way to talk to Cas so that he would listen, or learn how to listen to him in a way that would help me communicate my needs more effectively. What I *did* discover was that I wanted a different life.

I knew it was only a matter of time before I ended my marriage and began living with dignity. But that happened much later.

Brooklyn, New York, May 1992

The week after Mother's Day, our seventy-three-year-old neighbor, Gemma, was bludgeoned to death. There had been family violence in both our homes. I kept silent about what was happening in mine, but a few weeks before her death she opened up to me.

I'd known the gentle grandmother had an alcoholic son-in-law, but I hadn't known he was being investigated by child services regarding allegations of incest. He had threatened his wife, Gemma's only child, that if she testified against him, she would be sorry, very sorry. My neighbor was also troubled that her eldest granddaughter had recently married a heroin addict, and that he had been sneaking into the house at night to steal from her. With such a grisly example so close to home of what could happen if abuse escalated, I was fearful when Cas was out and agitated when he was home. The homicide report mentioned "robbery" as the motive, but there had been overkill; it appeared to have been personal. The effects of multi-layered abuse and dysfunction were dismissed by investigating detectives, though, as "routine family squabbles."

Caspar's anger issues worsened after our neighbor's murder. Financial problems with his demolition business, and his lack of formal training in business management, made him dependent on others for guidance. His chief advisor was his accountant, a bar buddy with a gambling problem. Frayed nerves, long hours at work, and the means to upgrade from Johnnie Walker to Chivas Regal accelerated his drinking and violent outbursts.

Five weeks after Gemma's death, Caspar came at me in a way that sent me running for the door. Given the rage he was in, if he had caught me, he might have seriously harmed or even killed me. The look on his face, the flared nostrils, the threats he made, and the aggressive chase fueled by hours of drinking before he returned home to a sleeping child and a disgusted wife, only disappeared after he hurled his cold dinner into the backyard through the kitchen window.

I sat crying on the back steps, hoping none of our neighbors had seen or heard the latest outburst. I had to find a way of getting Cas back into therapy and look at his rage. If he refused again, maybe I could enlist his brother to talk with him. Charles was a sober, gentle guy, but I wondered if he had the wherewithal for an intervention. He joked around to the extent that it was hard to know what he was actually thinking. Lately, I noticed how his anxious humor always enabled him to avoid confrontation.

I knew Cas would be remorseful and make amends with little gifts and niceties. He'd offer to cook dinner or take us out to eat. He'd probably finish the rock garden that the demands of my work had forced me to put side. But despite everything I was learning in therapy about living with an angry alcoholic, I wanted instant gratification.

So after Cas passed out in a drunken stupor, I removed the broken window screen and the scattered dinner from the backyard patio. I put on my robe and slippers and made myself two ham-and-cheese sandwiches, resentful that, once again, Chris would wake his father in the morning, asking why he'd gone to sleep with his clothes and shoes on.

As the night wore on, I made popcorn and watched *Casablanca*. While Ilse cried because Rick had insisted she leave with Victor for Portugal, I was scraping the bottom of a pint of Cherry Garcia. Then I laid out three small stacks of index cards for review, and after completing the first stack, made a trip to the bathroom to purge. After my next binge, I poured a bottle of Chivas Regal into Cas' work boots. Before I got into bed, I took a triple dose of Ex-lax.

This macabre behavior went on and on in our home during my son's childhood.

Chris slept through this tirade, but he was awake for many others. He was sitting at the table when Cas critiqued a meal by throwing it on the floor. This made him laugh, probably from nerves. There was the night he watched television in the next room while Cas tightened his grip on my throat. He saw his father throw the garbage pail across the kitchen. He burst into tears when he heard me threatening to call the police. And he stood by his father's side the night I did call.

A dean at the Brooklyn Academy met with Cas and me, and explained our son was "at risk." She told us, "Christopher instigates mischief any chance he gets. He tells his classmates terrible things about their mothers, things aimed at poisoning their relationships. In my fifteen years at this school, there has never been anything like it." Caspar excused himself. He needed to go outside for a cigarette.

She continued, "It's the kind of behavior we will not tolerate. Whatever its source may be, it is damaging his emotional well-being. A number of kids have been shunning him. He's becoming friendless. His return here next September, I am sorry to say, is contingent upon his being treated by a therapist. The headmaster will require proof of his visits. I am sure you understand. Please convey our decision to Mr. Simonelli—he seems to have disappeared."

I found Caspar outside the car, smoking. "What took you so long, Arianna? What did that bitch have to say? You know I have a ton of appointments this afternoon. Come on, let's go."

When I took Chris for counseling, Cas told him, "It's your mother who needs counseling, her and that lesbian-looking dean of yours. You're okay. I was the same way in school. There is no problem here, only a couple of crazy women."

Chris loved his father. Moreover, in his childish mind he saw him as the only one who understood and came to his rescue. Women, especially his mother, he believed, had no business making a fuss over every little thing.

"These therapists are phonies," Cas continued. "Like I said, it's not you who is the problem. Tell the therapist what he wants to hear. Play along, pal, okay?" When Chris began stealing money from his wallet, Cas blamed the therapist for "screwing with his son's head."

Gemma's death changed me. It made personal safety a priority, for myself and for Chris. Now when Cas acted out his rage or acted inappropriately with Chris, I took it more seriously, saw the effects more clearly. And something else had happened: I'd become disgusted with myself for not having put an end to this sooner.

Brooklyn, New York, July 1992

The three of us spent July 4, 1992, alone. During dinner, Cas said nothing, only that the chicken was undercooked and the potato salad was "swimming in the cheap mayonnaise you buy." He drank heavily. The only jollity came when he found Chris looking through one of his *Playboy* magazines. He sat next to him, commenting on the pictures. When I protested, they both laughed and called me crazy.

The previous week the therapist had been shocked by my panic attacks and acute anxiety over Chris' mimicking his father's behavior. "Arianna, what your husband is doing may be harmful to you, but he seems to be intentionally sabotaging Chris' development. The *Playboy* incidents, for example, are acts of emotional incest. I will leave another message at your husband's office, urging him to join us for at least one session."

That July 4, I went to bed early. With the sound of firecrackers in the background, I reread parts of Ovid's *Metamorphoses*. I drifted off to sleep thinking about how joy often turns into tragedy.

In many of Ovid's stories the gods are angered by excessive grief: Orpheus, Niobe, Cyparissus, all ravished by their misfortune. Why had their suffering incurred the wrath of the immortals? It had to be something more than hubris, the stock explanation for divine vengeance. Could it be the gods have no patience for whining? The following Monday, I made an appointment with a divorce lawyer.

I should have done so much sooner, but I decided then that it was time to leave Caspar.

New York, New York, July 2005

Today, my office is a safe place for students in unsafe situations. After listening to their stories, I refer them to the campus women's center, where they are put in touch with a counselor or the appropriate community service. I heal a little more every time someone I've taught becomes a women's center intern, an activist who organizes events and workshops, such as a recent one aimed at raising awareness about signs of abuse.

One intern, Amina, approached me after the workshop. As she'd done several times before, she thanked me for referring her to the director of the women's center. Then she said something I hadn't expected. "Professor Naso, you'd be surprised how many students are victims of abuse but have difficulty breaking away from the abuser."

I had never shared the dark side of my past with a student before. Haltingly I admitted, "Yes, Amina, I know; I've been there, too. And stayed way too long." Of course, I left the student center grateful for the chance to validate my student's work. But the recognition that we were working on the same team was something else, something that, for me, has to do with what Gabriel Garcia Marquez called "living to tell the tale."

Silence equals death—if not totally, then for some part of the body, mind, or spirit. Still, fear and shame continue to keep victims connected to their abusers. As I write this, I am remembering the fresh young faces of former students who stayed too long.

CHAPTER 10
Displaced Persons

O, bountiful rain,
Touch a tree newly risen,
Swaying once again.

London, 6 July 2005

B Y ONE O'CLOCK, I WAS STILL WORKING on the manuscript, but the buzz from my mid-morning cappuccino was gone, so I packed a student paper and headed toward the Boulevard Deli for a working lunch. Turning onto Wellington Street, I came face to face with Kevin Youssef.

Years earlier, when I was researching my dissertation at Dr. Williams' Library, Kevin had patiently and skillfully guided a very anxious me through the collection. If it hadn't been for his knowledge of seventeenth-century texts, I might have returned home *sans* research. A new project brought me back to Dr. Wills, as everyone calls it, during the summers of 1996 and 1997. That was when I learned we shared a passion for David Lodge's novels and each had a son, an only child in his teens.

We used to sit in the park outside the library after closing time, talking about our lives, about our kids—two strangers sharing secrets without an agenda, only the need to open up about the pain of parenting a talented but troubled teen on drugs.

Parents with this dilemma are like members of a tribe. We are bound by the frustration that comes with seeking solutions to problems our children deny they have. Outsiders either shun or pity us; either way, they don't want to become us. Members of our tribe inhabit the same emotional territory. And we have our own language, so there is no need to explain what the incessant turmoil looks like. We depend on each other for survival.

"Kevin, it's so good to see you. You look great. How are things with you?"

"Arianna Naso, I can't believe I'm talking to you after all this time! How long is it? Five, six years since you worked in Dr. Wills?"

"More like eight years. But we waved at each other when Kermode spoke at the British Library two years ago. Remember? I looked for you during the reception, but you weren't there."

"Ah, yes. A quick exit following a message from my ex-wife, one of those never-ending family crises. I remember we used to share stories about our boys. Well, if you can believe it, my Ben is still living at home. It is just the two of us now. Denise and I divorced about five years ago. He's twenty-seven, and, well, he still hasn't gotten his life on track. Doesn't like to work, problems with drugs, personality issues he can't or won't address."

I shook my head, resisting the urge to unleash my saga. "I know— we are not out of the woods in New York. Chris still has issues."

Issues, I thought. What a benign word. Sounds more like media speak than the reality Chris lives with.

We gave each other a nod of understanding and compassion. I started to tell him about *Angelina's Story*, but my heart sank when he looked at his watch.

"Oh, Ari, I want to. . . . Listen, I was supposed to meet a colleague at Charing Cross ten minutes ago, so I must run. But I would love to have dinner and catch up. Well, as much as you can catch up eight years over dinner. What do you say?"

"Sure. I'll be in London for another week. Tomorrow will be a hectic day, but I could do dinner after I finish at the BL Friday about 6:00."

"I'm still at Dr. Wills, so how about meeting 6:15 at the North Sea Fishery? Do you know the restaurant? It's on Leigh Street."

"That's great. I'll see you then."

What I didn't say was that I hoped our catching up might go beyond dinner. Several years older, Mick Fleetwood-like ponytail gone, Kevin still had the boyish charm I remembered. The first time I met him, we were both married. And even though I was divorced when I returned a few years later, my emotional damage had all but neutered me.

That was then, and now is now. Wellington Street brightened as I imagined us walking back from dinner on Friday along Kingsway to Waterloo Bridge. We'd stop for a moonlight view of the Thames. If I sensed a connection, I'd invite him to my room for a tea.

Remembering that the following night was a late night at Self-ridges, I made a mental note to head there after I left the Library. Dinner with Kevin called for a new outfit and maybe some earrings—long, sparkling earrings that sway when you move. Amused by my thoughts, I muttered, "How '80s is this?" I was cautiously hopeful.

The Boulevard Deli, an Italian *trattoria* in the heart of Covent Garden, had a misleading name but great food. As usual, it was crowded.

"*Ciao, cara,*" I called out to Claudia, the waitress who always brought an extra coffee on the house and asked questions about Manhattan clubs my students were better equipped to answer.

"Ciao, Arianna, give me a few minutes. I'll have a nice table for you."

"That's fine, no rush." Then I remembered the unfinished manuscript and my weekly telephone therapy session. When would I learn to say what I *really* meant?

By time Claudia brought my chicken and salad, I'd begun reading the final paper Donna Greco had handed in after the conclusion of my spring Italian American Literature course. Eager to bring closure to last semester's chores, I made a mental note to e-mail a change of grade to the English Department. Moments of closure come by slowly in academia. Here I was on the verge of completing two tasks, if I watched the time.

Donna Greco
English 345 Italian American Literature
Spring 2005
Professor Arianna Naso
Final Paper

ON MY ITALIAN AMERICANESS
Journal Entry - 11 April 2005

"I didn't know these things were talked about! What a trip!" That is what I kept repeating to myself on the R train back to Brooklyn. Tonight, Prof. Naso brought our Italian American Literature class to the Cornelia Street Café. One Saturday a month, a writer reads to the Italian American Writers' Association in the charmingly dingy basement of this Greenwich Village landmark. The reading is followed by audience members coming up for their five minutes of open mike fame.

Tonight's featured speaker was a poet, Vittoria repetto. Her poems made me think of the joy and the pain that comes with being an Italian American woman. Vittoria is a large woman, whose voice conveys mixed emotions and a determination to be herself and be respected. One poem keeps running through my mind, because it concerns an overbearing father serving up great food, insults, and prickly love. Can't remember its name, but I loved the image of his offering dishes like ravioli, gnocchi, and torta to his daughter, while he repeatedly tells her that she is fat. It blew me away—Fat was the refrain; fat was the button he pushed. What would be my refrain if I wrote a poem about my family's weekly Sunday gathering? Tramp, puttana, who do you think you are? These words would capture the mental battering I have to endure while they tell me how much they love me.

I heard my own dilemma when one of the five-minute open-mike speakers read from a short story-in-progress. Her main character, Benedetta, is a young Italian American woman being held hostage to gender expectations, written by whoever was the Medieval predecessor of Emily Post. A San Francisco flower child, Benedetta is being urged to marry the wealthy older man who owns the restaurant where she, her father, and older brother work. After their shift ends, she and her family walk home together. She is expected to help her mother with the housework and care of the younger children. The family laughs at her dreams of going to college. They warn her that too much reading will make her insane. The restaurant owner has become a regular at Sunday dinner, and the family treats him like a celebrity. Benedetta is fearful her family will lose its income if she refuses to marry him.

The man is a pervert and a sneak. But she remains silent when the edge of the tablecloth covers the withered hand that strokes the inside of her thigh. Bit by bit she senses the gulf between her will and the reality of her life. One morning, she *packs a small bag and takes a Greyhound to LA.*

That's all the speaker read, but I felt a sense of relief when her character got away. She took charge, even if it meant she had to give up her family.

I have often heard how life imitates art. And tonight when I got home, as expected, I was questioned about what I was doing out so late in the Village. Weird looks on my parents' faces when I tried explaining the readings at the Cornelia Street Café. "Who was there? What did you eat?" I explained that the readings were connected to what I am learning in my Italian American Literature course, but my mother cut me off and asked if there was any good Italian music there or if I met any "nice Italian boys." I didn't answer, just opened the refrigerator and grabbed a wedge of cheese and three slices of bread.

"Watch the crumbs! I just mopped the floor! And don't go bringing any food into your room. All that sitting around and eating while you read, the room is starting to stink. With your filthy habits, you'll never get a husband."

"Yeah, that would be a shame. Guess I'll just have to become a lesbian or a puttana, so I can prove you right."

Then my father chimed in. "Watch how you talk to your mother. Remember, as long as you are living under our roof, you'll do as we say."

So here I am writing in my journal, belly so twisted I couldn't eat the sandwich I made if my goddamn life depended on it. The run I took to exorcise my parents' bullshit didn't help. Every one of my fears ran alongside me.

I am too fat.

I am not smart enough.

Maybe they are right, I am my own worst enemy.

Someday I will lose everyone who loves me.

I dress like a tramp.

Men will only use me for one thing.
I act as if I am ashamed of my family.
When I turned the corner and saw my house, I made my-
self throw up. Now I was in control. But I know that's really
sick. I need to move away before I either hurt myself badly or
lose myself to my family's fantasy of what a good woman
looks like.

I decided to begin my paper with a memory of one of my recent anxiety attacks, because it gives meaning to the personal history I am about to relate. Reading Italian American literature, in particular Diane di Prima's *Recollections of My Life as a Woman* and Louise De Salvo's *Vertigo: A Memoir,* has not only helped me frame my story by examining its cultural context, it also taught me that my story isn't over. The memoir I will write at some future-but-as-yet-undetermined date hopefully will be inspiring to some Italian American lost soul like me. But for now, this is my story told in di Prima's experimental style.

In the early 1900s, my great grandparents left Sicily and Naples for New York. I've been told how brave my maternal great-grand-mother was traveling to American alone, in search of a new life after her mother died in Palermo. She met Enzo, her future husband, my maternal great-grandfather, on the boat coming over. She married at age sixteen and had her first child the next year. While she worked as a seamstress in a neighborhood factory, my great-grandfather worked in the Brooklyn Navy Yard. As for my father's side of the family, I know very little about their life in Naples. I never asked and my family never volunteered any information. This is how it usually is with Italian families.

We are a close-knit, loud, and opinionated family, except for discussions about politics or religion. They are taboo subjects in our home and must never be discussed at the dinner table. I don't get it, but I usually play along. Breaking the rules and not sticking together just doesn't cut it.

Every Sunday we have a huge dinner that includes pasta and about six other courses. We gather at my grandmother's dining room table, across the room from the plastic-covered sofa she placed there as a bride. Over the couch hangs a picture of the Pope with a palm crucifix wedged behind it. My grandmother says a novena for me every night, hoping I will "get my life in order." At twenty-four I am still the baby in the family, and I was told that I can only lose that status by having a baby myself.

When I was younger, I was told I should go to college and become an independent woman. But now, all I hear from my family is, "When are you going to get married and have a baby?" They constantly remind my twenty-nine-year-old sister, Nicole, her biological clock is ticking. Instead of encouraging her pursuit of a Ph.D. in Chemistry and admiring her work as a high school science teacher, they talk about needing to dance at her wedding. My sister, Anna Lise, has been labeled "the rebel." Why? Because she runs a small business from her Greenwich Village apartment and dates around. She laughs it off when they warn her that because she is so bold, no one will ever want to marry her.

No matter how far women may go, it is nothing compared to having a husband, children, and a house in the neighborhood. My family wants to know why I don't have a steady boyfriend. Why don't they understand when I say I am afraid to commit to one man? I don't blame them; I hardly understand it myself.

MEMORY:

I am sixteen years old; it is another sleepless Saturday night for me. I have my radio tuned to Z-100 while I read *Wuthering Heights*. Although I think *Jane Eyre* is much more romantic, I am intrigued by the dark forbidden love between Cathy and Heathcliff. As I am reading where Cathy cries out, "Heathcliff," I hear the front door slam and my mother yelling. I close my book and turn down my radio. She and Anna Lise are arguing. These fights always end with my mother beating my sister with a hair brush, leaving her crying on the bathroom floor. My sister came home drunk an hour and a half late. In general, she disregards all rules my parents set. Although I am two years younger, I want to take care of my sister. But I have my own issues; I rebel in my own secret way.

I must admit it: My drug of choice, my addiction, centers on sex. I know this is dangerous, but it never stops me. It doesn't stop me from going to a bar and picking someone up for the night. I like being physical with a man, like the pleasure it brings me. This is my high; no matter how hard I try, I cannot stop. While reading Louise De Salvo's *Vertigo: A Memoir*, I learned she had a similar experience. Like me, young Louise saw sex as a way of getting "free of it all" (174). I felt a sense of relief when I read this, but the tears really started coming as I read her reflection upon her teenage years. She writes: "Sex is the one thing in my life (besides reading) that feels good, and can usually be counted upon to please me. It lets me forget how miserable life is. It doesn't cost anything. . . . The trouble with sex, Susan [her friend] says, 'is that although it is cheap, it's also dangerous'" (150).

I am reminded about my escapades, think about how I am acting out my frustrations with myself and my family's expectations, and the freedom I feel while I am having sex. I forget everything: I am focused only on him and how good it all feels.

When I was sixteen, I was not allowed to date, but I started seeing my friend's brother. Mark had been like an older brother to me for many years. He told me I was funny, beautiful, and smart. Mark was always there when I was sad or needed someone to make me laugh. He encouraged me to work hard in school, so I would be prepared for college. Eventually our parents found out. They did everything in their power to keep us apart, saying I was too young to be in such a serious relationship, especially with someone who was twenty-one, five years older than me. Time and again I was reminded that he was about to graduate college and start a career, and that I was only a junior in high school.

That fall, when he found a job, he began a relationship with a coworker. Everyone but me was thrilled when they married. And I am not sure until this day that I am over him. Mark was my first love, the first man I slept with, we had made plans, and in the world I come from, he was supposed to become my husband.

Diane di Prima's *Recollections of My Life as a Woman* speaks to my being held hostage to the codes and silences of Sicilian women. Central to the code is standing by your husband without question, remaining loyal in spite of the conditions and personal consequences. Her opening chapters make clear that a young woman is taught to take care of a man and bear the burden silently (di Prima). This may explain why, given my upbringing, I am always looking for a man to complete me and make things better. When a woman breaks the silence and leaves an abusive man, she faces consequences.

A few years ago, my mother's sister, my aunt Catherine, decided to divorce the man who, as my grandfather explained, "Had put food on the table for the past twenty years." A heavy drinker, he'd end each beating demanding she keep quiet about it "or else." As expected, my grandparents responded to the news by reminding Aunt Catherine that divorced people are excommunicated from the church. "You'll burn in hell for this!" Grandma said. "And, God forbid, what will people say?"

"Mama, I've been so miserable in this marriage. I need to get out there and find some happiness, find a man who makes me feel loved and safe." Aunt Catherine's feelings were ignored, and her parents told her that she would be their death. How could a family that sees itself as loving and supportive act this way? Apparently, saving face and strict adherence to inflexible, outdated rules, is what really matters.

Looking back on the lives of Sicilian women, di Prima reasons that they "fell prey to the delusion that there was something a man could do for them that they could not do for themselves" (224). Things may go badly, but they needed to stay, no matter what. This, she explains, creates a gnawing "lack of self-esteem," witnessed by women throwing themselves away for "a smile or a song." In her own case, even though she was an accomplished poet, di Prima regarded the writer Le Roi Jones as her superior. For a period in her life, she allowed him to control her mind and her body.

Feeling as if my life had been in a downward spiral since, at sixteen, I lost the man to whom I had "given myself," I read di Prima as if she were speaking to me. Her experience of moving past painful relationships, where she conformed to the Sicilian code she had learned as a child, encourages me to find a way to develop my own individuality, my own talent, whatever it may be.

MY CHICKEN WAS GETTING COLD, so I decided to finish reading Donna's paper later. The reminder of the ambivalence over educating women that still exists for some Italian Americans left me feeling a little anxious. The glow I'd felt after seeing Kevin was being replaced by a cold feeling of emptiness and the urge to fill myself with more food, a lot more. Turning to one of my old coping mechanisms, I ordered a small mushroom pizza to go, acting as if it were normal to eat a second lunch right on top of the first. Misery was snaking its way into my psyche.

CAS HAD COMPLAINED that I was becoming less spontaneous, "You're always far away with some idea or other." It was true. After long hours at in the library or at my desk, I was more serious, less jokey. Bantering had been a big part of how we communicated. In retrospect, I realize we had mistaken familiarity for intimacy. We'd mercilessly tease each other about our vulnerabilities.

"If you could move some belly fat to your behind, you'd be one fine woman."

"Don't mention my belly, and I won't comment on your thighs."

I'd like to think that Cas' sadistic streak initiated this behavior. But in the beginning of our relationship, I'd engaged in it more than I protested. Then, especially as I moved forward with my graduate work, I had realized what sadomasochistic discourse looks like. I became uncomfortable with the familiar banter and turned silent when Cas made comments that bothered me. At the same time, I was captivated by the stunning imagery and moving language in the poetry of Dante, Petrarch, and Shakespeare. Although I realized most couples don't speak to each other in rhymed couplets, I was turned off by the put-downs and rude language that characterized my relationship. Someone had changed expectations, and it hadn't been Cas. It had been me.

It was true that my father and Caspar encouraged my education, but, like me, they were unaware of how education can separate people. They helped me financially but resented the ideas I brought home. My emerging self-reliance and independent thinking was odd behavior for a woman, a sign of arrogance that challenged tradition and what they regarded as "common sense."

Children grow up and individuate, finding a gulf between their new identity and the one that has been scripted by family history. In my case, working towards a Ph.D., and the self-reliance it awakened, stood in stark contrast with my family's distrust for "fancy ideas." When I talked about something I was learning or attempted to engage them in a discussion of some new idea, I noticed one or the other quickly changed the topic.

Perhaps unwittingly I distanced myself from my working class past for a lifestyle where open discourse and criticism are taken for granted. Sure there were congratulations when I landed a professorship and began publishing, yet there were changes I had not anticipated. And there were ever-increasing demands on my time. Often, an editor's deadline or stack of student papers resulted in my cutting short visits with Cas' family or with Sadie and my father.

I was living in two very different worlds: I spent my days in a department where autonomy and challenging authority is the norm, and returned home to comments like "What's the use?" or "You can't fight City Hall." Over time, my core beliefs separated me from the more conservative members of my family. I had become one of those women about whom they said, "Who the hell does she think she is?"

As far back as I could remember, my father had told me that I talked too much. His critique of what he considered my second most serious character flaw (defiance was the first) grew as I became more involved with my academic work. He'd often remark that I cared too much about my plans, was too interested in the profession he called my "job." Like Casper, he hated it when I corrected him, saying it was more than a job, it was my passion. They often reminded me of the nuns at my elementary school who ridiculed my plans for the future.

My father told me he was tired of listening to me congratulate myself about becoming a professor and engaging in research. "Remember, it's just a job. Leave your work there when you go home. And never forget where you came from. Sometimes it seems, Arianna, like you want to become smarter than your father, smarter than everyone else." And I was afraid to question his resentments or look at my role in creating them.

It bothered me most when Sadie chimed in. "Ann Fugenti—" the daughter of her friends, Valerie and Anthony, she'd often remind me— "has already gotten a job in the Financial Aid office at Brooklyn College. And she did this without having to get a degree. It's a good job, better than teaching. She doesn't have to take work home. Where is all this research business going to get you?"

I got through many visits with Sadie by medicating myself with large amounts of food (she was an excellent cook), tense that, any moment, I'd react to her negativity and become the next daughter to be banished.

A headache coming on, I might have stopped the painful reminiscence but willed myself to mull over the past a while longer. Remembering being the core of any memoir, I told myself, "Think back to the events behind the pain, to the experiences you'll soon turn into words. Damn, you've made a career of telling students, 'Show, don't tell.' Now, muster up the courage to be honest. Just don't fall into self-pity, tempting as it will be."

And so I continued to think about my saga, the tale of the bad Italian American daughter. Ideas for the memoir project had begun surfacing.

I thought about how Dad had ridiculed the soup I brought to the Farina's house as a gesture of support over the death of their daughter, Nancy. In fact, the soup was thin and tasteless. I had rushed to put the chicken soup together after returning home from a doctoral seminar on Middle English poetry. Cutting and chopping ingredients for the soup, I'd become increasingly absorbed in the cassette of the class, periodically shutting it off to take notes. Distracted, I'd added an extra quart of water and four tablespoons less of salt. I had totally forgotten about adding parsley and pepper to what became a tasteless soup.

Instead of just adding some salt and pepper or pushing aside his bowl, Dad had amused the mourners with the irony of how I could read and write the "damn hardest and most confusing literature on God's earth, but can't follow the simplest cooking instructions."

He had to pity Caspar for marrying his handful of a daughter. I was a "good egg," he added, "but there is no getting through to her." The not being able to get through to me—what it took years of therapy to appreciate as personal integrity—he understood as defiance. He had told the mourners, "Arianna has always had a mind of her own and refuses to listen." Next to him was Sadie, laughing loudly, offering second helpings of her daughter Chickie's eggplant parmigana.

Caspar would always smile politely during these moments. Stroking my arm, he'd tell me, "They're only joking." But he never voiced his support of me or did anything to counter the behavior.

Years of hurtful remarks about my education accumulated into iceberg-sized resentments. At her sister Laura's 30th birthday party, a family friend asked Cousin Butchie if she too planned on getting a Ph.D. As if she'd been waiting for a chance to vent her animosity, she shot back, "Oh, no—one in the family is enough."

I was wounded, but flashed a smile. There sat Caspar, laughing while he sipped his third Rob Roy. Later that evening, when I asked what he'd thought about Butchie's remark, he said "Maybe one Ph.D. *is* one too many."

AT FIRST, CASPAR ENCOURAGED my graduate work and dream of becoming a college professor. But as my dream became a reality, his encouragement all but disappeared. He told me it wasn't right for a wife to be so opinionated; it wasn't attractive.

Quietly detaching should have been my response. Today, I realize I made matters worse when I became defensive, citing the wisdom of one critic or other. Sarcasm was my weapon of choice. "From which ancient school of thought did you get that idea? Sounds like you have a lot in common with the people who thought up witch dunking." I knew my responses were tinged with my own brand of meanness, but I was still too naïve to understand how diminished familiarity is a step in the process of crossing cultures.

My transformation had begun as I had become totally focused, perhaps driven, by the end of my junior year. That fall, I had met Professor Henry Leibowitz, known to everyone, including his students, as Harry. A labor activist and expert on the oppression of the working class in America, he had recently been awarded a grant to recruit and educate undergraduates in an experimental, interdisciplinary program he had designed. The goal of the program was to prepare socially conscious, well-read community activists. There was funding for an administrative assistant. They needed someone to serve, as Harry explained in a slightly sexist way, "Like a benevolent floor lady who keeps things in order." I was offered the job.

Dad warned me that my part-time sales job at B. Altman provided me with security. He said he appreciated the goals of Professor Leibowitz' program, but explained how such well-meaning ideas usually wind up summarized in some report and filed away. In the end, however, he was persuaded when I pointed out that, since the job was on campus, I'd be traveling directly from home to school and back again. *That* he liked.

Whenever WBAI called to interview Harry about some critical topic or other, he'd extemporize for as long as they liked—usually longer. Often he did so while eating part of some colleague's lunch or munching from a bag of potato chips that belonged to one of the adoring students sitting at his feet. He knew why institutions had risen up and how they failed. With equal parts of anger and compassion, he'd explain why people had been robbed of their chance to earn a decent living and function as members of a healthy community. Critiquing the work of intellectuals including Studs Turkel, C. Wright Mills, and Noam Chomsky, and equipped with voluminous knowledge of the practical and theoretical foundations of society's problems, he was a rising star.

Listening to him and his colleagues intensified my passion for learning and the chance to gain insight into my own history. I yearned to know why things were the way they were. Now, both in class and at work, I was learning how to ask important questions and understand how language, especially literary language, was a product of the society that had created it, a commodity that reflected the means and mores of human production. Subsequently, books were no longer just fictions, verses, or essays. They had subtexts and subtleties that raised questions about an author's political beliefs and view of the world and its people.

Like a virgin bride just discovering the joy of sexual climax, I'd been awakened. Learning became more than pursuing a degree; it was transforming my social and political awareness. I couldn't separate myself from what I was discovering. For most Italian American women of my generation, it was dangerous when you crossed over from the kitchen to the podium. So when I brought up a discussion of how the 14th-century Peasant's Revolt later resonated in the writings of Karl Marx and the Italian Antonio Gramsci, I heard the familiar refrain, "We don't talk politics at the dinner table."

I'd rebel by going for a walk alone when it came time to make the espresso and take out the inevitable bottle of Sambuca. While I walked, I wondered where one was supposed to discuss these topics. During one Sunday walk, I wove a stream of consciousnesses about how religion and the wrongs done to European peasants had created the legacy of bigotry and disempowerment that pervaded my family's sense of their place in the world. My internal chatter actually deepened my understanding. I came back in time for dessert. I enjoyed my espresso and Sambuca.

These days, the deafening din of non-political, non-religious banter table talk has been replaced by blaring television sounds of spectator sports that command the attention once given to male elders. Instant replays have replaced oft-told stories of guts and glory. But it serves the same function: It drowns out talk of anything controversial or that requires action.

THE GENERATION BEFORE MINE had seen few divorces, and the marriages that broke up were explained away as "Louis' being in show business," or Clemmie's being "such a nag she drove her Charlie to start a secret family in Chicago." Save for a few exceptions, the Italian American households I had known as a child were filled with love and mutual respect. Perhaps this was because the women in my family ran domestic affairs competently and with good cheer. Money might have been tight, but they stayed at home and made do, not like those brazen American women they condemned for dressing up, leaving their children with strangers, and neglecting their housework.

At one gathering, Great-Aunt Daisy recalled a situation concerning Millie, Cousin Patsy's wife. The unfortunate woman was driven into the workforce by the dire circumstances of her alcoholic, dysfunctional home. The only steady income had been Patsy's meager disability check. But this is not how Aunt Daisy remembered the story.

Millie "puffed herself up with pride because she found a job in some big shot Manhattan law office." Aunt Daisy recalled a visit to Cousin Patsy, who'd been "sick with his cirrhosis." He told her: "Daisy, I am embarrassed you had to come here and see this mess. *La Signora* Millie has turned this place into a pig sty. After she dolls up every morning, she leaves me a plate of food, as if I am a dog. Ten hours later, she comes back complaining how hard she worked."

"What a mess the place was," Aunt Daisy said, "You think she would have enough shame to clean up before she took off in the morning. I am sure her boss would have understood if she came in a little late. She was needed at home."

Compare Giorgio had been listening on the other side of the open kitchen window. Washing a handful of figs he'd just picked off Grandpa's prized tree, he chimed in, "Millie got away with murder neglecting her responsibilities. *Povero* Patsy, God rest his soul."

Aunt Vickie added, "Yeah, but before he died, just around the time his mind started to go, he let her have it good. Their Tony told my Junior how, one night, while his father was talking about the spots on his shot glass, his mother starts mouthing off about being given an assistant at the law firm, so she could attend a course on legal research at NYU. Millie starts bragging how the company was going to pay for the whole thing. Patsy asked her, 'You a lawyer now or something?' After giving him one of her sarcastic looks, she turns her back to him while he's still talking. Patsy takes off his belt, and that was that. By the end of the week, she quit that damn job and found one closer to home. That's when she started working in the A&P on Kings Highway."

Comare Mary shook her head. "Oh, that Patsy. Millie was giving him a hard time, but to do a thing like that. After all, she was trying to help out. His disability check wasn't covering much more than the rent. And to tell the truth, I think he drank more than he got in that check. Come on, I don't like to hear things like this. Let's talk about something else."

During the late '60s, Italian American working-class women were entering the work force beyond the factory labor or take-home work the first generation had been forced to settle for. Opportunities were opening up for women on other fronts, too: in education, in politics, and in their personal lives. But at home I encountered what my teachers referred to as "European gender roles." There was a split in the Italian American community, it seemed, between those who accepted—although they may not have embraced—the changes, and those who believed traditional family values were being undermined. It took me years to fully understand how the fear of powerful women is the legacy of the misogynistic tradition that goes back beyond the ancient Greeks who colonized Southern Italy.

One day, the family was gossiping about some "Sicilian *puttana*" who had forgotten "who she was" and taken over the management of a local pharmacy. Naively, I attempted to introduce the debating skills I was learning in a speech course. I had not yet cultivated an appreciation for tact and timing.

"What *is it* with you all and women in power? What are you afraid is going to happen if a woman becomes the master of her mind, her body, and her destiny? What about the remarkable women who've gone beyond traditional gender expectations? Do you know women like Golda Meir serve as prime ministers now? And there have been Italian women, like Maria Montessori and—"

"*Basta,* Ari!" Dad yelled, mixing another shot of Sambuca into his espresso. "Enough with this women's. . . . What is it? This *women's lib* thing they're poisoning you with at that college?"

Cousin Hugo took the bottle from Dad and jumped in. Pouring some Sambuca for himself and Cas, he commented, "I don't know what's happening to you, Arianna Naso. Are you turning into some sort of man hater?"

Cas was smiling. As always, he held back his nasty remarks until we were alone. In front of the family, he'd sit there quietly, as if a harsh word never passed his lips.

CHAPTER 11
Trans-Atlantic Therapy

Story of my life,
Happiness lost, now regained.
Moving past the shame.

WHEN I BEGAN HUNTER COLLEGE in 1967, a group of re-form-minded faculty had been planning a Women Stud-ies major. At first, I was confused about why faculty across the country were fighting for a diversified curriculum. But my instructors made crystal clear the many ways in which the traditional canon was elitist. The culture wars they supported—the literary move-ment inspired by the struggle for civil rights—led to the establishment of ethnic, class, and gender studies programs. Although I was little more than a parlor activist, I was on a scholar's journey of hard work, reinvention, and experiencing the tug of war between acculturation and alienation.

What initially struck me about my professors was their breadth of ideas and interests, but what impacted me most was how they taught by example. Some spent their summers in Chile, taking part in

Paulo Freire's program where modern agricultural methods were taught to peasants; others joined the Peace Corps, performing service in faraway places. Almost everyone rode the buses at one time or another to Washington, marching for women's and civil rights and to protest the war in Viet Nam.

A professor from another college, Armand Schwerner, spoke to us about the Ku Klux Klan's murder of his nephew, Mickey, and fellow activists James Chaney and Andrew Goodman, a Queens College graduate. Field workers for the Congress of Racial Equality charged with helping register black voters, the three had met in Mississippi during Freedom Summer, 1964. Listening to Prof. Schwerner talk, I realized how traveling beyond the familiar was more than something that happened in books or on the news. Could I risk security and my family's approval in the name of civic responsibility? Would I have been strong enough to sacrifice my life as Chaney, Goodman, and Schwerner had done?

The faculty told us, their students, to reflect on what we were learning and "pass it on." "How are you going to serve your community?" They set meetings to organize anti-war and civil rights marches, and some opened their homes for consciousness-raising meetings that expanded the limits of what I believed I was allowed to think and say and do. My activism was limited to participating in student sit-ins to provide free and open access to CUNY and equal pay for women faculty. At the time, I was too entrenched in my comfort zone to venture further afield.

Still, everything I believed in came into question. And it left me feeling alienated, displaced, wherever I went. With my view of the world broadening and my social conscience coming alive, I felt like a stranger at home. At school, I was seen as an outsider, a newcomer from the Italian American working class. As both an undergraduate and as a graduate student, I was never taught by an Italian American; at least, no one spoke about their Italian heritage or had an identifying surname.

I'm glad that I didn't give up, even when I felt like I was swimming in the wrong pond. Unknown to me at the time, many other Italian Americans were feeling marginalized in academia. A few years into my graduate work, I learned the Italian American faculty and staff at the City University of New York had filed a class action suit claiming discrimination. Their allegations were substantiated, and in 1976 the University recognized Italian American as an affirmative action category for hiring and promotion.

THE PRESENT SMACKS OF THE PAST, however, when it comes to who deserves to be in academia and who doesn't. This past January, I participated in a British Literature search at one of the CUNY campuses when an Italian American applicant caused a sotto voce stir.

The candidate, Dr. Maria De Mario, had been short listed following the Modern Language Association Conference interviews. When she came to campus, she made no effort to hide her Bronx accent. Maria De Mario is one of those academics who either do not know or do not care that her working-class Mediterranean origins are turning her into a Caliban in front of educators whose teaching and writing condemns any form of bias.

At the interview, I felt my stomach tighten when I noticed the New Historicist sharing a smirk with the Structuralist in response to what they mistakenly perceived as a parochial point of view. While discussing her research, the candidate jokingly credited the Sisters of Mercy at St. Catharine's Academy for cultivating her interest in gender politics. The interview fell apart when everyone facing the Post-Colonialist raised their eyebrows after Dr. De Mario said, "I flushed out ideas."

The Deconstructionist whispered, not-all-that softly, "Fleshed out," bringing the faculty's behavior well beyond bad manners. And I know enough about semiotics to realize the interview was over the moment the chair reached into her Burberry backpack and came out with lip gloss.

Over afternoon tea, while the committee discussed the candidate, the Post-Modernist, who couldn't recall Dr. De Mario's name, let alone that she had a Ph.D. from Cornell, referred to her as "that Italian woman from the Bronx."

It was decided she would not fit in. She was voted "not viable."

"Could someone explain why she won't fit in?" I asked. The Formalist commented on how her teaching presentation had been lackluster. The Deconstructionist added Dr. De Mario was much less clear about her research and publication agenda than she had been at MLA. (The next year the duo lobbied for a candidate who was fired during his first semester because he came to class drunk.)

"But what does that have to do with fitting in?" I asked.

Unaware or unconcerned about his ironic response, the Marxist said, "Well, do we really want our students to be taught by someone so inarticulate? Aren't they getting enough of *that* role modeling at home?

I reminded the group that the "that" to which their colleague was referring was protected by their university's affirmative action guidelines. "Do you realize these deliberations are tainted with an anti-Italian American bias?" But the committee was not swayed; they insisted the next four candidates had more impressive credentials. The chair commented that Dr. De Mario had been invited to campus because she had been the only affirmative action applicant.

In a letter to the committee and their dean, I explained how the candidate had been treated unfairly. But although the College Diversity Officer reminded the committee about its commitment to Affirmative Action, he told me there weren't sufficient grounds for a grievance.

The search committee experience was one of many occasions in academia where Italian Americans have been treated with suspicion, scorn, or both. Before I was tenured—during that precarious time when the astute keep stoically silent—a Multiculturalist periodically approached me with the question, "What exactly is it that makes Italian Americans different from other Americans?" At the time, the Multiculturalist had the ear and the friendship of the department chair. Holding my cards close to my untenured vest, a move vulnerable outsiders have historically been forced to make, I withheld a sarcastic response.

The week before the chair presented me to the college-wide tenure committee, several colleagues and I were reviewing the scoring rubric for the College's Writing Assessment Test, or WAT, as it was called. Collegial banter that day centered on the syntax and idiomatic expressions the group found common among papers written by students with Italian American surnames. A Compositionist said these papers are "Wop WATS." The remark made the Multiculturalist look like the injured party, since I sat there silently containing my outrage.

On the way home, I stopped at Waldbaum's for Cherry Garcia ice cream and a package of plastic spoons. I ate the entire quart before driving out of the parking lot.

It was only after the security of tenure that I felt confident enough to rip off my safety mask. And these days, the attitude towards Italian Americans in academia is more accepting, but, as in the case of the candidate at the nearby campus, there are those who believe we are somehow less than your average academic. True, there are more Italian American faculty at the College, but I can't help but notice how quick they are to point out northern Italian roots or mixed heritage. As for the attitude towards Italian American students, frequently they are compared to characters in *The Sopranos*, or serve as the butt of some inappropriate remark. A former dean tried to amuse a group of faculty by telling them that "salmonella" was actually the name of a tutor in the Tutoring Center.

Thankfully, I have two new colleagues who own their southern Italian heritage. One proudly talks about a family trip to his grandfather's village in Basilicata. The other brought a ballet company from Sicily to the college, making sure the event was free and open to the community. But I wonder what she thought when a colleague reacted to music she'd brought to our holiday party with the condescending question, "What's with the Italian music?"

How are Italian Americans viewed by their colleagues? Mostly okay. But on occasion, gestures of excessive gregariousness or mercurial behavior quickly get attributed to an ethnic predisposition. A while back, an Italian American colleague from the Biology department, with an impressive publication record and superior teaching evaluations, filed a grievance after being denied promotion. The promotions committee had questioned the quality of her research, although a colleague doing comparable work had recently received their approval. The Biologist accused them of unfair treatment.

When her appeal was denied, she called the union. The dean with the salmonella gibe called her in. He warned her to stop "acting like a wild Neapolitan." The grievance she filed with the union went nowhere, so she hired a lawyer, who filed charges of ethnic discrimination. But after years of postponements and increasing marginalization at the College, she dropped the case.

Sometimes I wonder if she too sits in her car filling the black hole in her psyche with ice cream and resentment.

AS I HEADED BACK TOWARD THE STRAND, I thought about Italian American women, who are still being haunted by the ghosts of tradition and the three-headed dog that guards the gate of entry into academia. Needed to talk about this with Neil. But not today. For now, I was committed to understanding more deeply how my violent marriage affected my eating disorder.

For the past seven years, my therapist, Neil Venditti, and I have met every Wednesday at 10 a.m., or on the phone at 3 p.m. if I'm in London. Happily, British Telecom's calling card promotion significantly lowered the cost of our weekly 45-minute phone session. In his gentle, probing way, he helps me dig into memory and talk about how much I've endured on my personal journey. As a child I sensed a desert behind my father's eyes. As a woman, it took a long time to break free from Caspar. Every once in a while Neil reminds me that I "turned all those challenges into triumphs."

After enduring decades of trauma, my recovery had a slow, uneven start. It took time for me to learn how to set healthy boundaries with people who can't or won't filter their remarks. "Well, you're a big shot now living in Manhattan." Or, "Believe me, I know that restaurant in Los Angeles. It's among the best. Your son won't last working there for more than a week." Now that I'm living a more balanced life and have broken through my thick wall of denial, I am starting to see myself and others more realistically. Neil has helped me realize such remarks concern the speaker's problems, not mine.

Unless there is some pressing "issue," I sometimes worry about not having enough to say. But, word by word, he guides me into the depths of my memory, so I might live in the present mindful of, but not crippled by, the past.

Living with what my therapist and several doctors have identified as post-traumatic stress disorder, I frequently experience anxiety that borders on panic. Gaining a deeper understanding of how my anxiety created self-defeating behaviors—overeating, overworking, excessive spending, excessive worry, hyper-vigilance, and bouts of isolating—has led to making better choices.

Drawing on skills I've successfully employed in my professional life, such as compartmentalizing, now, when things become overwhelming or people behave unreasonably, I detach. Small doses of controlling or angry people is all I can tolerate. Rather than win a battle, I stay focused on my integrity and compassion. I walk away to think things over before opening my mouth. More times than not, I can "drop the rope," as an Al Anon friend used to say, in what is becoming an emotional tug of war.

It was 2:15 by time I got back to the Strand Palace and opened my laptop. Just forty-five minutes left to work before I called Neil. For the past several weeks, we'd been exploring my food issues. Should I use the time before I rang him up proofreading or preparing for the session? I split the time in half between my two projects: the manuscript, and the self that I am revising.

I thought back to some hurtful events.

Leaving a marriage was still a taboo in my family. Although they had known about Cas' drinking, I had not told them about the violence and intimidation I lived with. This had been a mistake, and consequently, some family members had told me I was crazy to leave such a great husband.

My father, however, supported my decision. He told me that he had known for a long time that I was unhappy, but "kept quiet about it." Unexpectedly, he called one night to tell me that, if Cas ever laid his hands on me, he'd be "one sorry son of a bitch." But aside from Dad, and an occasional word of support from Nina, there were subtle put-downs about single women, independence, "college people," and those who strayed from the Catholic Church.

Worse still, my Leone cousins regaled Cas' legendary drinking quips. They'd laugh about the time he coached cousin Joanie at her 21st birthday party on how to not to lose your seat at a crowded bar. It was as if he was still at the table when they remembered his comical expressions, like calling empty liquor bottles "dead soldiers." Chris laughed too when Aunt Mel and her daughters memorialized his father's drinking behaviors. Then he'd turn to me with flat-lined lips and stone cold eyes.

I felt betrayed, but I was also angry at myself for not talking about the abuse. There are still times when I think I should have come clean. Where was my self-confidence? How would they have reacted, I wonder, if I told them about the violence? Would they think more of me if they knew that, after one attack, I worried that, when I didn't show up at Grandma's for dinner, I had ruined the family's holiday? The truth is they should have trusted my decision and not have said hurtful things, especially in front of Chris. Had I realized how their behavior was damaging him further, I would have spoken up. But living with constant anxiety, I probably would have done so with unbridled anger and made things worse.

Before I turned to proofreading the manuscript, I made a mental note of a dozen things that were better in my life since my divorce, all the while resisting the urge to dwell on Chris' situation.

DAMN, IT'S ALMOST 10:05 his time, I thought. Hope his line won't be busy.

Maryann: *Hi, Neil. It's Maryann. How are you?*

Neil: *Good, but the important question is how are you? Are you still getting those headaches? And how's your stomach been?*

Maryann: *Negative, negative, I've had a week full of both. Actually they have been a little worse, especially the heartburn and the cramping in the lower left side of my stomach. If the appendix was on the left side, and if mine hadn't been removed three years ago, I would think there was trouble brewing. It is not always so intense, but it's a fairly regular nuisance. So I thought about what we discussed and took action. I made a note to set up a visit with the gastroenterologist the day after I return to New York. It is on my calendar, first thing that morning. I also have been journaling a record of what I feel in my intestines and the events, thoughts, and eating that precedes the episodes.*

Neil: *That's good. What are you noticing?*

Ari: *Well, Sunday night I went to a nearby hotel that has a carvery. I ordered prime rib and a baked potato, fully aware that that cut of meat, and the butter I'd find hard to resist, might upset my stomach. But I caved in. After a few bites, I asked for a cup of hot water. Needed to soothe the cramping. As if it weren't bad enough, I started remembering the time a prime rib dinner landed me in the hospital.*

Neil: *Want to tell me about it?*

Ari: *I thought back to an argument we had a few months before we separated. It was a Thursday night, around midterm time of a spring semester. That morning, Cas and I had vented to each other about our mountainous workloads. He'd suggested we eat out that night, so we'd return home early, get Chris settled in, then have the rest of the night to catch up on work. He said he'd be home by 5:00, and we'd leave for the restaurant by 5:30. Cas was making much more money than me at the time, so these dinners out were usually his treat. Generosity? Control? I'm not sure. Back then I never thought about such things. It was easier to just go along with what he wanted.*

Then about seven o'clock—after I had bathed Chris and was serving him dinner—in walks Cas reeking of liquor. He ordered that I get Chris' jacket and the three of us leave for the restaurant. I pointed out that it was a plan he had ruined when he decided to spend two more hours drinking. He became furious. The dance began between my self-righteous indignation and his anger over what he saw as my lack of tolerance for "what he had every right to do."

By 7:30 I was red faced with rage, and he was making one threat after another. Then in one swoop he pushed everything off the table. Only a moment before, Chris had grabbed his dessert and taken refuge in his room. Strewn across the floor was a mix of food, milk, and a plastic Star Wars dinner set. Our dog, Feste, alternated between standing by my side and licking up the remains.

After he showered and drank some coffee, Cas came downstairs as if nothing had happened. He announced his mother was on her way. I should get dressed and "take that look" off my face—that's how he'd respond to my unhappiness.

At the restaurant, we shared an order of baked clams and a Caesar salad; Cas had a Rob Roy followed by a glass of Chablis. The more he drank, the more he demanded I admit how much better I had it than my friends, how ungrateful I was.

As I did far too often, I drowned out the tension by eating non-stop. I endured the litany of accusations and threats, swallowing my raging anger along with chunks of garlic bread, followed by mouthfuls of mashed potatoes and prime rib. The combo moved down my esophagus to my stomach, where, I suppose, all the tension, rage, and disappointment turned a $29.95 meal into intestinal damage. Sounds like a geography of my dis-ease.

Neil: *Indeed. Why not go on; it might help to tell the whole story.*

Ari: *Well, I was afraid to say my insides felt like they were about to explode, so I ordered cup of tea while Cas took his time downing an espresso and two complimentary shots of Sambuca. My cramping got worse.*

During the middle of the night, Cas carried Chris to the car, dropped him off at his mother's and took me to the hospital. The ER doctor thought I had appendicitis, but it turned out to be the start of diverticulosis and IBS. "Nervous stomach," he said. "You're such a young woman. And with such a loving husband here. What could possibly be bothering you?"

Neil: *In the restaurant, where he wasn't likely to throw one of his temper tantrums, why were you afraid to tell Cas your stomach was in so much pain?*

Ari: *Ah, well, the food. . . . He'd get on me about my weight fluctuations, about how much I just ate and how selfish I'd become now that my stomach was full. I didn't want to hear a rant about how I had made him rush through dessert.*

Neil: *What feelings do you recall from that night? And what are you feeling now?*

Ari: *Shame.*

Neil: *When? Then or now?*

Ari: *Both, shame, shame, a stomachful of fucking shame.*

"Tums or Zantac?" That was the question I grappled with after the session dug up more than I needed to remember. I took one of each, wishing there was a medication for resentment. "Deep breath. I must stay well and complete the manuscript." Mumbling—I did a lot of mumbling as I paced the floor in my hotel room. "Fucking stomach. I just spent a whole phone card. . .I feel worse than before I called. Need a little self-care; need to walk off this stress. And this pizza I ordered for no sane reason, I'll offer it to the homeless woman I saw sitting outside the hotel."

CALMNESS BEGAN RETURNING as I pressed a warm washcloth over my face and ran some Bumble and Bumble brilliantine through my hair after massaging my scalp. The fresh smell gave me the sensation of a new beginning. I reminded myself that I was entitled to the life I was carving out.

Small pleasures are the joys you can count on. The "wow" experiences come by so infrequently, but the little things, like getting a whiff of the brilliantine while riding down in the elevator for a walk along the Thames, brings a feeling of centered well-being.

I smiled as I walked past a postcard I noticed on the rack in the lobby. It read, *Keep Calm and Carry On.*

And that's how I felt, sitting on a bench in front of the National Theatre, meditating. I savored the serene river that had swallowed the fires of so many wars. It rippled in the glow of the warm July sunlight. I became one with the moment.

The sky was cloudless, and the wind was still when I walked by the Tate Modern. Rows of delicate trees lined the entrance to the former turbine station that houses Rothkos, Giacomettis, and Pollacks. On the grass sat picnickers, talking and laughing. Their youth rendered them carefree, gay. "No need to eat my baguette in a hurry," they seemed to say. "There is plenty of time. The art will wait. The sky will remain blue, so I can linger here a while longer." They were in sync with the world. It was theirs to savor.

Looking at them, thoughts of Chris seeped into my mind. Why couldn't he be here, healthy and having a good time? I realized it might help to write him a letter when I felt less fragile. Writing to him, even if I had no mailing address, I learned, can be therapeutic. But there are times when I experience a toxic effect from writing. Better now just to enjoy the sight of young people picnicking on the grass. So I kept walking. Despite the prime rib memory tailspin, I was making progress.

I walked back towards the Strand over the Millennium Bridge, calmed by what I took in, remembering how much I enjoy being in London, the city where I come to work and play.

Before I left for the Royal Opera House that night, I finished proofreading the manuscript. It was off to Jed in the morning. Walking past the mirror in the hotel lobby, I smiled back at myself.

"Job done. Hopefully, job *well done.*"

I ARRIVED AT COVENT GARDEN early to read about Auber's *La Muette de Portici*. The opera is set during the 1648 Neapolitan revolt. For nine days, Tomasso Aniello, a popular fisherman the locals called Masaniello, had led an insurrection against the greedy Spanish governors. In graduate school I had studied Masaniello's revolt, so I was curious about Auber's adaptation.

The guidebook explained that the opera re-imagines the conflict as having been ignited by the seduction of Masaniello's hearing-and-speech-impaired sister, Fenella, known as "the Dumb Woman of Portici." Brewing hostilities ignite when Alphonse, the Spanish Duke of Arcos, violates her. After various twists and turns, the chain of disorder comes to a climax. Fennella responds to the news of her brother's death by committing suicide as Vesuvius erupts and the Neapolitan populace cries out for God's mercy. A note in the souvenir guide explains how, in 1830, a performance of *La Muette* in Brussels set off the revolt that led to independence from the Dutch.

Ah, the power of art, I thought. It can disturb what needs disturbing while soothing your soul. During the performance, I was captivated by the images of revolt, murder, and volcanic eruption set in motion by the violation of a woman so powerless she did not have a voice to scream out her pain. Trapped by silence, Fenella climbs into the crater of the smoldering mountain. Both the volcanic mountain and young woman—emblems of Naples' colonized misery—are transformed into fiery rain.

The experience was stunning. The intensity of Auber's music underscored the powerful act of rebellion. Using nets draped on an ancient wharf, the set designer had recreated Portici, the Neapolitan fishing village. A *papier-mâché* Vesuvius was ablaze during the tragic finale. Fenella stood at the rear of the crater while lava fashioned out of silk strips rippled in the foreground. In death she became one with the Neapolitans' dashed hope for liberty.

The opera, with its Southern Italian setting, gender, and class issues, was the perfect place to celebrate the completion of my work, my Italian opera. But three hours of staged tragedy and intense music in the stifling opera house left me feeling feverish. I walked east along Fleet Street. The cool night air felt good, refreshing. "Damn," I wondered, "when will the British get air conditioning right?" The almighty Royal Opera House, and there was no breeze.

Moonlight illuminated St. Bride's churchyard, where so much history had taken place. Had John Milton ever walked there? Maybe one day in 1673 he came face-to-face with the rising playwright Aphra Behn. I imagined him criticizing Behn for the bold female characters she created, which were being played by women actors. She might've pointed out how his characterization of Eve in *Paradise Lost* would prove destructive to women.

Amused by my fantasy, I headed back towards the Strand. What would I have added to the conversation if I'd been there? Then I thought about patriarchy and its role in violence against women, and how so many continue to suffer in silence.

BUT ALAS, WHILE MOST OF LONDON SLEPT, and I was lost in reverie, there were others who spent the night of July 6, 2005, finalizing a horrific plan. They'd arrive in the morning to set London ablaze. What memory of violence, what anger did they harbor against this city and the innocents toiling in its fields? So complicated are the wrongs that create infernal revenge.

Yet tonight, no tragedy could stifle the will to survive of one who courageously transcended hellish despair. Chris had set out to escape the clutches of drug addiction. How permanent his recovery might be, or the date of some future relapse, could not cloud that night. For now, he was safe from the ravages of that lifelong battle. And like some classical hero, he had begun traveling home. As for me, my grief was about to be vanquished, if only for a while.

Back in my hotel room, an orange light glowed in the dark. British Telecom had delivered a heavenly message.

CHAPTER 12

Nearing Home

Needing to remain,
I move through night's smoky ash
Towards light and you.

OLD WAYS OF THINKING die a slow death: a late night message means bad news. Seeing the phone's blinking light, I thought how miserable I'd feel hearing Kevin say he couldn't meet me for dinner. Maybe that's why at first I didn't recognize Chris' voice.

Hi, Mom, it's Chris. Uh, my father told me you went to London and left this number.

I've been thinking about calling you for a while now. How are things with you? We should talk. Yeah, there's a lot we need to talk about, and I hope when you come home we can do that. Okay? Just please don't bring up my father and the drinking shit. You. . .I've been so angry with you, but you always said a therapist might help, and now I think, what the hell, we should give it another try. Instead of missing each other's phone calls, write to me. My friend, Maureen, lives in the same building as Dr. Keegan, so you have the address. I bounced around a lot after moving from my father's office. Then Maureen offered me a room in her apartment. It's okay for now. Let me know what's going on and when you'll be back. Maybe you can send one of those Mind the Gap postcards. So I'll see you soon. And oh, by the way, I'm sober. Been going to NA meetings, too. Bye.

I replayed the message four times.

THAT NIGHT, I DREAMED OF FIRE RAGING INSIDE A THEATER. *It took a while to find an exit, but instead of panicking, I was captivated by the fire's brilliant shades of orange, red, and yellow. I remained near the exit, focused on the spectacle. Out of the flames, a phoenix took shape. Vultures circled around it, threatening to attack. The fire's roar made it impossible for me to caution the regenerative bird.*

Then I saw Chris. I noticed he was smiling and seemed in good health. He walked towards me, carrying a cup of tea. "This is for you, Mom. I've been holding it for so long. I hope it's not cold." As he entered the burning theater, I opened my mouth to warn him, but nothing came out. I was powerless, yet I knew it didn't matter. Swooping down beneath the vultures' reach, the phoenix carried Chris back into the daylight, holding him the way a stork does a newborn child. Before I could take him into my arms, I woke up.

Thursday, 7 July 2005, 7:20 a.m.

My plan had been to get up by 7:00. But I stayed in bed for an extra twenty minutes thinking about Chris' phone call, the dream, and what I'd say in the note I'd write over breakfast. Although I remembered only fragments, the dream had been filled with hope. The bits I recalled were warmed by simple acts of kindness.

Since I was off schedule, I'd forego walking to the British Library but still make time for a quick run. Hearing from Chris had brought up a lot of feelings and memories. A run, even a brief one, usually grounds me. Distracted by my thoughts, I left the hotel without the package addressed to Jed. On the way to the café, I bought a large Mind the Gap postcard; now all I needed was the right words.

My dear Chris,

It was wonderful to hear your message. I can't explain how good it was hearing your voice. It's been so long since we spoke, and so much has happened. But for now, I'll just say I'm fine, taking care to put more balance in my life. I came to London for a Christopher Marlowe conference and some research at the British Library. I'm also editing the book I've been writing, the biography of my great-grandmother, your great-great grandmother, Angelina Longo. Walking around the city, I think of you and all the places we visited together. A few of your favorite places are gone, but the man who sells the ice cream cones with the Cadbury 99 Flake remains across from Russell Square Park. The philosophy bookstore you like in Covent Garden is there, still surrounded by swarming tourists and great street musicians.

What is most important in my life right now is that you sound happy. Yes, I agree, when I get home we should find a therapist who can help us rebuild our relationship. I will be back next Thursday. But if you find someone in the meantime, go ahead and make an appointment. I am open, and I am ready.

Thanks for sharing the good news of your sobriety and recovery in NA. Taking care, and breaking free from what holds us back, are the best gifts we can give ourselves. It's wonderful that you are doing this for yourself. I wish you all the good things in life even more than I wish for our reunion, and believe me, that's great deal. See you when I get home. Can't wait! Hope you like the Mind the Gap postcard.

More later and much love,
Mom xxoo

I RAN SOUTH OVER WATERLOO BRIDGE in the direction of the National Theatre. Tempting as it was, I did not climb down the big cement steps and continue the run along the south bank—a painful decision to make on such a beautiful morning. Instead, I turned around and ran towards Kingsway, encountering only green lights along the way.

My legs felt strong. The backpack containing my laptop became lighter as my endorphins kicked in. I accelerated my pace. If the streets weren't so packed, I could have run all the way to Euston Road and the British Library. Eager to keep moving, I took the stairs instead of the elevator down into the depths of Holborn Station, power-walking along the corridor leading to the northbound platform of the Piccadilly Line. The sign above the platform read, *Train Arriving in 3 Minutes*. It was 8:20 a.m.

Finding an empty seat during the morning rush hour was not the only lucky break I'd have that day.

AN ADVERTISEMENT CAUGHT MY ATTENTION, and I smiled thinking of what Jed would say if he were there. Time and again when the workload at the college felt oppressive or life became more difficult, we joked about escaping to the tropics. It never failed to amuse us when one phoned the other announcing a collect call from Bora Bora. Seeing the aqua blue lagoon set beneath a flawless sky took me beyond the joke into a world of natural beauty and sensual serenity.

I pictured myself relaxing with a book on a tropical beach. The book was solely for pleasure, not for work. I wasn't scheduled to teach it the next day; it simply engaged my mind without the pressure of creating questions for my students or sharing impressive insights with my colleagues. No, I was reading for myself, feeling relaxed, lying there naked save only for a thin coating of sunscreen.

My mental imagery shifted. I saw myself walking towards a white hut and stepping into a hot tub, where a faceless man handed me a cold drink. Yes, lots of coconut and lime. All he wore was a smile. A soft breeze hugged our shoulders; waves broke in the distance.

As the train slowed down at Kings Cross, I looked again at the Bora Bora advertisement. Next trip, I thought, there'll be more romance. But, hum. . .there's still dinner with Kevin tomorrow. We'll see. Work, play, relationships—important to keep things in balance.

Would the line inside the Kings Cross Post Office be as off-putting as the crowd outside the underground station? I had a long list of "to-dos" before completing my work at the Library. Crossing Euston Road, I remembered that I'd forgotten the package for Jed.

"Shit. Should I go back and get it, or wait until tomorrow to send it off?"

Determined to have closure and enjoy some free time, I headed back down the stairs at King's Cross Station. It was 8:48 a.m. when I boarded the fourth car of the Piccadilly Line train heading south towards Russell Square. The height of the rush hour, the train was packed.

In the first car was a 19-year-old father whose wife was pregnant with their second child. A convert to extremist ideas, Germaine Lindsay had reinvented himself as Abdullah Shaheed Jamal. The rucksack he carried gave him the appearance of a student or a vacationing office worker *en route* to a hike in the country. But Jamal was part of a calculated jihadist mission. His rucksack contained two home-made organic peroxide-based devices. In a moment, he'd activate them. Righteous murder, including his own, Jamal believed, would deliver him to eternal glory. Horror was about to derail my plan. But for many of my fellow passengers it created much worse.

I stood holding onto the overhead strap, eyes closed, worrying about the time. "Better let this mistake go before I end up with a tension headache. Too much good happening to ruin the day."

When I opened my eyes, I faced another advertisement for Bora Bora Island—resplendent in shades of green and blue, a bright contrast to the bleak carriage car. Reentering the portal of my earlier reverie, I was thrown backward following a tremendous bang that set off a horrific chorus of screams. Something hit me in the face; blood made its way down my nose to my top lip.

The lights went out, but it was the endless rush of smoke that turned day into night. Pellets of broken glass whirled about. For a moment, bloodied bodies tangled in the chaos startled me less than the overhead strap that had been ripped from its fastening, standing erect in my hand like the grip of a sword whose blade had melted away. I knew I must stay calm, stay awake.

The weight of people flailing about was oppressive. Breathing was all but impossible. I was grateful my inhaler was inside my pocket, but it made little difference. "How long," I asked myself, "before help arrives? Will there be more explosions in the meantime? Is this how I'm going to die?" Unsure whether or when help would come, each minute seemed like an hour. Finally, rescue workers arrived and led those of us who could walk into the tunnel and finally out into the light.

Walking through the tunnel, I brushed small pieces of glass from my face and hair. The nosebleed had stopped. Except for the wheezing, my injuries seemed minor. I noticed a man wrapping his tie around his nose and mouth, and did the same with my scarf.

No one pushed or shoved. We moved along, a steady stream of survivors, soot-covered bodies leaving a site of unimaginable danger. Another woman and I locked arms with an elderly man standing frozen in shock. Together, we walked on until we reached an emergency exit in the King's Cross tunnel. Someone placed his hands on my shoulders, welcoming me as if I'd just finished a race. "Atta girl, you made it." Finally, I felt safe enough to cry. The tears cleansed my eyes and calmed the adrenaline rush that had kept me going when I could hardly breathe.

My eyeglasses had been smashed by a fellow passenger's briefcase. Had the plastic lenses which had been loosened from their broken frames protected my eyes from the airborne glass in those first moments after the explosion? Whatever the case, I was thankful. I felt a little dazed but declined an emergency worker's suggestion that I join those being taken to hospital. My only wounds were surface scratches.

Feeling somewhat relieved by the water I was drinking and the Albuterol that was clearing my airways, I gave the police an account of what had happened, my personal information, and where I could be reached. A passerby told me there had been another explosion, a bus on Upper Woburn Place, so I walked along Tottenham Court Road towards St. Martin's Lane and the Strand.

I caught a glimpse of my soot-covered self in the lobby. The concierge asked nothing other than, "Are you alright, madam?" But he took me by the arm and escorted me to my room. "If there is anything you need, madam, do not hesitate to call down. In the meantime, I will have the restaurant send up a tray of tea and some biscuits. Our way of saying, 'We are happy you survived that nasty debacle.'"

My back was aching, but I was too wound up to sleep. After a hot shower, I made several phone calls to New York. Later, I walked to the post office on William IV Street and mailed the post card to Chris and the manuscript to Jed. My mind kept racing: *Life. So fragile, so unpredictable. This morning I thought how strange that on the same day I'd mail a note to Chris and my completed manuscript to Jed. What a surprise. As for the horrific event that led me here...well, that's beyond belief. But here I am.*

For the rest of the afternoon I sat by the Thames and meditated.

Needed to honor my feelings, to regain at least some calm. I decided to wait a day or two before journaling the carnage I witnessed. Going there in writing might bring me further into the memory than was safe to go right now. First, I needed to talk it out, grieve, and get support.

Instead of shopping at Selfridges that evening, I decided I'd go the 7:00 p.m. Al Anon meeting on Shaftesbury Avenue. And before I did, I'd call Jed again. Maybe if we set a play date, it would make the prospect of going home more tangible. I needed that now.

Before walking on, I thought it might help if I performed a ritual. So I took one of those big octagon-shaped fifty-pence pieces, my favorite English coin, and threw it in the Thames. A small gesture of giving, of gratitude. As I did, I whispered, "Thank you."

MUCH STILL TO DO. Life plans. Next week I will be back in New York. Chris and I will begin the hard work of rebuilding our relationship. Maybe Neil could help us find a therapist. But Chris will have to feel safe with the whole process of selecting someone he can open up to. Then we can begin the work. My heart says it will be a long road, but we are both survivors who have the gift of time. I will support his recovery in the healthiest way I can, and not diagnose, lecture, get angry, cry, or plead, all the things it's so easy to turn to when you are desperate to stop someone's pain, as well as your own.

But the heart is often unrealistic. The bitter truth is that more often than not, addiction and emotional problems are immune to loving intentions. Giving advice, even the best advice, frequently provokes angry outbursts, always results in resentment. After all, recovery is an inside job. These are diseases that continually confront the afflicted and their loved ones with challenges. And when blessed recovery takes place, it does not mean that the challenges or temptations or faulty thinking have disappeared, that they are gone forever. They will remain; they can only be managed.

Typically, there are relapses, often devastating ones. They rob your loved one of his safety, dignity, and serenity. During those periods, you are often seen as the enemy who is part idiot, part creator of all that's gone wrong. Loving relationships with addicts and those with emotional issues require changed thinking and revised priorities. In order to survive, you must become selfish, doing so with confidence and without shame. Earlier today, amidst the shattering explosion on the Piccadilly Line, I took care of myself first. If I had done otherwise, then I might not have been able to take someone's arm and walk beside him through the smoky tunnel. In life there are many smoky tunnels with people in need of support.

Thoughts racing from the excitement of the last twelve hours, the glorious and the horrific, I continued my affirmation. *I will get back to my home Al Anon meeting and thrive in the loving company of friends. I will set boundaries to maintain my serenity. In a few weeks, my book will be on my publisher's desk. Soon, I will begin another project, a memoir. As for the hardships on both sides of the Atlantic, maybe I should be grateful: They have provided my life and my work with texture. They have given me a story to write.*

I am a survivor. This story is a work in progress.

ACKNOWLEDGEMENTS

I want to thank the friends, colleagues, family members, and neighbors whose encouragement and support enabled me to complete this fictionalized memoir. The list of names is too long to include, and I fear omitting someone whose name might have temporarily slipped past my weary mind. I hope all those who've reached out know how much they mean to me for this kindness, and for so much more.

I am grateful to the College of Staten Island/City University of New York, the most excellent of intellectual communities, for providing me with stimulating work. The core of that community is of course the students, and to those I've taught, in particular those in my Italian American Literature course and Women and Literature course, thank you for the feedback regarding identity, displacement, and reinvention. Among my former students, Tolana Nicholson and Simeonette Mapes, whose lives were cut short by cruel circumstances, deserve special mention. Both personally and professionally, I am grateful for the work of my colleague Ellen Goldner, Director of the College of Staten Island's Bertha Harris Women's Center, for helping students become proactive against abuse.

Sincere thanks to Barry Sheinkopf and Full Court Press for turning my story into the book I dreamed about for almost a decade. My work with Peter Murphy's writing group, which met during the summer of 2013 at the University of Dundee, Scotland, provided me with excellent insights and suggestions. Mellissa Seecharan, my colleague and former student, provided invaluable editorial assistance. I also thank Sal Venturelli, Mary Ann D'Aquila, and Bill La Frosia for sharing their family memories, Joshua Longo for making available the news articles concerning Michael Longo's tragedy, and Kathy and Joe Feola for the map of southern Italy that now covers this book.

My fiction has been informed by materials available through the generosity of the Church of St. Michael the Archangel, Rutino, Italy; the New York City Vital Records Office; and the archives of the *New York Times* and *Brooklyn Eagle*. Among Italian American women writers whose contributions enrich contemporary literature, the work of Louise De Salvo and Diane di Prima have been my personal beacons. I also wish to acknowledge the late Jerre Mangione for his seminal work on the Italian American experience in America, Vittoria repetto for her poetry, and Milan Rai for his account of the July 2005 London bombings, as well as for his commitment to peace.

On the home front, my catpanion, Colette, kept me company during the endless hours I spent at the computer. In 2008, we both underwent treatment for cancer, yet we're still here. And for both of us—if I may be presumptuous—that is sheer joy. The members of my Friday night Al Anon meeting (you know who you are!) have my heartfelt gratitude, as does Michael Zampella, Joanne Clark, and the medical teams at Memorial Hospital and NYU Langone for the healthier life they've helped me create.

Christina Tortora helped me understand the grammar and inconsistencies in spelling characteristic of southern Italian dialects on both sides of the Atlantic. I have taken much license in the story and claim responsibility for possibly complicating things further. Terry Rowden's discerning feedback helped me through the later stages of this work. The friendship and guidance of Arnie Kantrowitz, former chair of the English Department at the College of Staten Island and my dear comrade in arms, has guided this book from its inception. His compassionate wit lifted me up many times when remembering turned painful.

Lastly, to the many courageous men and women I've encountered who've convinced me that joy is possible despite one's present circumstances, *grazie mille*!

—M.F.
New York, December 2014

About the Author

Born and raised in New York City, Maryann Feola writes biography, historical and literary criticism, essays, and reviews. Her biography of the early Quaker, George Bishop, was published by Ebor Press, England, and Syracuse University Press. She teaches literature and women's studies at the City University of New York/The College of Staten Island. Much to her delight, Maryann Feola resides in Battery Park City.

CPSIA information can be obtained at www.ICGtesting.com
Printed in the USA
LVOW07s1642040515

437168LV00002B/456/P